A COTTAGE *Wedding*

A HEART'S LANDING NOVEL
FROM HALLMARK PUBLISHING

LEIGH DUNCAN

A Cottage Wedding
Copyright @ 2020 Leigh D. Duncan

Print ISBN 978-1-952210-45-7
eBook ISBN 978-1-947892-61-3

www.hallmarkpublishing.com

Chapter One

$\mathcal{J}$ASON HEART TUGGED ON THE door of I Do Cakes and stepped into the bakery. A sea of voices rolled over him like a wave, drowning the merry tinkle of the bell that announced his arrival. He brushed an unseen fleck from his starched white shirt while he took a second to regroup. The noisy crowd had thrown him off-stride. Even though he was right on time, owners and managers of the town's businesses already crowded the dining area. Chairs at the small tables were filled. Along the back wall, people had already laid claim to the best spots for leaning against the pink-and-white striped wallpaper. No matter. Unlike previous meetings that had gone on for hours, this one was just a formality—a final review of the agenda in preparation for the arrival of the Executive Editor for *Weddings Today*. He headed for the closest empty space.

"Jason. Here. Sit by me." Mildred Morrey beckoned with an age-spotted hand. "It's about time you got here," she groused, though the lines in her face softened into a smile. The owner of Forget Me Knot Flowers removed a gargantuan purse from the chair beside her. "I've had to fight off three people who wanted this seat. One more, and you were out of luck."

"Sorry. I meant to get here earlier. I was waylaid by an anxious bride on my way out the door." Jason bent his long frame into a pretzel and squeezed in between the woman who'd taken him under her wings ages ago and Cheri Clark, the owner of the area's premier bridal salon.

"Are you ready for all the chaos?" Mildred asked once he'd gotten settled.

"You don't really expect it to be as bad as everyone says, do you? After all these months of preparation, I'd expect everything to go pretty smoothly." For a town that put on more than two hundred weddings each year without a hitch, playing host to one woman ought to be a snap, even if she was one of the most influential people in the industry.

"I keep forgetting that you've never been through one of these."

Jason's throat tightened with a familiar ache. He coughed dryly. During the last review, his dad had still been in charge of the Captain's Cottage. At fifty-five and otherwise healthy, David Thaddeus Heart had complained of indigestion in the weeks leading up to the editor's visit. The diagnosis—pancreatic cancer—had been handed down at a doctor's appointment shortly after Heart's Landing had once again been named American's Top Wedding Destination. Over the course of the last two years, Jason had learned a lot about running one of the country's busiest wedding venues, but every once in a while, something came up that he'd never handled, like the magazine's biannual competition.

"We all miss your dad." Mildred played with an earring that dangled among her silvery curls and cleared her throat.

"He was a good man," added Cheri.

"Thanks. He was always sprucing up something. I bet he'd have enjoyed all the changes we made this spring." Jason glanced out the bakery's front window. With the magazine's evaluation looming, practically every storefront in town had been treated to a facelift. But the heart of Heart's Landing was, as always, the Captain's Cottage.

Jason's mouth tugged to the side in a

wry grin. "Cottage" was hardly the word for a house the size of the one his great-great-great-grandfather and the town's founder, Captain Thaddeus Heart, had built. Fourteen bedrooms and two enormous ballrooms took up only a small portion of the home a scant hour southeast of Newport, where wealthy families like the Astors and Vanderbilts had once vacationed on their own enormous estates. Many of those mansions had fallen into disrepair, but the Captain's Cottage looked better than it ever had. Working around a schedule crowded with weddings and celebrations, the housekeeping staff had polished the one hundred twenty-five-year-old hardwood floors, carefully dusted every globe in chandeliers the size of small cars, vigorously shaken out rugs, and repaired even the tiniest nicks and smudges. Outside, white masonry walls gleamed in stark contrast to black shutters and trim. The season's roses had been trellised along the veranda, and every plant on the acres surrounding his family's ancestral home had been carefully manicured.

Mildred nudged his shoulder. "The pressure to retain our number one ranking is intense. Then, there's the fact that Regina Charm is handling the evaluation herself this year. She isn't the most pleasant person to deal with."

"Humph. You can say that again. A cold fish, that's what she is."

Jason smiled at Cheri. "Don't hold back, now. Tell me what you really feel."

The woman's face colored. "Oh, I shouldn't talk about our clients like that. But Regina pushed all my buttons."

"Mine, too." Mildred's voice dropped to a whisper. "She has that whole New York vibe working for her—aloof, snooty. Nothing was good enough for her when she was planning to get married here. And once her dreams of having a Heart's Landing wedding hit a snag—"

"When did that happen?" And why was he just hearing about it now? Jason threaded his fingers through hair that brushed his collar. It sounded like Regina Charm was a real piece of work. No wonder everyone in town was on edge.

"A year ago this spring. Remember the leak at your place?"

How could he forget? He'd taken a rare weekend away from his responsibilities at the Captain's Cottage last April. While he was in Boston, a bad storm had taken out one of the estate's massive oaks. To make matters worse, the uprooted tree had broken a pipe. Water had backed up into the Blue Room, causing severe damage. Among the many phone calls he'd swapped with Alicia,

5

the venue's event coordinator, he seemed to recall a vague reference to a bride who'd been less than pleased that her ceremony had been shifted to the larger, more beautiful Green Room. But by the time he'd arrived back in town, Alicia had worked everything out. Or at least, he'd thought she had. "You're saying that was Regina's wedding?"

"It would have been. She and her fiancé called the whole thing off." Mildred sighed heavily. Though the breakup had nothing to do with Heart's Landing, the town prided itself on delivering a perfect wedding to every bride. On those rare occasions when they weren't able to meet that goal, it hurt. Even a year later. "Let's just say, I don't think she'll be looking at us through rose-colored glasses."

Jason stifled a groan. "I hope we're up to this."

Thank goodness repairs to the Blue Room had finally been completed. He'd hired Ryan Court, the best restoration contractor in the business, and had personally overseen every detail. Not that he'd needed to. Ryan had done an excellent job of painstakingly restoring the wainscoting to its original beauty. Refurbished with new drapes and paint, the second-largest ballroom had once again become a popular spot with the brides who chose the Cottage for their ceremonies and receptions.

"You'll do fine." Mildred patted his hand. "I'm sure you dealt with your fair share of CEOs and celebrities in Boston."

She had a point. He'd started out as the booking agent for a small comedy club and moved up to manager of one of the area's largest convention centers. Over a span of ten years, he'd worked with the most popular bands and artists on the music scene. But all of that paled in comparison to the importance of the next ten days. Placing second or third in the *Weddings Today* competition was not an option. Maintaining their spot as the first choice for brides from one end of the country to the other was critical to the success of every business in town.

At the front of the room, Mayor Greg Thomas rapped firmly on the hostess stand. The low buzz of conversation died down.

"If I can have everyone's attention." Greg hitched a pair of khakis higher on his round belly. "We'll run through the agenda, item by item, and get this over with. I know you all want to get home to your families, and I don't want to keep you a minute longer than necessary. Let's dive right in, shall we?" He glanced at the notes he'd spread across the makeshift podium. "Regina Charm is due to arrive at three PM on Friday afternoon. She'll

Leigh Duncan

go straight to the Captain's Cottage. Jason, why don't you take it from there?"

"Yes, sir." Jason unfolded his legs and stood. Around him, the familiar faces of people he'd known his entire life nodded their encouragement. Everyone in the room shared one thing in common. Their livelihoods depended on a perfect score from *Weddings Today*. Determined to do his part, he cleared his throat.

"Much like it was done in the Captain's day, the entire household will turn out to greet Ms. Charm. I'll assume Thaddeus's role, as usual, but I've asked my girlfriend Clarissa to fill in for Evelyn." Well, not exactly. He and his cousin Evelyn had appeared at quite a few weddings and receptions dressed as the Captain and his wife, Mary. But when Clarissa had heard that the Executive Editor for *Weddings Today* would be in town, she'd begged to play a leading role. Which reminded him, he needed to confirm Clarissa's travel plans. He jotted a mental note and continued. "We've set aside the Azalea Suite for Ms. Charm's use while she's in town. It's the largest of our bridal apartments and has been recently updated. Once she's settled in, we'll turn her over to you, Mr. Mayor, and get ready for the meet-and-greet at six that evening. It'll be in the Green Room. You're all invited, of course."

He took his seat as the mayor nodded. "That's good. My only concern is in the timing. Since Ms. Charm opted to drive up from New York, rather than take the train, I'd be watching for her to arrive any time after noon. She's known to throw things off schedule a bit. Shows up early for interviews. That sort of thing. She likes to test people's reactions."

When a murmur of agreement passed through the room, Jason nodded. So, Regina Charm liked to spring surprises on her hosts, huh? Well, she wouldn't catch him napping. He'd post one of the house staff on the widow's walk bright and early Friday morning. They'd sound the alarm the moment a car turned onto the long, curving driveway that led to the Captain's Cottage.

Greg cleared his throat. "Everyone should have Ms. Charm's agenda." From a list that included practically every business in town, the editor had selected the places she'd like to see, as well as events she wanted to attend. It was more than enough to fill a crowded schedule. "Like I told Jason, Regina is prone to surprises. If your shop isn't on her list, she still might pop in for a quick visit. Stay on your toes."

One by one, the mayor called for brief reports on the plans to entertain the editor. From Something Old, Something New on

Bridal Carriage Way to the bed and break-fast on Union Street, owners had arranged for tours of their businesses. Restaurants in the area had signed up to host Ms. Charm and her party at so many breakfasts, lunches, and dinners that the woman was in danger of needing an entire new wardrobe before she headed back to the city. Invitations to several weddings had been issued by brides who were eager for the opportunity to have their special day mentioned in *Weddings Today*. Plus, plenty of leisure activities had been planned in case the editor wanted to take advantage of the warmth of early summer. Last, but certainly not least, Regina would be the guest of honor at a special presentation of the Heart's Landing pageant. Usually performed in the fall, the play portrayed the time Captain Thaddeus had braved a hurricane in order to make port in time for his wife's birthday.

"I guess that sums it up." Mayor Thomas rubbed his hands together. "I'll be on call to serve as Ms. Charm's escort and answer any questions she might have throughout her visit here. One final word. I don't have to tell you how important this competition is for our town. With ceremonies taking place 365 days a year here in Heart's Landing, we pride ourselves on delivering the perfect wedding to every bride. But hard times lay ahead if we lose the designation of America's Top Wedding Destination. If anything goes awry, and I mean even the smallest hiccup, I'll expect to hear from you right away."

Greg scanned the room, his blue eyes meeting and registering agreement everywhere. Satisfied that his team knew what to do, he grinned. "All right now, we've got this. Let me hear that good old Heart's Landing spirit. What do you say?"

Jason, along with everyone else in the room, lifted an imaginary glass of champagne. He chimed in with the rest in the familiar toast. "The best is yet to be!"

"Yes, it will." Greg ran a hand over his bald pate. "Okay, folks. Time to head home now and get some rest."

Jason couldn't agree more. If Regina Charm was half as difficult to deal with as Mildred and Cheri said she was, everyone in town would need to keep their wits about them during her visit.

Chapter Two

ON THE FOURTH FLOOR OF the *Weddings Today* headquarters, a flourescent light hummed in the ceiling over Tara Stewart's desk. The air handlers for the towering office building in lower Manhattan kicked into high gear. Tara pulled her cardigan tighter as tasteless, odorless air spilled cold into her cubicle. Her chair emitted an annoying squeak when she tipped forward, but her focus on the image on the computer monitor didn't waver. She traced a finger over one of a dozen photographs. Grabbing her magnifying glass from the pencil holder, Tara ignored the bride's smiling face, the ostentatious cascade of flowers clutched in a pair of perfectly manicured hands, the fortune in diamonds that sparkled from her neck and ears. Instead, she panned the lens slowly over the wedding gown. "Well, if that don't beat all," she whispered.

Her breath on hold, she unearthed several designs from the scattered stacks on her desktop. Ideal for summer weddings, the gowns had been featured in last November's edition of *Weddings Today*. She thumbed through the pile until she found the one she wanted and treated it to the same scrutiny she'd given the image on her computer. A smile tugged at the corners of her mouth. There was no doubt about it. Kate Steven had worn a Sophie Olsen original when she'd walked down the aisle on an exclusive Long Island estate. Remorse stirred in her chest. Tara batted it down. She'd worked at *Weddings Today* long enough to learn that climbing the corporate ladder meant stepping over someone else. In this case, Kate Steven.

This is big. Really big.

Paper rustled as Tara's fingers trembled with the thrill of being the first to stumble onto a hot story. Afraid she might drop the magnifying glass in her excitement, she returned it to the holder. What next?

"Van?" She swiveled toward her cubicle mate and one of two dozen other junior staff who were hungry for a byline in the nation's top wedding magazine. "I need a second pair of eyes on this. Do you see the same thing I do?"

"What's up?" Three feet away, Vanessa Robinson ran a hand over the wiry, jet-colored hair she'd tamed into sleek braids. She spun toward Tara. Her dark eyes bright with expectation, she studied the screen beyond Tara's shoulder. Van's mouth formed a round O. "Are those pictures from Kate Steven's wedding?"

"They are. They just landed in my inbox." Among her many tasks as a cub reporter for *Weddings Today*, Tara wrote the tag lines that accompanied candid shots from the dozen or so weddings featured on the collage page of each edition.

"Oh, my word! I never thought I'd see an A-Lister like her relegated to the back of the magazine."

"I know, right?" Tara nodded. The wedding of a spokesmodel for one of the country's biggest designers would normally receive top billing. But any hopes of splashing Kate's picture on the cover of *Weddings Today* had been dashed when the bride had insisted on an uber-private ceremony and had turned down the magazine's request for press credentials. "See anything else odd?"

"Well, Kate looks gorgeous, but that's nothing new." The supermodel was knocking on the door to forty, but the camera still loved her flawless skin and shiny golden hair. The not-so-blushing bride had chosen a slinky off-white gown that draped the curves of her six-foot frame like it was made for her. "I love the cut of that dress. It's so dreamy and..." Vanessa fell silent, her eyes narrowing as she traced the lines of the gown on the screen. Her hand and her jaw dropped. "Isn't that a Sophie Olsen? What's she doing in that?"

"I was asking the same question myself. Did she think no one would notice?"

"How could they not?"

"Exactly." Kate Steven had been the face of the Donna Marsha brand for five years. Her choice to walk down the aisle in another designer's wedding gown was an unforgiveable slight. "I smell a story."

Tara pressed her thumb into the soft flesh under her chin while she tapped her forefinger against her upper lip. The shiver of excitement she'd felt moments earlier turned into a rumble. This could be "the one." The story that proved she'd been right to leave Savannah and follow her dreams to New York. The story that warranted a byline and a teaser on the cover of *Weddings Today*. If she played her cards right, it might actually help her erase the dreaded *junior* from her title and propel her into an office of her own. One that had a door and four walls that reached all the way to the ceiling. Unlike her current space in the bullpen, where cubicles topped out at mid-chest and privacy was a pipe dream.

Not that she'd be around much to enjoy her new digs. No. Once she became a full-fledged senior reporter, she'd be too busy covering far-flung celebrity weddings or protecting the magazine's readership from unethical vendors—the kind who promised the moon and delivered nothing—to actually sit behind her desk and stare out the window at the dull, gray cement exterior of the building next door.

Wasn't it about time something big came her way? Her parents had expected her to follow in her sisters' footsteps and join the family business. When she'd chosen a different path, they hadn't been able to hide their disappointment. She'd been trying to prove herself in their eyes ever since. But it had taken longer than she'd expected. Oh, she'd known she'd have to pay her dues. The day she'd broken up with her high-school sweetheart and moved to New York, she'd sat down at the tiny kitchen table in her fifth-floor walk-up and had a frank, heart-to-heart chat with herself. This was her time, she'd decided. If she was going to succeed and make her parents proud, she had to buckle down and get serious. And that meant setting her personal life on the shelf. One day, she'd find her Mr. Right. For the foreseeable future, though, she'd concentrate on making a name for herself. She'd focus on writing about weddings and not dreaming about her own.

And that's exactly what she'd done.

In the two years since she'd landed a job at *Weddings Today*, she'd written dozens of articles on such not-so-fascinating topics as the differences between Point D'Esprit and Chantilly lace. She'd dutifully touted the advantages of serving sparkling wine over champagne in companion pieces for a senior reporter's article on receptions. She'd done all the legwork and consolidated the research for her higher-paid and more respected bosses on Reporter's Row.

She hadn't expected it to be easy to get ahead in such a competitive market—and it hadn't been—but surely her time had come. The more she thought about it, the more certain she grew that a juicy tidbit from Kate's wedding was just the ticket she needed to propel her career in the right direction. She jiggled her computer mouse, but the laptop had put itself to sleep, something it did whenever she ignored it for too long. With a good-natured grumble, she logged back in. She sent the image of the model wearing the inappropriate dress to the printer and scooped up the photo of the Sophie Olsen.

"What are you going to do?" The wheels of Vanessa's office chair rumbled as she returned to her half of the tiny cubicle.

"The first step is to convince Ms. Charm to let me look into it." The Executive Editor for *Weddings Today*, Regina Charm had to approve any story her junior staff deemed worthy of investigation. "Once I get the go-ahead, I'll do the research. Talk to Kate. And Donna Marsha. Or, at least, their assistants." She had to admit that the odds of a junior reporter getting face-to-face time with two of the biggest names in wedding fashion were nil, even for an important story like this one. And wasn't that always the way? In a bizarre version of *Catch-22*, she had to have a big scoop to boost her up onto the next rung of the corporate ladder, but to get it, she needed access to people who wouldn't give the time of day to lowly junior reporters. "Somehow, I'll get to the bottom of this and learn why a spokesmodel for one brand would wear a competitor's dress."

"When you put it like that, I don't see how Ms. Charm could turn you down. You think she'd let you write the entire article?" Vanessa drummed her fingers on her chair's armrests. "Do you know how jelly I'll be if she does?"

She did. For one glorious split-second, Tara envisioned a teaser on the cover of the next edition, a two-page article inside with her name prominently featured. The story she'd write would be so well-researched and well-written, Ms. Charm would practically beg her for regular contributions. From there, the sky was the limit. Featured articles. A monthly column. Promotions and accolades.

But first, she had to plant her foot on the next rung. She slipped the photos into one of the magazine's blue binders and tucked it under one arm. "Wish me luck."

"You don't even have to ask. You've got this."

"When I do, drinks are on me at The Scribe." Two doors down from the magazine's headquarters, the watering hole served as the staff's most popular gathering spot. Tonight, she'd walk into the bar where framed covers of *Weddings Today* hung over the booths, and everyone would congratulate her on her first big assignment. Thinking of the welcome she'd receive, Tara sighed.

Her visions of grandeur dimmed a bit when Vanessa's full lips parted. "You know I'd love to, but I can't. Charlie and I are going to Bed, Bath and Beyond to create our registry as soon as I get off work."

Pretending she didn't care, Tara nodded. "Some other time, then."

She turned toward the opening between their desks. A little over two years ago, she'd have traded her eyeteeth for the kind of relationship Vanessa shared with her fiancé. But that was before. Before she'd discovered texts from other girls on her former boyfriend's phone. Before she'd given up on dreams of white picket fences and had set her sights on something more attainable. Climb the ladder of success, that was her new goal. Landing this story was the next step.

She shrugged out of her cardigan and snugged the tail of her blue shirt into the waistband of gray slacks. Her shoulders back, head held high, she marched past the rows of cubicles that held dozens of other junior reporters and interns. The glass-fronted door at the end of the corridor loomed like the entrance to the lion's den. Which, considering her boss's mood of late, wasn't a bad comparison.

Momentary doubt flickered. Tara doused it and kept her feet in motion. At the door, she curled her fingers over sweat-dampened palms and knocked on the jamb.

"Ms. Charm? Do you have a minute?"

The ultra-thin woman in a standard-issue, shabby-chic black suit looked up from photographs paper-clipped to articles written by senior staffers. She removed a pair of reading glasses—today's frames were bright red—and pinched her nose. "Come in, Tara. Do you have those blurbs finished for the composite page?" The nasal tones of a Long Island native whipped through the air. "I need them by Friday."

"I just have to add Kate Steven's, and I'll be done with them. But I spotted something very interesting in the photos from her wedding."

"Yes." Regina Charm's inflection didn't rise a bit.

Tara stepped forward, her pulse racing. This was her big chance. It could be months—years, even—before another opportunity like this one came along. She had to grab the editor's attention.

"Yes," she said firmly. "As you know, Kate is the spokesmodel for the Donna Marsha line." The designer was the second-most popular in the industry. "But for her own wedding, Kate chose"—she paused for effect—"a *Sophie Olsen!*" Stepping forward, she slid the printed image onto her boss's desk. "I want to probe deeper into that, find out why Kate would make such a statement."

"Something about this has your reporter's nose twitching?" Her thin lips curving into a barely amused smile, Regina twirled her glasses by one stem.

"It does." She nodded.

"Not bad."

Her heart leaped. These days, "not bad" was considered high praise on the floor where her boss rarely had a kind word to say about anything. She crossed her fingers. This was it, the moment of truth. Had she won the editor over?

"But it's not for us." Regina folded her reading glasses and set them aside. "Our subscribers aren't interested in a quarrel between the creatives and their faces. Our readers are women who are planning their weddings or hope to be soon. They want to know what's hot in next season's gowns. Is strapless on its way out? Are empire waist-lines making a comeback? Which fabrics are popular right now? They expect us to answer those questions for them and leave spats like this one to the gossip rags."

"But I thought..." Tara's heart sank straight down to her toes while heat climbed the back of her neck.

"I know what you thought. But no." Regina aimed a nail the same color as her glasses at the picture. "That is not for us. You've been with us for two years. I'd think you'd know that by now."

"Yes, ma'am. Sorry to have bothered

you." Not only was Kate's story *not* her big break, Regina's subtle jab told her she'd better bring her focus more in line with *Weddings Today* or start looking for another job. Prepared to make as gracious a retreat as possible under the circumstances, she backed away from the desk.

"On the other hand…"

At the sound of her boss's voice, Tara's retreat halted. *What now?*

"I do admire your attention to detail. Even some of the more senior reporters might have missed the dress." Tension in the room mounted while Regina treated Tara to an intense study. At last, her boss tapped the folded pair of glasses against her desktop and nodded. "Close the door and take a seat."

Her emotions bouncing like a yo-yo at the end of a string, Tara gulped. Though she couldn't recall the last time something good had come out of a private chat with the Executive Editor, Regina had just handed her a compliment. Of sorts.

"What can I do for you, Ms. Charm?" she asked, deliberately adopting a bland tone.

"I'm sure you're aware that we're in the middle of our bi-annual review of the most popular wedding sites throughout the U.S. The town that receives the highest marks will be on the cover of our August edition, with a four-page spread inside."

Tara blinked and scurried to keep up with a conversation that veered in a direction she hadn't expected. In an industry worth 72 billion dollars a year, roughly twenty-five percent of brides and grooms chose a destination wedding. Earning the title of the most sought-after location meant a serious boon to the winner's economy. The entire office had been buzzing with speculation, but she had nothing to do with the contest, so why had Regina brought it up?

"For the past ten years, that honor has fallen to Heart's Landing. You've heard of it, haven't you?"

"Oh, yes." Practically every young woman in America had dreamed of getting married in the quaint little seaside town a stone's throw south of glitzy Newport. There'd been a time when she'd pictured herself standing on the veranda of the Captain's Cottage reciting her vows. But she'd put aside those thoughts in order to concentrate on her career. She traced the crease in her slacks.

"Personally, I think the people there have grown so complacent, they've let things slide." Regina's gaze drifted to a large plate-glass window that overlooked busy lower Manhattan. "That was certainly the experience I encountered last year. My fiancé and I

24

would never have called off our engagement if it hadn't been for the way the staff at the Captain's Cottage mishandled our arrangements."

Tara swallowed a nervous gulp. It was no secret that Regina's wedding to Wall Street investor Robert Hutchins had fallen apart mere weeks before the event. The editor had been in a foul mood ever since. Not that Tara or any of her coworkers dared discuss the matter within Regina's earshot. Now that her boss had raised the subject, though, how was she supposed to respond?

Recalling how devastated she'd been when she discovered her long-time boyfriend's roving eye, Tara shoved all the warmth and sincerity she could muster into one sentence. "I was so sorry to hear about the breakup, Ms. Charm."

"Don't be. I'm over it." Dismissive, the editor waved one hand. Her attention shifting, she focused on Tara. "Don't let anyone tell you different—true love is just a fairy tale. It doesn't exist any more than Snow White, Cinderella, and Prince Charming do. Now that I've discovered the truth, I'm better off, believe me."

Tara clamped her mouth shut over a protest that was sure to rile her boss's feathers. The few times she'd spotted Regina and Robert at company functions and charitable events, she would've sworn the couple had been truly happy together. In the year since the pair had called off their wedding, the editor had grown more cynical every day. If that was better off, Tara wasn't sure it was much of an improvement.

"Enough about my life." As if she realized she'd been swapping confidences with a lowly junior staff member, Regina straightened. "Let's get back to the subject at hand—Heart's Landing. This year, the magazine wants a special, in-depth look at the entire town. They've allocated ten days for visiting every business and venue, sampling the fare from the various caterers and restaurants. Normally, as Executive Editor, I'd handle the evaluation personally." Regina cleared her throat. "However, I don't believe Heart's Landing deserves the title any longer. I think it's time to pass the torch to another contender."

Tara nodded. According to whispered gossip around the water cooler, Regina had planned a wedding that would outshine the royal wedding of a lesser noble. Her fury had been a force to reckon with when things hadn't turned out exactly as she'd envisioned. Now, it seemed, she placed the blame solely on Heart's Landing.

"I'm sure you understand how that puts me in an awkward position. It wouldn't look

right for me to give the town a scathing review. People might accuse me of letting my
own experiences color my perception. Nothing could be farther from the truth."

In what could only be construed as a demand for support, Regina arched one carefully drawn eyebrow and cast an expectant
look across the desk.

Recognizing her cue, Tara nodded.
"You're far too professional to let your own
feelings influence your work."

"Thank you for saying that. Still, *Weddings Today* needs to maintain its impartial
standing. That's where you come in. I want
you to go to Heart's Landing in my place.
You'll handle the entire evaluation. Can you
do it?"

Tara gulped. Her? In charge of judging
the incumbent in this year's contest? This
was more than taking a step up the corporate ladder. It was grasping the shiny bronze
star on the top of the tree. "Yes, of course,"
she blurted, despite the clanging of an inter-
nal alarm.

*Careful. Opportunities like this one come
with strings attached.*

"This might sound like we're putting a
lot on your shoulders, but your job will actually be a simple one. You'll fill out the check-
lists, visit all the must-see locations, snap
pictures for the magazine, attend weddings

and, in general, give everyone the impression that you're performing a detailed evaluation. In reality, you'll only be taking a cursory look at the town. Needless to say, I don't expect, or want, a glowing report. Do I make myself clear?"

"Perfectly." Tara pressed her fingers together. Okay, so this might not be the plum assignment it had sounded like at first, but it was still a great opportunity.

"The real part of your job is a little trickier. Heart's Landing has held the title for so long, it's going to take something substantial to knock the town off its pedestal. That's where your unique skills as an investigative reporter come in."

Tara leaned forward, her nose for a story on alert.

"Your real purpose while you're there will be to debunk the lies that form the very foundation of Heart's Landing's claim to fame. For nearly as long as the town has existed, rumors and whispers have circulated about the town's founder. Not everyone is convinced he was the paragon of love and faithfulness people have made him out to be. I want you to dig into the history of Captain Thaddeus Heart and find out the truth about him."

Tara sucked in a breath. Now this was

the meaty kind of assignment she'd been hoping for.

"You've heard the stories, I'm sure. How the good captain supposedly loved his wife so much that he sailed home for her birthday every year. That he battled a hurricane in order to make port on time. Like we're supposed to believe that." Regina gave an indelicate snort. "Then, there's the heart-shaped stones mounted all over town. Locals claim Captain Thaddeus personally chiseled them as birthday presents for his wife." She examined one blood-red fingernail. "Rocks—how perfectly droll. That, in itself, speaks volumes about the true nature of his relationship with his wife."

Looking up, she continued, "I've requested access to the captain's logs and records. Everything you need to expose his story as nothing more than a fairy tale will be available to you. Think you can do it?"

"Of course, Ms. Charm. I'll do my best."

"You must know how important this is, Tara. Debunk this myth, and you're on your way up in the world. Fail, and well..."

"I won't." She didn't need anyone to spell it out for her. Succeed, and she'd get that promotion she'd been angling for. She'd remain on staff at *Weddings Today*, have her own office, write the kind of stories she'd dreamed of writing. Fail, and at best, she'd be stuck in the bullpen for the rest of a very short career.

From a drawer in her desk, Regina retrieved a business card and scribbled on the back. "Here," she said, sliding the paper across the desk. "That's my private number. This conversation stays strictly between you and me. You're not to tell anyone—especially anyone in Heart's Landing—about the true nature of your assignment."

While Tara slipped the card into a pants pocket, her boss retrieved her reading glasses and slipped them on. Regina's focus dropped to the pages she'd been examining when Tara had entered the room. "Be sure to get those collages to me," she said without looking up. "Spend the next couple of days wrapping up your assignments in the office. You'll need to take your company laptop, of course. Someone from the travel department will explain how to get reimbursed for your expenses—I'll have them get in touch with you. You'll catch the train on Thursday. No one in Heart's Landing expects you until Friday, but that's the point. Remember, you always get a more honest picture when you catch your subjects off guard."

Tara stood. "I won't let you down, Ms. Charm."

"I'm sure you won't." Regina removed the paperclip from one of the stacks on her desk and picked up a red pen. With bold strokes, she relegated someone's work for the week to the recycle bin. "That will be all for now."

Outside her boss's office, Tara leaned against the wall to catch her breath. Guilt prickled her scalp. She swallowed, then swallowed again. Raising the issue of Kate Steven's dress had backfired and, for a minute there, she'd been afraid Regina would tell her to clean out her desk. She exhaled, happy it hadn't come to that. Getting fired would only confirm her parents' opinion that moving to New York had been a big mistake. Besides, Regina had offered her a way to redeem herself. To succeed, though, she'd have to destroy the foundation of a town that had staked its reputation on providing the perfect wedding for every bride.

Could she do it?

She squared her shoulders. She had to. This new assignment could give her everything she'd been working toward—the chance to make a name for herself, establish her career at *Weddings Today*, and prove to her family that she'd made the right choice by moving to New York. And if she didn't do it, Regina would find someone else to handle the task. She snapped her fingers.

The job was as good as done.

Chapter Three

OOD PANELING THAT HAD DARK-
ENED with age lined the walls of
Jason's office at the rear of the
Captain's Cottage. Near the door, history
tomes crowded the shelves of a bookcase.
Atop it sat one of the many artifacts taken
from the merchant ship his great-great-
great-grandfather had named after his wife,
Mary Shelby Heart. Through fair skies,
following winds and rough seas, the brass
clock had kept near-perfect time, a job it had
continued to do for more than a hundred
years. The minute hand clicked into place
with a faint tick.

Jason propped his iPhone on its stand
on the worn surface of the teak desk that
had been in the family for generations.
He checked the camera angle and smiled.

Perfect. Any second now, the phone would ring, and Clarissa's face would appear on the screen. Thanks to the miracle of modern technology, the miles between them would disappear. They'd laugh and talk of building a future together like they used to do before he'd inherited the Captain's Cottage and left Boston.

Well, almost like they used to do.

No matter how often he told himself that their long-distance relationship was working, his heart complained that a series of texts, phone calls, and Facetime visits weren't at all the same as actually being together. He longed to breathe in air scented with Clarissa's perfume. Twirl a lock of her hair around his finger. Help her with her sweater. Feel the occasional brush of her hand on his arm. He missed that, all of that. And no wonder.

Nearly two years had passed since he'd come home to Heart's Landing. Despite all his experience managing convention centers throughout Boston, it had taken a while to get the hang of running a venue that hosted a dozen weddings each week. Now that he had, he loved doing his part, along with everyone else in town, in giving brides and grooms their perfect day. But the work was demanding. He'd only managed a few, quick trips back to the city, the last of which had been cut short when Clarissa had cancelled their plans for a picnic on the Common and had gone into the office. As a result, three— no, four—months had slipped by since he and Clarissa had shared a meal or taken in a movie together. But after several false starts, she was finally coming here.

A whisper of self-doubt rode the wave of anticipation that jittered through him. Was he doing the right thing by letting her help him with the *Weddings Today* review? It was sure to be a stressful time, and he had to admit, he wasn't sure their relationship could withstand the pressure. His cousin Evelyn could have filled the role of hostess; he'd been performing with her for so long now that they had the routine down pat.

But when she'd heard that Regina Charm was handling the evaluation personally, Clarissa had insisted on taking Evelyn's place. He only hoped his girlfriend understood how crucial this review was, not only to him, but to the entire town. After how badly things had gone with the Executive Editor's own almost-wedding, it was doubly important that Heart's Landing put its best food forward this time.

Tapping his toes in time to an old sea shanty, one of dozens carefully recorded in Captain Thaddeus's journals, Jason deliberately shifted his focus to the upside. Maybe it was a good thing Clarissa had timed her first visit to Heart's Landing to coincide with the big review. He'd wanted her to see his hometown—and all it had to offer—at its best, and it had never looked as beautiful as it did right now.

A low buzz sounded from his cell phone. Straightening, he punched the button, accepting the call. On the screen, Clarissa's familiar face appeared in the frame.

"Hey!" His heart warmed. It didn't matter that she was running late, as usual, or that he'd spent the last ten minutes woolgathering while he waited for her call. She was on the line now, and almost before he knew it, she'd be here in person. That was the important thing. "It's good to see you! How are things in Boston?"

"Busy as usual." Clarissa's focus remained glued to something beyond the camera's angle. Papers rattled and came into view. She held up one sheet. "Make the changes I've marked and get this back to me before the end of the day. Close the door on your way out." She slipped the paper into a waiting hand. "Sorry," she said, not sounding the least bit apologetic as she finally glanced at her phone. Her lips curved upward into a smile that didn't quite warm a pair of cool blue eyes. "I had a little something that couldn't wait. But I'm all yours now."

As good as that sounded, Jason knew better than to hope for a lengthy conversation. He'd been trying, without much success, to finalize the details of Clarissa's arrival for several days. He'd even connected with her once, only for her to be called away shortly after they'd exchanged greetings. Not that she was entirely to blame. He'd had his own share of emergencies to deal with. Everything would be fine as long as they both remembered that managing a long-distance relationship required patience and compromise. And doubly so for successful couples.

Now, though, Clarissa's often-delayed visit to Heart's Landing was just around the corner. He was sure it would do her a world of good to step away from the crushing routine of her hectic life in the city. Starting the day after tomorrow, they'd have nearly two weeks to reconnect and strengthen the bond between them. Complete strangers had fallen in love in less time.

"You're looking good! Everything going well at work?" He hoped so. As an account manager at one of Boston's most prestigious firms, Clarissa's mood ebbed and flowed with events in her office.

"Yes. In fact, Rick—you remember Rick Handon, don't you?"

Jason nodded while he squelched an urge to ask when she'd started calling her boss by his first name. During his last visit to Boston, Clarissa had respectfully referred to the ad agency's owner as "Mr. Handon."

"He was so pleased with how I handled the press releases for the Ballor merger that he turned the Craigen account over to me. You know Craigen's, don't you?"

"Who doesn't? It's one of my favorites." Though the city fathers of Heart's Landing had been vigilant in preventing chain stores and restaurant franchises from gaining a toe-hold, Jason stopped in at one of Craigen's popular eateries whenever his errands took him to nearby Newport. "Their lobster rolls are the best. That's really good news for you. Congratulations!"

"It is, but"—Clarissa ran long, thin fingers over the dark hair she'd captured in a tight chignon—"it's a lot of work. I need to develop an entire new ad campaign before I meet with the client next month."

"Oh, so this will be more of a working vacation?" Disappointment crept through Jason's midsection. He quickly squelched it. Who was he to complain when he had his own responsibilities to attend to while Clarissa was in town? "I'm sure we can free up some time for you."

Elbow on the desk, he propped his chin

Leigh Duncan

on one fist. With a few clicks, he brought up the agenda for the next week. Dinners, outings, weddings, and festivities crowded the schedule. It would take some work to clear an hour or so here and there, but he'd do whatever it took to make Clarissa's trip a productive one.

"Let's see. There's the assembly on Friday afternoon—that's a must." The arrival of the Executive Editor from *Weddings Today* was a grand occasion. As was the custom in the 1800s when Thaddeus and his wife Mary had thrown lavish parties on the estate, the entire staff would line up on the driveway to meet their important guest. "You won't want to miss the cocktail party that evening, and we have a big day on Saturday when we'll accompany Ms. Charm on a tour of Heart's Landing."

He exhaled. Carving time out of the hectic schedule was going to be tougher than he'd thought. "We could cancel the hike later in the week, but everything is in bloom right now. I'd hate for you to miss it. I thought we'd hit the beach one day, too. And don't forget, we have starring roles in the pageant next Saturday."

"Hmmm." A soft chiming drew Clarissa's focus away from the phone. She fiddled with something on her desk before she faced him again. "Getting this account is a huge opportunity for me. I can't afford to be away from the office right now. I'm sorry, but I'm not going to make it."

"At all?" He had to have misunderstood. She wouldn't, couldn't, cancel out completely. Not on the eve of the most important event to occur since he'd inherited the Captain's Cottage. She knew how important Regina's visit was.

"I know it's disappointing, but honestly, darling, it's better this way. I have so much work to do to get ready for this presentation that I won't be able to focus on anything else. Plus, I have to be near Rick—he needs to approve every decision. So, you see why I can't go out of town." Blue eyes flashed as Clarissa smiled brightly. "Why don't you come here instead?"

"You're cancelling out a promise you made weeks ago, but you expect me to walk away from my obligations to visit you in Boston?" The suggestion was beyond ludicrous.

"You won't come to see me?" Annoyance tightened Clarissa's lips.

Jason shoved down an angry retort and took a breath. If he had any hope of salvaging the situation, he'd have to appeal to her sense of fair play. "This was your idea, Clarissa. You insisted on coming now so you could meet Regina Charm. You're leaving me high and dry here."

"Oh, please." She rolled her baby blues. "You make it sound like the world is coming to an end. Evelyn can take my place."

His cousin would usually be glad to step into the role. But with the review looming, her responsibilities as the Cottage's book-keeper and supply manager had doubled. "She's already pitching in wherever she's needed. I can't ask her to do any more."

Any hope that Clarissa would recon-sider died when her blue eyes hardened. "It sounds like you're forcing me to make a choice I didn't want to make."

He gave her one last chance. "I'm just asking you to keep your promise. All the arrangements have been made. People are—I'm—counting on you."

But apparently she didn't care. His heart sank. He ran one finger along the edge of the desk. If things had gone well during Clar-issa's visit, he'd hoped to pop the question and slip a ring on her finger. That wouldn't happen now. A woman who couldn't commit to ten days certainly couldn't commit to a lifetime.

"Look." Clarissa glanced over her shoul-der at the closed door behind her. Satisfied that they wouldn't be overheard, she sighed. "We haven't been on the same page in this relationship for a while. All those broken dates? Those cancelled trips? You have to admit, we've drifted apart."

He bit his tongue. As much as he wanted to deny it, he'd known that things had become strained between them. But he wouldn't point out that she was the one who'd broken date after date and cancelled one trip to Heart's Landing after another. Swapping recriminations and accusations wouldn't help them salvage what was left of their relationship. "That's one of the reasons I was looking forward to this visit. I hoped we'd reconnect, rediscover what we'd lost."

"What's the point when we're headed in opposite directions?" She leaned forward. "My career is taking off. Yours, though..." She shook her head. "How you could walk away from the life we had in Boston? I never understood that."

She'd known from the very beginning that he'd inherit the Captain's Cottage one day, though neither of them counted on it happening so soon. But if she wanted to believe that he was at fault, he'd take the hit. He came from strong, seafaring stock. His shoulders were broad enough to carry the load.

"It's over between us?" he asked, just to be clear.

"I always thought you'd get tired of living

41

there and come back, you know. But that hasn't happened."

No, and it wouldn't. He'd found his sense of purpose in Heart's Landing. Studying the past had always been important to him, and now he actually had the chance to play a small part in history by giving brides their perfect day. He'd developed the kind of friendships here that he'd never had in the big city, where people spent so much time rushing from one thing to the next that they rarely slowed down long enough to talk, really talk. He loved the slower pace, the quiet streets, the fog that carried the tang of the ocean. He wouldn't trade what he had here for a thousand years anywhere else.

"I guess this is goodbye, then." There was no use in drawing things out. Clarissa had made her decision, and it wasn't him.

"I guess it is. I'll, uh, I'll see you around." Staring into the phone, she brushed her fingertips beneath dry eyes.

"Yeah. See you around," he agreed, though he wouldn't hold his breath. He shook his head when the screen went black and automatically shoved a hank of hair off his forehead. So this was how it felt to break up with the person you thought you'd spend the rest of your life with. He leaned back in his chair and closed his eyes, waiting for the heartbreak to wash over him. When the stabbing pain didn't come, he sighed. He supposed he and Clarissa had really been saying goodbye to each other ever since he left Boston. Six months ago, when she'd cancelled her first trip to Heart's Landing, he'd known on one level that things were never going to work out between them. Somehow, his heart had gotten the message long before his head—and yeah, his pride—had understood it. That had to be the reason why the breakup didn't hurt as much as he'd expected. Not that it mattered. He didn't have time for heartache.

In less than forty-eight hours, the Executive Editor for the nation's most popular bridal magazine was going to arrive on his doorstep. From the moment she passed the Heart's Landing city limits sign until her departure, every single detail of her trip had to be absolutely perfect. A goal that was going to be nearly impossible to achieve, considering the huge monkey wrench Clarissa had thrown into the town's well-laid plans. He'd need help if he had any hope of getting things back on track.

In the hallway outside his door, heels tapped on the ancient hardwood floors. Jason shook his head. He should have known. Just when he thought he'd have to track her down, the very person he needed to talk to was on her way to his office. How did Evelyn do that? Ever since he was a kid, he could count on his cousin to show up at the slightest hint of trouble.

Seconds later, an impish face peered around his door jamb. "Hey there. I thought I'd pop in to say hello to Clarissa. Looks like I'm too late, though. You two lovebirds have already wrapped things up?"

Jason inhaled slowly. "Turns out, *breaking* up doesn't take very long at all."

"No." Evelyn let out a low whistle. "You called it quits? I didn't see that coming."

"Neither did I." His neck suddenly felt tight. He worked the knot in his tie loose and gave it a yank. Colorful silk in a pattern he'd never have chosen puddled onto his desk. *Huh.* He should've suspected things weren't going to work out for them when he'd opened the gift Clarissa had sent for his birthday last October. Holding the gaudy cloth over his trash can, he let it drop.

"Are you okay?" Evelyn peered at him, her brown eyes filled with concern.

"Other than the fact that she bailed at the worst possible time, I think so. I thought it'd hurt more, but frankly, I'm more irritated about her leaving me in the lurch than anything else."

"Well, I never liked her. Not even a little bit." Evelyn's hand sliced through the air.

"As for the review, you know you can count on me."

"Can you handle the extra load? You're already doing so much." He searched his cousin's face, relieved at the serious look that darkened her eyes. He ran a hand through his hair. "I promise. I'll make it up to you."

"Well, I wouldn't turn down a day at the spa when all this is over." Evelyn's gaze softened. She sank onto one of the office chairs and slung denim-clad legs over the arm. "Honestly, though, there's no need. We're family. We help each other out. It's what we do. Besides, we can't afford to mess up this thing with *Weddings Today*. It's too important for Heart's Landing. I'll go over everything online, but what's first on the agenda?"

He'd tinkered with the schedule enough that it was etched in his brain. "Regina Charm is due to arrive late Friday, but I've been warned that she likes her little surprises, so we'll start watching for her first thing. We have the big reception that evening—the mayor and business owners from town will be here. You'll want to dress for the occasion." Evelyn's usual jeans and a T-shirt weren't going to pass muster. "Then, there's the Smith wedding on Wednesday night and the pageant next Saturday."

"Okay. We're doing the whole Mary-and-the-Captain routine for those?"

"Yeah." The two of them often received standing ovations when, dressed to the nines as Captain Thaddeus and Mary Heart, they performed at weddings. Jason snapped his fingers. In preparation for Clarissa's arrival, he'd had a replica of Mary's gown cleaned and pressed and hung in the closet of the guest suite in the family wing. He waited a beat, half expecting the searing heartache he'd heard others talk about after their love lives shipwrecked. When the only thing that hurt was his pride, he winced. He and Clarissa hadn't had the kind of love that would last a lifetime. He could see that now. He probably ought to be thanking his lucky stars that he hadn't proposed to her, but he couldn't help wondering when—or if—he'd ever fall in love.

"You were saying?"

Evelyn's voice reminded him that life went on. "Would you mind grabbing the dress from the Opal room?"

"Sure. No problem." Evelyn swung her feet to the floor. "Why don't I get my notebook, and we can go over everything in detail, just to make sure I'm up to speed. We can work over lunch. I'll order in. Do you want anything special?"

"Nah. Whatever you get is fine. As long

as it's not a Craigen sub." He paused to mentally cross an item off his list of favorites. He'd never eat another one of those as long as he lived.

Chapter Four

"NEXT STOP, HEART'S LANDING. HEART'S Landing, next stop." In a black suit and vest, a short-billed hat clamped on his head, the train conductor rocked from side-to-side, making his way down the aisle of the coach car.

Eager for her first glimpse of the town, Tara looked up from her laptop. Her back ached from sitting hunched over for so long, but she hadn't wanted to disturb her sleeping seat mate so, other than a quick foray to the dining car, she'd worked the entire seven-hour trip.

Too bad corporate credit cards were off limits to junior reporters—even ones on important, secret missions. Otherwise, she could have rented a car and gotten here in half the time. She rolled her shoulders and flexed her toes. It was just as well. Relying on public transportation would allow her to take a closer look at the services Heart's Landing provided.

She powered down the laptop that had put itself to sleep again and slipped it into the carry case at her feet. Beyond the window, fields and low stone fences gave way to Cathedral Heights, a neighborhood of tidy houses that boasted more than the usual amount of gingerbread trim. In the distance, a church spire soared above slate-roofed buildings. Slowing, the train rolled through a street crossing at Boutonniere Drive. They crawled past Procession and Honeymoon Avenues. At last, with a screech of brakes, the car rocked to a stop at the Champagne Avenue Station. Tara grabbed her backpack and purse, slung her camera bag over one shoulder, and edged past the woman who snored softly in the next seat.

On the loading platform, she snapped a couple of quick pictures while she drank in warm, fresh air that carried the faintest trace of the ocean and brought back a flood of memories. Her parents had packed up the SUV and driven from their Savannah home to Tybee Island nearly every weekend through the summer and, most years, well into the fall. But it had been too long since she'd been close enough to the beach to get her feet wet. The smell of Heart's Landing reminded her of the long walks she used to take along the shore. She could use one of those right now to work out the kinks after spending the trip researching everything she could find online about Captain Thaddeus Heart. She made her way to the luggage rack, where she traded a baggage claim for her suitcase. Lugging her bags, she headed for the small train station.

She remained on the lookout for anything that might lower Heart's Landing's score in the competition, but she couldn't find fault with the cute hearts and flowers that adorned the door handle. Nor with the string of hearts that lined a cheery wallpaper border above freshly painted mint-colored walls.

"Excuse me," she said, stepping to the window where a lone clerk sat behind a glassed-in counter. "Where can I get a cab?" This wasn't New York City, after all, where hailing a taxi was as simple as raising her arm.

"You headed to the Union Street Bed and Breakfast, are ya? Marybeth and Matt will send a van to get you." Inquisitive brown eyes took her measure as the clerk waited a beat. "Or there's a shuttle that'll take you to the hotels on the north side of town. It runs every hour on the hour." With a glance at the clock, she added, "The next one will be here in ten minutes."

Tara smiled, soothed by the rounded vowels and softened R's of the clerk's accent. It was nice to get a real answer to her question, too. She'd grown used to abrupt replies in bustling New York, when people deigned to answer at all. "I appreciate that, but I'm not going to either of those places. I'm headed to the Captain's Cottage."

The clerk aimed a quizzical look at her ringless finger. "Newly engaged, are ya? If you're planning to hold your wedding there, you couldn't find a more beautiful setting. Is Alicia expecting you? She and her assistant Jennifer schedule all the events at the Cottage. You just tell them Georgia sent you." The clerk brushed a finger under her name tag. "They'll give you the VIP treatment." Georgia smothered a laugh with one hand. "That's a little joke. All our brides receive the VIP treatment. Do you need some place to store your bags during your appointment? I'd be happy to keep them here if you'd like." Still talking a mile a minute, Georgia half rose from her chair.

"Thanks for the offer, but it won't be necessary." Tara waved the clerk back into her seat. "I'm staying there while I'm in town."

"Hmmm. Are you sure? They don't

normally have overnight guests. Unless..."
Georgia canted her head. Her expressive
brown eyes grew even warmer. "You're Clarissa, aren't you? Oh, my! The whole town's
been dying to meet you."

"Um, no. I'm afraid you have me confused with someone else."

"You aren't Jason's sweetheart?" Disappointment pooled in the woman's eyes.

"Jason Heart?" The owner of the Captain's Cottage. Tara had found several
references to Thaddeus's great-great-great-
grandson during her research. "I'm afraid
not, but I am meeting with him."

"That's too bad. For a minute there, I
thought I'd be the first one to welcome her
to Heart's Landing. But I guess not. Now,
where were we?"

"About that cab?" Tara brushed a hand
through her hair. The conversation with
Georgia had taken so many turns, she'd
almost forgotten what brought her to the
clerk's window.

"Oh, yes. Sorry about that. Let's see.
With all the hotels and the bed and breakfasts providing transportation for their
guests, taxi drivers don't normally meet the
trains. But I'd be happy to call one for you."

"That'd be great. I appreciate it." Tara
adjusted her purse strap at her shoulder.
She hadn't planned on having to play twenty

questions in order to get a simple cab ride across town, but she had to admit, it'd been nice to talk to someone who delivered customer service with interest and a smile.

"There's a bench outside the station. If you want to wait there, someone will be along in just a few minutes. Meantime, can I get you anything? Water? Coffee?"

The woman took going above and beyond to such a high level, Tara almost regretted turning her down. But she'd grabbed a bite in the dining car at lunch. As for something to drink, she had a bottle of water in her purse. Her suitcase rolling along behind her, she waved goodbye to Georgia and stepped smartly toward the door. Outside, a light breeze brought another breath of salt-laden air. Low-growing plants with fragrant pink and white blossoms filled nearby flower beds. Their perfume scented the air while she lingered by her bags.

Sure enough, not five minutes later, a yellow cab pulled to the curb. Tara barely had a chance to gather her things before a gangly young man doffed his cap her way. "I'm Chuck. You the lady who called for a ride?" Given the decided lack of other passengers standing about, he didn't wait for a reply but hefted her suitcase. In seconds, he'd lowered it gently into the trunk of the idling taxi and held the door open for her.

"Where are we headed?" he asked as Tara slid onto the back seat.

"The Captain's Cottage." She braced herself for another round of questions, but Chuck merely shrugged and climbed in behind the wheel.

"Welcome to Heart's Landing, America's Top Wedding Destination. Are there any stops you'd like to make along the way?"

"No, but I'd appreciate it if you took your time. I want to take it all in." Tara glanced out the window and frowned. How she was supposed to criticize tree-lined streets, buildings etched with hearts and flowers, and quaint houses that nearly bent beneath gingerbread trim, she didn't know.

"This is your first trip to Heart's Landing, then?" Pulling away from the train station, Chuck turned east onto Champagne Avenue. He gestured toward a two-story building where cedar siding had aged to a burnished silver. "That's the Union Street Bed and Breakfast. You can't go wrong staying there. Marybeth and Matt take real good care of their guests."

Tara noted the pristine white picket fence and the bright blossoms that spilled from window boxes. She'd be hard-pressed to say anything negative about the exterior of the inviting building. If the interior was as well-maintained, she'd consider staying there on her next trip to Heart's Landing. If there was another trip, she corrected. Once *Weddings Today* published her article, she doubted anyone in town would welcome her with open arms.

"Since this is your first visit here, I'll give you the nickel tour. On the house." Chuck leaned forward and shut off the meter. At the next intersection, he pointed to a statue in a pocket park. "That's Captain Thaddeus Heart. He founded Heart's Landing in the 1800s. There's a plaque at the base of the statue that tells all about him. You should check it out if you have the time." Pointing out other places of interest, he wove up and down city streets. Festive signs in front of buildings offered everything imaginable in the way of wedding supplies and services. At the end of the street, he turned onto Officiant Way.

"Captain Thaddeus sailed the trade routes between here and Europe for a dozen years or more. Each summer, he'd return home in time for his wife's birthday. The place where his ship put in is north of here, called Heart's Cove." He pointed to a bike path that followed the rocky coastline. "Makes a nice, scenic ride, if you're inclined."

Tara crossed her fingers and hoped there'd be time for a trip to the beach while she was in town. The only time she'd taken

the train from Penn Station to Long Island,
one glimpse of people sitting shoulder-to-
shoulder on the sand had been enough
to send her back to the station without
even dipping her toes into the water. Here,
though, only a few umbrellas dotted the
wide, empty beach, and birds, rather than
people, darted among the waves.

A little farther down the road, Chuck
headed north on Bridal Carriage Way. "This
is the center of Heart's Landing. Anywhere
else, it'd probably be called Main Street. But
we stick to a wedding theme."

"I can see that."

"As they say, when you got it, flaunt it.
And we got weddings."

Appreciating the humor, Tara smiled
broadly into the rear view mirror while the
driver rolled past restaurants and stores.
Hand-in-hand, couples roamed the tree-
shaded sidewalks, ducking in and out of
shops with whimsical names like Something
Old/Something New, I Do Cakes, and Forget
Me Knot Flowers. Everywhere Tara looked,
fresh paint glowed from the trim on red
brick buildings. Bright awnings beckoned
shoppers to linger at display windows. Asters, tiny pink roses, and milkweed dripped
from window boxes. Steeplebush and day
lilies sprang from strategically placed pots,
brightening the streets with dashes of color.

The town was every bit as picturesque as her research had indicated. In fact, it was better than she'd expected, and her lips tightened. Regina had been right. It'd be tough to find anything wrong with Heart's Landing.

Despite a green light, Chuck idled at Procession. Tara caught the faint sound of jangling metal, which grew louder as a pair of high-stepping horses pulled into view. From his seat on the white carriage behind them, a driver in black livery doffed his hat. A bride decked out in her wedding finery smiled out from plush, red-velvet cushions. Chuck returned the gesture with a friendly wave.

"The driver's Tom Denton. He's a good friend. They're headed to the church at the end of the block," he explained. "From there, he'll take the lucky couple to their reception. Which might very well be at the Captain's Cottage. We'll head there now so we don't end up photo bombing any of the wedding photos."

With that, Chuck turned onto Procession. At the end of the long street sat the fabled Captain's Cottage. Tara sucked in a breath. Impressive in pictures, the mansion looked absolutely gorgeous with the late-afternoon sun glinting off the pristine masonry. She struggled to take in the details, but there was so much to see, she didn't

Leigh Duncan

know where to look first. Blooming azaleas in bright reds, pinks, and whites peppered the lawn and perfumed the air with a spicy scent. Clusters of weeping willows dripped gracefully over a stream. Neatly trimmed hedges followed the curving driveway to a porte cochere deep enough to accommodate several arriving vehicles.

Chuck braked to a stop at the foot of wide steps that led to massive double-doors. "This is the end of the ride. Your fare will pop up on the card reader. Cash or credit is fine. There are business cards in the seat pocket. Take a couple. I'd be happy to take you anywhere you need to go while you're here."

With a swipe of her credit card, she balanced the ridiculously small bill with a generous tip. By time she retrieved the receipt, Chuck had toted her luggage up the steps and left her bags inside the front door. He returned to offer a hand while she exited the vehicle. She smiled at him. "Thank you for a wonderful tour." She tapped her purse. "I have your card. You'll probably hear from me again soon."

"My pleasure, ma'am." And with that, he was off, heading for the main road and presumably his next fare.

Tara peered up at the three-story house that had once been home to a seafaring captain, his wife, and their thirteen children. With its large, airy veranda and wings that spread out in different directions, the Cottage was certainly large enough to accommodate such a big family. Which was ironic, considering that an influenza outbreak in the 1890s had nearly wiped out the entire Heart clan. However, according to her research, a direct line of Thaddeus's descendants had called the Captain's Cottage their home for generations. Fifty years ago, things had changed when the captain's great-great-grandson had capitalized on the town's growing reputation and had turned the estate into one of the most popular wedding venues on the East Coast.

Her flats made soft, scuffing noises on the steps. Wishing she'd taken the time to change out of her travel clothes and into something a little more refined and appropriate for visiting such a lovely place, she stepped through the front door into the roomy foyer of a house that had known tender care for more than a century. She sniffed, inhaling a light, citrusy scent mixed with linseed oil. A larger-than-life portrait of Captain Thaddeus looked down on her from the wall across from the entrance. Though she'd seen the image in books, she took a moment to study the painting. From his feathered hat to his pointed shoes, he cut an impressive figure, but his face captured her attention. A pair of intelligent-looking eyes stared out from beneath thick brows. High cheekbones and skin lined by the sun and the wind surrounded a Grecian nose and finely drawn lips. Below, a square chin led to a jaw as well defined and straight-edged as the rest of him. The artist had posed the captain at the helm of his ship and had managed to capture him so much at ease that she could practically feel the salt spray or hear the wind whistling in the rigging and the cries of seabirds on the hunt for food.

The artwork was beyond intriguing. She could have stood there all day admiring it, but the rest of the house beckoned. Wide corridors stretched to the left and right. With an imaginary flip of a coin, she headed left. She hoped to ask directions to Jason Heart's office, but no one lingered at the coffee pots that stood on an elaborate sideboard in the dining room. A little farther down the hall, two sets of wide double-doors opened into a spacious ballroom. Massive chandeliers dripped crystals like icicles over what must have been an acre of hardwood floors. She felt a ping of disappointment that preparations for a wedding weren't underway, but the tall tables scattered throughout the room reminded her more of cocktail parties and casual gatherings. Leaving the ballroom, she moved forward, the soles of her shoes sounding loud in the empty corridor.

Where was everyone? Sure, no one was expecting her—she had, after all, followed Regina's orders and arrived a full day early. But the entire Captain's Cottage couldn't be sitting empty on a Thursday afternoon. Could it?

She poked her head into several other vacant rooms before a sharp right turn took her to a corridor with doors opening onto offices. A tasteful sign mounted by the first one on the left announced that it belonged to Alicia Thorn, Event Coordinator. Pens neatly arranged in a holder, a single tablet of paper, and a computer monitor sat on the well-organized desk. On the wall, today's date had been X'd out on a calendar that tracked weddings and appointments. Beginning to wonder if she'd need to call Chuck and have him drive her to a hotel after all, Tara moved on.

From somewhere nearby came the sound of someone humming. Drawn to the tune she recognized as a piece she'd sung with her church choir recently, she picked up her pace. Three offices down, she peered through an open doorway. Dressed in a simple T-shirt, her hair a mass of dark curls around an elfin face, a woman about her own age stared at a computer with rapt attention.

Tara knocked on the doorframe.

The humming stopped abruptly. The woman leaned out from behind the oversized monitor. "Hey! I didn't see you there. Are you looking for Alicia?"

Assuming she meant the event coordinator, Tara shook her head. "No. Actually, I was hoping you could tell me how to get to Jason Heart's office."

"Is he expecting you?" The woman frowned. "I didn't think he had any appointments on his calendar this afternoon."

Tara crossed the room, her hand extended. "I'm Tara Stewart from *Weddings Today*. I'm here to handle the magazine's evaluation of Heart's Landing."

If she'd wanted to surprise someone, she couldn't have planned it better. The frown on the woman's face deepened. She darted from behind the desk to meet her guest halfway across the room. "We weren't expecting you until tomorrow."

"I'm a little early." Tara tried not to squirm beneath an intense once-over. Despite the fact that her hostess was just as informally dressed as she was, she wished again she'd had the chance to swap her jeans and cardigan for something a little more professional.

"Humph," the woman said, folding her arms across her chest. "We were expecting Regina Charm."

"You've got me there. I'm Tara Stewart," she repeated. "Ms. Charm has been unavoidably detained in New York. She sent me in her stead." Though she'd love to emulate Regina's innate sense of style, Tara was pretty sure she could live in the Big Apple for the rest of her life without acquiring it. Still, she had to try. Imagining how the editor would react under similar circumstances, she aimed for a haughty tone. "I trust that won't be a problem?"

The question dangled in the air for a long moment. At last, the woman's mouth worked. As if it had never been there, the frown disappeared. "I'm sure it'll be fine. You caught me off guard, that's all. Wait till Jason gets a load of you. He's gonna flip his wig."

"Really?" Tara lifted her eyebrows.

"Forget I said anything." Grinning, she shrugged. "Me and my big mouth—that's one of the reasons they tuck me away in a back office. Mostly, I handle the bookkeeping and supplies for the Captain's Cottage. I don't get many visitors back here. I'm Evelyn, by the way. Jason is my cousin." Evelyn folded her hands together and twisted her fingers. "So, how long have you been with *Weddings Today*?"

"About two years."

Evelyn whistled. "You must be really good if they sent you instead of Ms. Charm. I'd like to have a job that sent me all around the country. I bet you meet a lot of celebrities, don't you?"

The young woman looked so expectant that Tara hated to disappoint her. The truth was, her inbox provided the only contact she had with the models and superstars who graced the magazine's covers. Unless she counted coffee runs—which she didn't—this was her first assignment outside the office. A tidbit of information she definitely did not plan on sharing with Evelyn. "Not many. But I'm hoping that'll change soon."

"We get them here every once in a while. Last Christmas, the whole town buzzed when Karolyn Karter and Chad Grant showed up for her cousin's wedding. You'll probably meet her while you're here. Jennifer Longely. Well, Bell now. She's a nice girl. Different from what we all thought of her when she first got here."

"How so?" She recognized the name from Regina's notes. Her boss had thought there was more to that story, as well, and had told her to be on the lookout in case she caught wind of a juicy rumor.

"Oh, you know." As if she realized she'd said too much, Evelyn retreated toward her desk. "I, uh, I should check Jason's schedule to see if he's in his office."

Unwilling to push her luck by probing deeper into something that wasn't at the top of her agenda, Tara let the matter drop. Karolyn Karter occupied a top spot on Hollywood's A-list, but her appearance in Heart's Landing was old news and definitely took a back seat to her current assignment. Besides, Evelyn's openness and candor might come in handy. So far, everyone she'd met in Heart's Landing had been gracious and accommodating, almost to a fault. Evelyn made a refreshing, forthright change of pace. Under different circumstances, they'd probably be good friends.

While Evelyn fiddled with her computer, Tara took the opportunity to look around. It appeared that, unlike Alicia Thorne, her hostess-of-the-moment was a bit of a pack rat. Stacks of papers and files crowded every inch of the bookkeeper's desk space. Cardboard boxes filled one corner of the small office. Like colorful tongues, swatches poked out of the sample catalogues that had been stacked along the walls and crowded the chairs.

"Looks like you're in luck. Jason doesn't have anything on his calendar. I'll let him know you're here...before I say something else I shouldn't."

"Sure. That sounds great," she said, though she wished she could see Jason's reaction first-hand.

Evelyn made the call. Then, leading the way, she headed for the office at the end of the hall. She didn't wait for an invitation but crossed the threshold like a woman on a mission. "Jason, I'd like to introduce Tara Stewart from *Weddings Today*. Tara, my cousin Jason Heart, the owner of the Captain's Cottage."

The figure behind the desk rose with a smooth grace. Tara got a quick impression of a man with the same regal bearing as his great-great-great-grandfather. Nor did the familial resemblance stop there. Tall and muscular, Jason Heart towered over her own five-foot-six-inch frame. A thick mop of jet-black hair barely brushed his shoulders. High cheekbones similar to the ones in the portrait in the foyer led to a sharply angled jaw. She extended her hand and stared up into slate-gray eyes the color of the sea beneath a cloudy sky. A touch of vertigo hit her when his palm grasped hers. It passed just as swiftly as it came when, after giving her hand a firm shake, his fingers dropped from hers.

"Welcome to Heart's Landing and the

Captain's Cottage," Jason said. "We're very glad to have you here. Although, you've caught me a bit flat-footed. I must admit I'm confused. We were told to expect Ms. Charm. Tomorrow. Has there been a change of plans?"

"I told Evelyn that Ms. Charm has been unavoidably detained in New York." Tara darted a glance at the woman who lingered nearby. "That's not entirely true."

"No?"

Two sets of eyes bore into her, but Tara had practiced what she'd say during the long train ride. "No. See, the thing is, Ms. Charm didn't want her own experiences in Heart's Landing to influence the town's chances in the contest. She was afraid that coming here again so soon after her breakup might stir up bad memories. She sent me to take a fresh, in-depth look at the place, but don't worry. Since Heart's Landing has consistently emerged as the magazine's top pick for ten years running, this visit is more a formality than anything else." She shrugged. "As for my early arrival, that's entirely my fault. My last project wrapped up sooner than expected, and I'd been so looking forward to the trip that I thought I'd just pop on up. I hope that's not a problem."

"Nothing we can't handle." Bright intelligence gleamed from Jason's gray eyes.

67

Tara couldn't be sure he accepted Regina's excuse, but he definitely wasn't buying the reason for her sudden appearance for a second and had the self-confidence not to care whether she realized he was on to her or not. "Of course, you're missing out on all the pomp and ceremony of the formal greeting party we had on tomorrow's agenda. And our mayor, Greg Thomas, will be disappointed that he wasn't on hand to welcome you himself. He's planned a tour of Heart's Landing for you tomorrow. With the packed schedule we have planned over the next ten days, he and his wife went out of town for the afternoon. I'm afraid you're stuck with me for now."

She could think of worse ways to spend the time than in the company of a man who reminded her so much of his swashbuckling ancestor, though it seemed like a far more prudent plan to keep her distance from someone who literally upset her equilibrium. She tugged on the hem of her wrinkled T-shirt. "I'd love the opportunity to freshen up after the long trip. Do you think you could have someone show me to my room?"

Jason's lips thinned. "We'll have so much going on over the next two weeks that we gave most of the staff the day off. There's only a skeleton crew on duty today. As I mentioned, we weren't expecting you before tomorrow." The skin around his mouth tightened. "I've pulled two of our best workers off their other tasks and told them to prepare your suite, but it might be several hours before they finish. I'm sorry for the inconvenience." All gracious apology and sorrow, he ducked his head.

This was exactly the kind of snafu Regina had told her to be on the lookout for. Tara supposed this was the point where her boss might have pitched a hissy fit and checked one of the many negative boxes on her judging form. But, as much as she wanted to please the executive editor, Tara wasn't Regina. Jason's well-mannered explanation had touched a soft space in her heart. She couldn't condemn him for not having everything ready when she'd sprung her arrival on him without any warning. Given the popularity of the Captain's Cottage, she should probably be thankful her room was available at all.

"There's a fully stocked salon reserved for our brides on the first floor. No one's using it right now, so you're welcome to it. As for the rest of the day, I can offer you several options. It'd be my honor to escort you into town and introduce you to a few of our more prominent shop keepers. Or give you a tour of the Captain's Cottage. Or, if none of that appeals to you, the dining room is at your disposal. You're welcome to work in there."

Thanks, but no thanks on that last one. She'd spent most of the train ride doing research. The prospect of sitting at a table and poring over her laptop when there was so much to see and do around Heart's Landing seemed like a perfect waste. On the other hand, if they'd planned on showing her about town the next day, throwing another monkey wrench in the plans might raise too many eyebrows.

"I vote for the Captain's Cottage. I'd like to see every nook and cranny," she said with a growing enthusiasm. Who knew what secrets she might unearth? "There's no need to take up your valuable time, though. I'm sure I can see myself around."

"I wouldn't dream of sending you off on your own. There are so many twists and turns in this old place, you might get lost and we'd never find you again."

There was that glint in his eyes again. The one that said at this particular moment in time, he wouldn't mind getting her out of his hair. But if he expected her to disappear, he could think again. She fully intended to put her best effort into this assignment. She had too much riding on it to do otherwise.

"Then, it's settled," Jason said when she didn't respond. "Let me take your bags to the

Prep Room. I'll meet you in the foyer in…" He let the words trail off.

"Twenty minutes ought to do it." She just wanted to splash some water on her face, run a comb through her hair and, at most, replace her rumpled shirt.

Jason gave a curt nod to his cousin. "Evelyn, wait for me here, please?"

The attractive owner of the Captain's Cottage was being far too accommodating. The last thing Tara wanted was spend the afternoon with a man who smelled like the ocean and caused her to lose her balance. But what else was she to do? She couldn't very well ask him to share his family's darkest, dirtiest secrets with her. Not when everyone thought she was here to write a puff piece about America's long-time favorite wedding destination. Not when, in fact, she was here to destroy the myth behind it.

After dropping Tara's bags off in her temporary quarters, Jason double-timed it back to his office. They hadn't even reached the official start of the *Weddings Today* evaluation, and already, things had gone horribly awry. But his years at the helm of some of Boston's largest conference venues had taught him not to panic when things wandered from the plan. He'd get everything back on track. His thoughts racing with ideas, he burst into the room.

"Okay, Evelyn. We have a lot of work to do," he said getting right to business. "First, get the word out that this Tara Stewart person has arrived early and isn't at all who we expected."

Evelyn traced one finger along the top of the bookcase. "Do you think that's a problem?"

"Yeah. Unfortunately." Jason stared out the door. This was exactly the kind of thing he'd been afraid of when he'd heard that Regina Charm's wedding had crashed and burned in Heart's Landing. It didn't matter that the town had nothing to do with the breakup. The woman would naturally feel they were at least partly to blame. "She's young and, I'll bet, inexperienced. It's out of line to send someone like her to evaluate us. It makes me think there's something more afoot. We still have a chance, but we can't hold back. We'll have to double-down on everything in order to make an impression and win her over."

Evelyn straightened like a woman who knew what was at stake. "Okay. I'll let everyone know. I'll call Mildred and Cheri first. Word will spread like wildfire from there."

"Good." Jason nodded. "Next, I need you

to find out everything there is to know about our guest. Who she is. Where she went to school. How long she's been at *Weddings Today*. Her position there. I want to know everything right down to her favorite foods and if she has any allergies. We can't afford to mess this up, and I'm flying blind here."

"Got it." A troubled look crossed his cousin's face. "She seems like a nice person, though, doesn't she? You don't really think she's here to sabotage us or anything?"

What did he think? Alarms clanged in his head like the bells of the *Mary S* after the lookout in the crow's nest spotted a pirate ship. One that might have more powerful armament or a hidden army stowed below deck.

Oh, Tara Stewart seemed capable enough, though he knew little more than her other than what he'd been able to observe. From the top of a head that rose above his shoulders to a pair of casual slip-ons, the lean, angular physique of a runner made him question whether she was as independent and driven as most sports enthusiasts. He hadn't been able to glean anything from the hair that hung like sheaves of spun gold to her shoulders where soft curls turned the strands inward. But a wide forehead free of lines and the lack of crows' feet around a pair of blue eyes told him she'd barely dipped her toes into her thirties. At best, she'd been with *Weddings Today* for a couple of years. Certainly not long enough to attain the seniority he'd expect from someone who'd been given so much responsibility. That in itself was a huge red flag.

Yet, she hadn't shown the least bit of anger or concern when they didn't have everything ready for her. If this had been a complete setup, he'd have expected her to turn on one heel, head off in a huff, and demand to return to the city as soon as possible, thus eliminating Heart's Landing from the contest. Instead, she'd gone along with their new plan. Which told him they had a chance of swaying her opinion. And if they could do that, maybe they could still win.

He squared his shoulders. What was he thinking? Of course, they'd succeed. Everyone in town, from the mayor to the boys who sold roses from plastic buckets on the corner, had spent weeks—months, even—getting ready for this review. All they had to do now was let the town speak for itself. Once Tara Stewart saw all it had to offer, Heart's Landing would retain its place at the top of the heap.

But there couldn't be so much as one more snafu. Not with the town's reputation hanging in the balance.

"Okay, let me know when you hear back

from everyone. Feed me updates about her as you have them." Jason slipped his phone into his pocket and fitted the Bluetooth receiver into his ear. He tapped the switch. Static crackled. "I'll be available."

"Will do." Evelyn reached for her own phone. "Where are you going to be?"

"We'll start in the attic and work our way down." He paused.

Evelyn cast a look at the ceiling. "You think that's a good idea?"

"She said she wants to see everything. Taking her up there will show her how deep our roots go in Heart's Landing. Besides, you can tell a lot about a person by the way they react to a little dirt and dust."

"Well, you'll find plenty of that."

He frowned. "Did you move all the log books and diaries to the library like I asked?" Regina Charm had sent a special request to have the journals on hand.

"Yes. Last week."

"Good. We'll end up there."

"Do you have any idea why she wanted to see his books? No one's ever asked about them before."

"Who knows? Maybe it wasn't Regina's idea at all. Maybe this Tara person is a history buff. That's part of what I want you to find out." He checked his watch. The allotted twenty minutes was nearly up. "I'm on the move. If you need me, or you find out anything, I'm right here." He touched the device in his ear.

Striding toward the entryway, he reviewed everything that had happened so far in a day that had taken a sharp turn away from the script. Tara Stewart's early arrival was no mistake, that was for sure. Regina Charm's itinerary had been copied and plastered on every bulletin board in town. He hadn't written the wrong date on his calendar. He didn't accept that Tara had simply decided to put in an early appearance on a whim, either. There was no earthly reason for her to show up a day earlier than expected, unless it was a trap to catch the town with its proverbial britches down around its ankles to see how well everyone handled the change.

But sending what appeared to be a junior staffer to do the job, that was an entirely different matter. Why would Regina Charm do such a thing? Was she honestly trying to remain impartial after her own wedding crashed and burned in Heart's Landing? That had been Tara's explanation. Did he really believe her?

He shook his head. He had to. The alternative—that no matter how well they performed over the next ten days, Heart's

Landing was doomed to failure—was too difficult to even think about.

Chapter Five

J ASON RESISTED AN URGE TO shake his head. He'd half expected Tara Stewart to return from her brief respite with the poise and self-assurance of a veteran reporter. If anything, with her hair in a messy topknot while she stood staring up at the painting of his swashbuckling ancestor, she looked even less experienced. The camera she'd slung over one shoulder lent her a serious air, but the loose blouse with slits on both arms definitely wasn't professional attire. Evelyn had referred to the style as a cold shoulder. He hoped that wasn't indicative of the journalist's mood.

"You bear an almost uncanny resemblance to him, you know," she said, turning toward him as he strode down the hall. "I bet you get that a lot."

"You're not the first," he admitted. "Evelyn and I put it to good use, though. We often appear at weddings and receptions dressed as the Captain and Mary. Sing a duet or two. Mingle with the guests. People like it." He shrugged.

"Your cousin has a good ear. She was humming the 'Covenant Hymn' when I came in. That's not an easy piece."

"You sing, do you?" The melodic lilt in her voice intrigued him.

"In my church choir." She half laughed. "Not on stage like you do. That must give you quite a thrill, to stand in front of an audience and belt one out. Do you enjoy it?"

Did he? He and Evelyn had worked out their routines in order to fill the needs of brides who loved the history of Heart's Landing as much as they appreciated Rhode Island's rocky coast or the town's beautiful wedding venues. He'd never really stopped to ask whether he actually liked performing or not. Not that it mattered. "I'm all for anything that makes our brides happy. We aim to provide each and every one of them with a perfect wedding. Around here, that's all that counts."

"I'll probably hear some version of that line quite often while I'm in Heart's Landing, won't I?"

Tara had an easy grace about her. The

prospect of spending time with her over the next few days was far less intimidating than he'd expected it to be with Regina. He relaxed enough to let a small chuckle escape. "It's who we are here. We wish all our brides a Heart's Landing love for the ages. Then, there's our town motto. You'll probably hear 'the best is yet to be' repeated so often before you leave that you'll find yourself chiming in with everyone else."

"Well, I don't know about that." Tara tapped the thin notebook she carried in one hand. "I'm supposed to remain at least a little bit impartial while I'm here."

He cracked his knuckles and hoped that was exactly what she'd do. Remain impartial. If she gave them half a chance, he had no doubt she'd soon realize that Heart's Landing's perfect blend of charm and sophistication made it the best place in the country for brides to get married.

"Why don't we get started? I thought we could begin at the top as long as you don't mind climbing a few stairs." A quick glance confirmed the sensible shoes on her feet. "The view from the widow's walk is spectacular. From there, we can work our way down to the ballrooms and the smaller wedding venues."

Tara met his questioning look with a distant smile that reminded him she'd come to Heart's Landing with a job to do. Though it would be easy to convince himself they could be friends, he couldn't afford to let his guard down around her. Was she here to praise them, like she said? Or to cut them to ribbons? Whatever her goal, it was up to him to uncover the truth. Intent on finding out more about what made her tick, he led the way from the foyer to the grand staircase.

Might as well get started. He lobbed an easy question. "Where are you from, Tara?"

"Savannah, originally. My folks own a restaurant near Forsyth Park. My dad makes the best shrimp 'n grits in the entire state. Whenever it's on the menu, people line up out the door. Mom runs the front of the house. She keeps my two sisters hopping."

He leaned closer, pleasantly surprised by the faint trace of a Southern accent that softened the corners of her voice when she spoke about her family. "You didn't want to go into the family business?"

"Nope. I can make passable dishes, but I wasn't born with my dad's talent in the kitchen. My sister Lulu, now, that girl can cook! She'll take over the stove when my parents retire. Maggie, she's my mom's right hand."

Tara's answer struck him as just a little too polished in spite of her off-hand manner. Wanting to uncover the whole story, he probed a bit deeper. "No place for you? Is that why you moved to New York?"

"In part. Everyone says I was born with a pen in my hand. From the time I could print the alphabet, I've known that writing was my calling. When it came time for college, my folks wanted me to major in the business. They weren't thrilled when I studied journalism at the University of Georgia." Almost like an extension of her team's name, she peppered the conversation with a quick, *Go Bulldogs!* "Afterward, I landed an internship at *Weddings Today*. I've been there ever since. This assignment is my big chance to prove to my parents that I chose the right career." She canted her head. "But listen to me going on and on about my life when I'm the one who's supposed to be interviewing you."

She was a smart one. She'd caught on to him a lot faster than he'd thought she might. Going forward, he'd have to respect her intelligence. "What do you want to know?"

"Have you always lived in Heart's Landing?"

"You mean, have I ventured any farther than Newport?" he teased. "Yes. I spent ten years, give or take, in Boston after getting my Masters. Cornell. Hotel Management," he added, wondering if she'd be impressed. "No matter where I lived, though, this has always been my home. Running the Captain's Cottage is more than a job. It's a legacy. Passed from one generation of Hearts to the other. I'm proud to carry on that tradition." Reaching the first-floor landing, he ran his hand over the wooden railing much the same as his great-great-great-grandparents might have done. The familiar, smooth finish felt cool to his touch. He'd always known the Captain's Cottage would play a big part in his life's work. The various positions in Boston had merely provided an ample training ground for what was to come.

"And now you manage all of this." Tara paused to scribble in her notebook. When she looked up, she asked, "Was that the plan?"

"I thought I'd stay in Boston for a while longer. I managed conference centers and arenas there, and I liked the work. The people were interesting, and every once in a while, I rubbed elbows with superstars. But when my dad died, the timetable shifted."

"I'm sorry." Tara's voice dropped. "How long has it been?"

"A little less than two years." He stopped to clear his throat. More and more often, the good memories outweighed the bad. Still, the pain of losing him so early lingered, even after all this time.

"And your mom?"

He shook his head. "She died in a car accident when I was seven. It was just my dad and me after that."

"That had to be tough."

Was that an honest sympathy he heard in her voice? Much as he'd like to believe it was, he didn't know her well enough to tell whether the comment came from her heart or if she was simply mouthing a standard platitude. "So many have it so much worse," he said, meaning every word.

Though his childhood hadn't been ideal, he wouldn't choose another one. Connie, their head chef, had watched over him like a mother hen. She and the other cooks had always encouraged him to help himself to a cookie or a snack on his way through the kitchen. He'd learned woodworking skills and the fine points of preservation from helping his dad make repairs around the Cottage. The pond in the back made the perfect place to ice skate in the winter or catch fish in the summer. The kids he'd slid down the banister with on snowy afternoons were still his closest friends. So, maybe he hadn't had a mother, but he'd definitely been loved. Lately, though, he'd begun to wonder if his mother's loss had had a bigger impact on him than he'd thought. Was that the reason he hadn't been able to find happiness with

Clarissa or any of the other women he'd dated?

A thought for another day, he mused.

They reached the third floor, where railings overlooked the cavernous space below. Reaching for the key he'd taken from the rack in his office, he explained, "We keep the attic locked because, well, it's an attic. Mostly, we use this area to store seasonal gear and other items no longer in use. I'd be happy to bring you up here any time you'd like, but we don't really want anyone wandering around unescorted. Can't have someone getting hurt if they bump a shelf and it falls over, can we?" He didn't wait for an answer.

He slipped the key in the ancient lock and gave it a sharp twist. With a whisper, one of a pair of double doors swung open to reveal a room that stretched out in either direction and covered the main part of the entire house. He took a deep breath as he preceded her over the threshold. The attic's cool, dry air had always reminded him of history and stability. Shelves crowded with appliances and bric-a-brac from days gone by filled a quarter of the space. Covered in cloth, furniture pieces loomed out of the shadows. Farthest from the exterior wall stood built-in cases filled with books.

"This place is amazing!" Tara's soft gasp

stirred motes in the shaft of light that poured through one of the evenly spaced octagonal windows. "It's like a museum." She sneezed.

"A dusty one. Watch you don't brush up against something and ruin your clothes. We probably could do a better job of keeping things spic 'n' span up here, but people so rarely come to the attic, it's hardly worth the trouble." He took a handkerchief from his back pocket and handed it to her.

"Thanks." She pressed it briefly to her nose. "But I thought you said we were heading to the widow's walk."

"We are. That door opens onto it. I thought you wanted to see everything." He pointed across the room where chifferobes and armoires held clothes that dated back several generations. "This is all part of the history of the Captain's Cottage."

"Impressive. Mind if I look around a bit?"

"Take your time. We're supposed to get some rain later this afternoon, but I think we're safe for now."

He idled by the door, unable to prevent a grin from stretching across his face while she silently pored over items on the closest shelves. When she made her way to the tall wardrobes, his smile widened while she traced her fingertips across the metal tags. Stopping at one, she pulled out a beaded silver dress. Foot-long fringe dripped from the hem.

"That belonged to my great-grandmother. She wore it when she danced the Charleston to Paul Whiteman and His Orchestra," he recited from memory.

"Your great-grandmother was a flapper girl?" Tara's eyes shot up.

"Among other things. Socialite, homemaker, businesswoman. She single-handedly kept this place afloat during World War I. Converted both the ballrooms downstairs into workrooms and enlisted every woman in town in the war effort."

"Wow!"

"She was quite the character." Thinking of all she'd accomplished in an era where women had often been seen and not heard sent a rush of pride through his chest. "I was just a child when she passed, but even into her late eighties, she had a sharp wit."

Tara carefully returned the gown to the closet. "She sounds like someone I wish I'd met."

"Her diaries are on one of those shelves." He pointed toward the built-in bookcases on an interior wall. "I'm sure we can find them if you want."

"I'd like that. Not right now, though. There's so much else to see." With the eagerness of a true explorer, she started toward the door that led to the widow's walk. "I bet the view is terrific from up here."

"It is that." He strode past her, his hand reaching for the set of keys. Putting his shoulder to the heavy wood, he pushed. The door squeaked open. A stiff breeze blew into the room. It carried the fresh scent of ozone and salt. He'd checked the weather before they'd come upstairs, but apparently a forecasted evening storm had come ashore earlier than expected. "Shoot. I think we're out of luck."

Rain fell in gentle sheets in front of him, turning the distant ocean a gray-blue. Water dripped from the eaves onto the slate tiles. Closer than he liked, lightning arced from the sky to the waves. Disappointment rolled through him. The view from the widow's walk was spectacular in the sunshine. Not so much in the middle of a storm.

"I guess we'll have to save this for another time. It's not safe to go out there now. The tiles get very slick when they're wet." Hoping Tara wouldn't be too frustrated, he crossed his fingers.

"Not a problem. It's still a pretty view. Tell me about the widow's walk. What's its purpose?"

"Before the radio was invented in the Twenties, wives and loved ones watched the seas for arriving ships. Captain Thaddeus was a merchant sailor—he plied the ocean between Boston and London. There were huge profits to be made in bringing silks and teas from the Indies, returning with bales of cotton or tobacco. But it was a harsh life, too. Filled with dangerous storms, slack winds, the occasional pirate, even. He always made it home in time for his wife's birthday, though. October 21st. Starting in late August, Mary spent so much time out here watching for him, she literally wore footsteps in the slate tiles."

"If I recall the stories, she also tied herself to the railing at one point, didn't she?"

So, Tara knew more than she let on. Or she thought she did. Good thing he had an advantage she didn't possess—as a teen, he'd pored over the ship's logs and the Captain's journals until he practically knew them by heart.

"Not exactly," he corrected. "In 1897, when the Captain's ship was overdue, a late-season hurricane struck. She had the servants lash her to the posts. She was sure he'd shipwreck at Heart's Cove." He pointed to a jagged outcropping that was barely visible in the rain.

"Was it a bad storm?"

"When you're at sea in a wooden boat, there aren't any good ones." He'd gotten caught out on the open water in a squall when he was fifteen. The experience had given him a wary respect for the ocean. "This particular hurricane sank the *Triton* off Pinar del Rio. One hundred-eighty-eight men died that day. Fortunately for us, the storm died down a bit before it hit Block Island. By then, the winds had dropped to below sixty miles an hour."

"The Captain made it home, I take it?"

"He did. A good thing, too. Otherwise, I wouldn't be here. Mary gave birth to a son nine months later. He became my great-great-grandfather."

He closed the door and led the way across the room. "We'll come back another day when it's bright and sunny." By then, he hoped to learn whether or not Tara had a hidden agenda.

The tall man on the staircase beside her exuded poise and charm, but Tara sensed a vulnerability beneath his cool exterior. Did he feel threatened by her presence in his house? Silly question. He'd be a fool not to, and she had the unshakeable feeling that Jason Heart was no one's fool. He was well aware that, with the stroke of a pen, she had the ability to change the face of Heart's Landing until the next review. Or longer.

Unfortunately, that was exactly what she was here to do and, in her position as a junior reporter, she didn't have much of a choice. Which was a shame, because everything she'd seen so far told her the town deserved to hang onto its designation as the best wedding destination in the country. From the gently rolling hills surrounding Heart's Landing to the vast ocean at its back door, from the quaint shops and tree-lined streets to the many restaurants she'd spotted during her taxi ride and the people who'd made her feel welcome despite her unexpected appearance, every detail had been picture perfect. And that was before she'd stepped foot in the Captain's Cottage. Which was truly show-stopping.

She trailed Jason down the flight of stairs, imagining herself making the same descent a hundred years ago. She'd have chattered with a bevy of girlfriends and sisters as they descended, each dressed for paying call on friends and neighbors in full satin skirts and blouses with big, puffy sleeves. Hats piled high with feathers and flowers. In the Roaring Twenties, she'd have made a grand entrance dressed to dance the night away wearing that incredible beaded frock she'd pulled from the wardrobe. After all this time, the silver fabric had still shimmered, the silk had rustled beneath her touch, the beads had clinked softly. Had she imagined the faint whiff of cologne that perfumed the air? She must have.

She cupped her jaw between her thumb and her finger. What had Mary worn during the storm? Had she stood at the edge of the railing, the rain pelting while her ribbons and bows rippled in the wind? Anyone seeing her there would think she'd gone mad, soaked to the skin with her long, black hair whipping about her. Clinging for dear life to the banister while she prayed for the safe return of her man.

Of course, that was a bunch of hogwash. Jason had all but admitted the story couldn't be true when he'd cautioned her about the dangers of venturing onto the widow's walk in the rain. Then there was the path Mary had supposedly worn. Tara didn't care how often the story had been repeated. Slate was hard. That was why they used it for roofing material. It was preposterous to think that Mary had worn grooves in the tiles. Not when the woman had had a dozen mouths to feed and an enormous household to run. In that day and age, someone—her housekeeper, if no one else—would've barred the door and kept the mistress from doing something that would end up getting her put away "for her own good."

She had to admit, though, the story was

intriguing. A real Heart's Landing love for the ages. Did Jason know it was a lie? Was that the reason for the streak of vulnerability she felt wafting from his wide shoulders? Or did it have to do with something else entirely?

She palmed one hand to her face. In all the excitement of her arrival, she'd forgotten the message she was supposed to deliver. She cleared her throat. "Georgia at the train station said to say hello. She thought I was someone else at first. She asked me to tell you she'd let you know as soon as Clarissa arrives."

"I didn't realize." Jason's foot hesitated the tiniest bit before it landed on the next step. "I'll have to give Georgia a call. She has enough to do. She doesn't need to waste her time."

Jason's abrupt dismissal tingled her reporter's antenna. "Who's Clarissa anyway? A friend?" *A girlfriend?* Not that it was any of her business.

"I thought so, but not anymore." He turned to her. "I might as well tell you. You'll probably find out anyway. Clarissa and I had been seeing each other for quite some time. She was supposed to be here this week to help with the evaluation. We were going to perform together at the Smith wedding on Sunday, and she had the lead part in the pageant next week. But business kept her in

Boston, and we've had a, uh, falling out. My cousin Evelyn will take her place."

The intensity of his gaze sharpened, but she only shrugged. One of the most important aspects of putting on a large event like a wedding was the ability to roll with the punches. Something always went wrong. The wedding cake tumbled off its pedestal. The bouquet wilted. The train ripped away from the bride's gown. A good staff addressed the problems with no one being the wiser. They served cupcakes adorned with tiny sparklers. They tossed the brown blossoms in the trash and had the bride carry her family Bible down the aisle. They reached for an emergency sewing kit and repaired the errant fabric. Being able to cope with a change in plans was an asset, not a detraction, and Jason's backup plan sounded solid.

"I'm sorry she cancelled on you," she murmured while he waited for her to say something more. "Sometimes there's no telling who's going to let you down."

"Yeah. Better to find out now than later, I guess." He paused at the landing. "I suspect she was just waiting for the right opportunity to break things off. It's true what they say—long distance relationships are impossible to maintain." He straightened. "The upside is that with Clarissa out of the picture, I'll have more time to devote to my responsibilities around here."

Tara had to give the guy credit. When she'd discovered the numbers of dozens of other women in her boyfriend's phone, when she'd learned he hadn't even listed her as one of his Favorites, she'd cut that relationship off at the knees. It had been the right thing to do, but it had still taken two boxes of tissues and a vat of ice cream before she was over him. Jason's breakup had to sting, too, but he wasn't moping around like someone who'd recently had his heart broken. Quite the opposite. She doubted he'd have mentioned it at all if it hadn't been for Georgia. Was that a guy's perspective? Or had he sensed something wrong in the relationship all along? Whatever it was, when she looked up, he'd moved on. She followed him into the comfortable seating area that filled a cozy nook on the floor below the attic.

In a gilt frame, a large picture mirror hung over a narrow table. The strategically placed counter made a convenient place for storing items ready to take downstairs. Books, photos, and a knitting basket gave the area a personal feel.

"Originally, this floor was reserved for guests," Jason said. "Once we opened the Cottage to the public, the family moved to the third floor. My quarters are on this side."

He hooked a thumb over his shoulder at a crooked corridor. "Evelyn's are on the other."

Tara glanced down a hall that seemed to stretch forever. "Do you use the entire space?" A dozen apartments the size of hers in New York could fit into each area, with room to spare.

Her question drew another healthy chuckle from Jason. "No. Most of the rooms are closed off to help keep expenses down. You wouldn't believe what it costs to heat this place in the winter. Summers are almost as bad, although this year, we've been lucky. It hasn't gotten too hot yet."

She'd noticed that on her way in from town. Thanks to an onshore breeze, temperatures outside had hovered near a comfortable seventy degrees. Regina had warned her that, because the short summers tended to be mild, many public places in Rhode Island didn't offer central air-conditioning. But the Captain's Cottage did. She was glad. For herself and for the women who chose this venue for their ceremonies. There was nothing worse than a testy, over-heated bride on her wedding day.

"We reserve one room for guests. We can open the others any time, of course. There just doesn't seem much point, considering Evelyn and I are the only ones left in the family."

It seemed a shame that after generations of Hearts had given the mansion such tender, loving care, there might not be anyone else to preserve the family's legacy. She flipped a page in her notebook. "What'll happen to the Captain's Cottage after the two of you are gone? Assuming, of course, neither of you marry and have children."

"I wouldn't rule that out for Evelyn." Jason's lips slanted to one side. "But it doesn't look like marriage is in the hand I was dealt."

She hardly thought that likely. Why, she could name a dozen women who'd jump at the chance to go out with a smart, educated owner of a successful business. Toss in the fact that, with his regal bearing and winning smile, Jason was easily one of the most handsome men she'd ever met, and she'd bet once the word of his newly acquired single status got out, every unattached woman for miles around would find some excuse or another to stop by the Captain's Cottage.

Her focus had drifted dangerously afield. She reeled it in and listened carefully to the rest of his explanation.

"Unless there are heirs, the estate will pass to the town of Heart's Landing. I assume they'll continue to run the Captain's Cottage as a wedding venue as long as it breaks even."

An awareness in Jason's gray eyes

mirrored her own growing concern. How long the estate remained profitable would depend in large part on her opinion of his home town. The weight of that responsibility pressed down on her as they descended to the second floor, where she spied her luggage waiting in the hallway. The sound of a vacuum buzzed through the closed door.

"It sounds as though they're almost finished with your rooms. That's good. I'd hate to inconvenience you any more than necessary."

"Please. It hasn't been a bother. I've enjoyed the chance to get familiar with the Captain's Cottage. You make a good tour guide."

At the compliment, a slight pink flush crept up Jason's neck. "I've given you our largest apartment, the Azalea Suite. I hope you'll be comfortable there, but if there's anything thing you need, don't hesitate to ask."

"If I could get the Wi-Fi password, that'd be awesome." She prepared to write it down.

The rosy tinge on Jason's neck crept an inch higher. He frowned. "We don't offer service up here. Just downstairs. You're welcome to use the dining room or the library any time you'd like. Both of those have a more than adequate signal."

No internet service in her room? That seemed odd, and she told him so.

Jason opened the door to a nearby suite. The first room featured a plush sofa, low lighting, and a wet bar. Beyond it, a wide sleigh bed stood in a luxuriously appointed space. "Brides use these rooms to prep for their weddings. After the ceremony and reception, the newlyweds spend the night. We took a lot of surveys before we eliminated TVs and internet service on the upper floors. Our couples consistently didn't want their brand-new spouses to get lost online. If they absolutely have to have service, they use the hotspot capability on their smart phones."

The explanation made sense, though she'd wished she'd known about the restrictions ahead of time. If she had, she would've upgraded her phone before she left New York. She'd been hoping for a desk where she could spread out her work without worrying about someone barging in on her and reading her notes. A place of her own. Behind a door, preferably one with a sturdy lock. The lack of service wasn't a deal breaker, though. She'd make do. She'd just have to be careful not to leave her work out where anyone could stumble across it.

For a while she and Jason wandered up and down corridors, poking their heads into suites that bore the names of flowers and had decors to match. The smallest, The Tea

Rose, made up for size with sumptuous furnishings. Gold-and-pink brocade topped the antique bed. Flocked print covered the walls. Airy and bright, it had a decidedly feminine appeal.

Stargazer lilies adorned the next apartment. Opulent purple asters, another. She tried to keep track of the number of massive claw-footed tubs but lost count somewhere after six. Each bath had been outfitted with heated towel dispensers and an array of lotions and perfumes, all the comforts of a five-star hotel.

"I'd be happy to stay in any of these. They're so spacious and inviting," she told her host. The grateful smile she received in return sent an unfamiliar shimmy through her middle.

On the ground floor, Jason treated her to a behind-the-scenes look at what it took to put on a big wedding. From the covered awning that promised to shield vendors and their wares from the weather to a wide incline that led to a roomy staging area, no detail had been overlooked. An Aga cook stove stood alongside the latest in kitchen gadgetry in an immense kitchen where the gleaming granite countertops and racks of copper-clad kettles would make her dad green with envy. She opened a pantry door and stared at shelves that were better stocked than some grocery stores.

"How does anyone make a sandwich in a place like this?" she asked. Which of the forty drawers of cutlery and tools held knives and forks? How would she ever find a loaf of bread?

Jason must have noticed her consternation. "Not to worry," he assured with his usual, unflappable charm. "Sweet rolls and two kinds of breakfast casseroles are served in the dining room each morning. We put out sandwiches and fruit at noon, cookies and snacks in mid-afternoon. We have a full-time chef on our payroll and at least one cook on duty around the clock." He smiled. "You wouldn't believe how many middle-of-the-night requests we fill for strawberries and whipped cream. If you want anything special, all you have to do is ask."

Judging from the size of the pantry and the side-by-side Sub-Zeros she'd spotted in the kitchen, Tara doubted she'd ever go hungry.

They moved on, peering into a series of rooms that could handle wedding parties ranging from an intimate gathering of immediate family to stately affairs for three hundred or more. Each had its own unique features. A hand-carved mantle in one. A breathtaking view of the ocean in another. On the veranda, the scent of roses floated thickly between wide columns covered with climbing vines. Just as she'd thought, the larger of the two ballrooms was being prepped for a party.

"A cocktail hour in your honor. Most of the local business owners will attend. They can't wait to meet you. It'll serve as the kick-off for the next ten days. Tomorrow night at six."

She noted the time. Glad she'd packed a few dressy dresses, she nodded.

They ended up at the library, where leather-bound books crowded a small table. "The Captain's journals and ship's logs," Jason explained.

Her fingers itched to begin leafing through them. As much as she'd enjoyed her tour of the Cottage, as much as she'd found Heart's Landing—and her host—to be utterly charming, she couldn't afford to let personal feelings stand in the way of doing her job. Her career rested on Regina's orders to debunk the myth of Captain Thaddeus. Unless she wanted to scrap any possibility of getting ahead at *Weddings Today*, she had to do what she'd set out to do.

"Mind if I stay here for a while?" she asked.

When Jason readily agreed, she settled down at one of the tables and took the first journal off the pile. Sure she'd find exactly what she needed in the old ship's logs, she began reading.

Chapter Six

"YOU SAY THIS TARA PERSON showed up a full day ahead of schedule? Why is she here? For the preliminary legwork or something?" A potent mix of disbelief and shock swirled in Greg Thomas's voice.

"It sounds as though she's handling the entire review." With the phone pressed against his ear, Jason flicked one end of the pen lying on his desk. Tip, clicker, tip, clicker. The pen spun in a dizzying circle.

"Ms. Charm, when will she arrive then?"

"I don't think she's coming." Jason resisted the urge to sigh. In the past fifteen minutes, he and the mayor had covered this ground twice already.

"At all?"

"That's what I've been trying to tell you."

Jason brushed his fingers through hair that would be due for a trim soon. His plan to catch the mayor up on all that had transpired since Tara's unexpected appearance in his office yesterday kept wandering from the script. The man stubbornly clung to the original plan. "Regina begged off. The person she sent instead—Tara Stewart—seems nice enough. She's sharp as a tack and has done her research. She knows more about Heart's Landing than she lets on."

The mayor sneezed. "Excuse me. Allergies. The wife and I spent yesterday picking blackberries." The conversation waited a beat while Greg gave his nose a noisy blow. "What do you think is going on?"

"I'm not sure. If I had to guess, I'd say things could go one of two ways. According to Ms. Stewart, Regina Charm feared that her own experience here in Heart's Landing might cloud her opinion and is simply giving us the best chance by sending someone impartial in her place."

"But you don't think that's it?"

An uncomfortable feeling stirred in Jason's gut. Someone at Regina's level should be able to set aside her own prejudices. Since she hadn't, it seemed far more likely that she'd tasked some innocent young reporter, like Tara, with carrying out her own agenda. Whatever that might be. "I wish I could say I didn't have my doubts."

"Humph," said the mayor, finally coming around to accept the situation. "I do, too. It'd be bad enough if our ranking slipped. We'd really take a hit if Ms. Stewart goes on the attack."

"Tell me about it." He knew perfectly well what was at stake. Not that he thought for a moment that Tara, with her guileless smile and clear blue eyes, would deliberately set out to destroy the reputation of a town she'd never stepped foot in before yesterday.

"Well, how'd things go then? You and she got along, didn't you? Do you think we can trust her?"

"It's hard to tell." Jason refused to sugar-coat things. "We only spent a few hours together. I gave her an in-depth tour of the Cottage. Her response was pretty positive." To be honest, Tara's reaction had been more enthusiastic than he'd have expected if she'd been sent here to do a hatchet job. "She seemed genuinely interested in the Cottage's history. We might have something in common there." As a child, he'd spent many a snowy winter's day hidden away in the attic, poring through the Captain's journals and logs. He'd imagined himself on the deck of the *Mary S*, battling pirates off the coast and sailing his ship safely through storms and

calm seas. In his teens, he'd worked alongside his dad, restoring floors and wainscoting, learning how to preserve the house he'd
inherit far sooner than anyone expected.
He'd minored in early American History at
college, and it was rare that he didn't read
a chapter or two of some historical treatise
before he turned out the lights.

"So you think she's telling the truth?
Oh, hold on a sec."

Jason held the ear piece away from his
head while the mayor cleared his throat.

"Okay. You were saying?"

"It's a little too early for me to answer
that. I barely know the woman." If the mayor
wanted someone to offer some insight into
what made Tara Stewart tick, he was asking the wrong person. After all, Jason had
known Clarissa for more than two years. Yet,
her betrayal had still blindsided him. He'd
do well to keep from making that mistake
again, for all their sakes.

"After the tour, then what did she do?"

"She was intrigued by the library." The
Captain's Cottage maintained a fine collec-
tion of early editions by American authors.
Occasionally, one of their guests would
suffer a bout of insomnia and wander downstairs in the middle of the night. The next
morning, the staff sometimes found them
curled up in one of the Queen Anne chairs

with an aged copy of *Little Women* or Emerson's *Essays* in their lap.

"You didn't take her out to dinner? Did you have other plans?"

"I offered. She declined," he answered shortly. The nerve of Greg, thinking he wouldn't properly care for a guest in his house, whether she showed up a day early or not.

"Don't get your feathers in a dander. I didn't mean to imply anything. My head feels like it's full of cotton."

Jason took a breath. "Sorry. Guess I'm more on edge about this than I thought." He gave his pen another push and watched it spin. The next week was bound to take a toll on everyone in town. He'd do well to keep that in mind. "The rain was coming down pretty hard about then, and she said she'd rather not venture out. We ordered in from Bow Tie Pasta." Known for its fine Italian cuisine, the restaurant had delivered enough lasagna, penne, and salad for an army. "Evelyn set everything up buffet-style in the dining room. We looked over the agenda while we ate and made a few adjustments." Tara's early arrival meant shifting the schedule forward a day. Afterward, she hadn't lingered, but had retreated to the library. She was still reading when he'd gone upstairs.

"I knew we could count on you, Jason. Now, what about today?"

He glanced at the old ship's clock on the bookcase. "She told Evelyn she had work to do this morning and would be down around ten. You're on tap to take her into town and introduce her to a few people."

"I'd planned to drop in on Forget Me Knot, I Do Cakes, and The Memory Box and introduce her to Mildred, Nick, and Helen. They're expecting us."

Greg had chosen wisely. Although they relied on everyone in the village to do their part, Jason and the mayor, along with those three prominent business owners had spearheaded the efforts to retain the town's number one ranking.

"But that was supposed to be on Saturday. I'm not sure I can get away from the shop today. What about the others?"

"Evelyn let them know about the change in schedule last night. They're fine." When Greg remained hesitant, he asked, "Is there a problem?"

"It's the Smith wedding. The bride is coming in this morning. She's decided she wants a different option for the vests. It'll take the better part of the morning for me to reorder." In addition to his duties as mayor, Greg owned Tux and Tails, the area's best tuxedo shop.

Jason called up the Cottage's master calendar. "That's awfully late notice." Featuring six bridesmaids and an equal number of groomsmen, the Smith wedding was one of a dozen-plus ceremonies that would take place in the mansion during Tara's stay in Heart's Landing. He rubbed his forehead and ran through a limited set of options. They couldn't very well leave Tara to her own devices this early in the game. Someone would need to show her around town, introduce her to all the right people, and make sure she felt welcome. It was equally important to attain sheer perfection in every detail of the Smith wedding, doubly so since Tara's engraved invitation to the event sat on his desk.

"It's fine," he said, instantly adjusting his own schedule for the day. "I'll go into town with her. If you finish up and can meet with us for lunch, that'd be great."

"We have one o'clock reservations at the White Dove Deli. I'll do my best to be there."

Whatever. In a town that prided itself on delivering the perfect wedding for every bride, Greg had his priorities straight. While the mayor took care of business, Jason would do his best to find out more about their mysterious visitor and whether or not she was lying to them all.

Heaven. She'd died and gone to heaven. Yesterday's delay while housekeeping had prepped her suite had been worth every minute. The staff had thought of everything, from designer soaps and lotions to a selection of snacks in the mini-fridge beneath the wet bar.

Tara pulled the Egyptian cotton up around her neck and ran a languid hand over the soft sheets. Scads of comfy pillows and a mattress that was sheer perfection had provided her with a solid six hours of deep, dreamless sleep. A definite improvement over the thin, fitful nights she spent in the city that never slept. Where taxi horns peppered the air, even in her fifth-floor walk-up, and her neighbor played his sax into the wee hours on the fire escape. No wonder she never quite felt rested there. Unlike here, where she ought to be exhausted after traveling all day, traipsing all over the Captain's Cottage, and working in the library until well past midnight.

When Regina had suggested she go through Captain Thaddeus's ship's logs with a fine-toothed comb, she hadn't realized it'd be such a massive undertaking. The good captain had worked the trade routes between Europe and the Americas for well over a decade and recorded something about every one of his days at sea. Last night, she'd managed to read only a single year's worth of entries. While she'd been able to skim past routine reports on the day's rations and weather or the status of the heart he was carving for his wife, she'd become engrossed by a few events. Like the day the *Mary S* had happened upon a pod of blue whales a hundred miles off the coast. The gentle giants had entertained the crew for hours before diving deep and swimming away. Storms and rain squalls had buffeted the ship often enough that they'd hardly required a mention. But every once in a while, the tri-mast ran afoul of a monstrous storm. Captain Thaddeus had been quick to give his crew credit for furling the sails and comporting themselves well during those harried days. She thought she might rather like him, if he were still alive.

Had Jason inherited his ancestor's strength of character? His drive?

The man was certainly the spitting image of his great-great-great-grandfather. Granted, she didn't know everything there was to know about Jason Heart. But she liked what she'd learned about him during the few hours they'd spent together. He radiated charm and good manners. Well educated, he'd spent years preparing himself for the daunting task of running the Captain's Cottage. His loyalty to Heart's Landing was one of his most endearing qualities, but more than that, he had a sense of place, of family, that was rare in this day and age of mobile-everything. If he lived in New York, he was the kind of man she'd be interested in getting to know better. But he didn't. For the short time she'd be here, she'd have to ignore the warmth she felt every time she thought of him.

Other things weren't as easy to overlook. Like the way her shoulders and chest tightened whenever she considered how her success might impact the Captain's Cottage— and the rest of Heart's Landing. If there was one thing she hated about her assignment, that was it. Yet, she couldn't fail. Couldn't walk away from the job, no matter who got hurt. Regina had given her one opportunity to prove herself. She had to succeed now that she finally had a chance to become a real journalist—the one thing she had her heart set on doing.

Every entry she'd read in the captain's logs so far supported Heart's Landing's claim that the town was built on true love. But there had to be something in the diaries and journals to disprove that story. She simply had to find it, and she would. Maybe as soon as today.

Dressed for the day in slacks and one of her favorite tops, she slipped on a pair of walking shoes and followed the scent of fresh-brewed coffee down the staircase. Brides and their families occupied several of the tables in the dining room. She chose an out-of-the-way seat in a corner. Once her laptop booted up, the internet service proved every bit as reliable as Jason had sworn it would be, and soon, the first of her daily reports was winging its way through cyberspace to Regina.

Her first task complete, she helped herself from urns that offered a variety of beverage choices. Sipping excellent coffee, she sorted through her inbox until she reached an email from Van. Her hand shook as she read the news that one of the hardestworking interns had been let go without a reference after incurring their boss's wrath over a minor matter. Her stomach tightened. Regina had made it very plain that she'd suffer the same fate if she failed to dig up some dirt on Captain Thaddeus.

Deciding that the situation at work warranted a second cup of coffee, she logged off. At the buffet, she surveyed a tantalizing array of breakfast foods while she refilled her cup. She was still debating between a yummy-looking egg dish and sweet rolls when a low murmur drifted in from the hall. Seconds later, Jason rounded the corner with two women close on his heels. The trio made a beeline for her.

"Good morning. Did you enjoy your first night in the Captain's Cottage?" Jason lifted a mug from the stand. "Is there anything you need to make your stay more enjoyable?"

Tara sipped her coffee while he fixed his. "Not a thing," she answered honestly. "I can't imagine a lovelier place for a bride and groom to spend their wedding night. You've really thought of everything."

"That's wonderful to hear," the dark-haired woman beside Jason put in.

Jason cleared his throat. "Tara, this is Alicia Thorne, the Cottage's Event Planner. Alicia, Tara Stewart. Alicia knows all about the weddings we'll be hosting here this week. You've been invited to most of them. I thought she might be able to help you select the ones you'd like to attend."

"It's nice to meet you, Alicia." Tara extended a hand. "Jason and Evelyn have had very nice things to say about you." She eyed the woman who'd been in charge when Regina's wedding had fallen apart. The white streaks that salted her otherwise dark hair and the laugh lines carved into her cheeks gave her a seasoned, experienced look. The flattering top she wore over navy blue slacks and low-heeled pumps completed an outfit that was both professional and approachable.

"We're thrilled to have you here, Ms. Stewart."

"Tara, please," she corrected, noting the warmth in Alicia's firm grip. "My mom is the only Ms. Stewart in our family."

"Tara." Even, white teeth showed in Alicia's smile. "And this is Jennifer Bell." She turned to a petite brunette who had doe-like eyes. "Jenny is my right hand. If you need anything while you're here, one of us will be happy to get it for you."

"You must be the newlywed Evelyn mentioned," Tara said, recognizing the name. "Congratulations!"

"That's sweet of you, Tara. Welcome to Heart's Landing." Jenny shuffled a stack of embossed card stock. "The Captain's Cottage hosts ceremonies every day of the week, but as you can imagine, the schedule gets a bit hectic on the weekends. We thought, if it was all right with you, we'd sort through these wedding invitations over breakfast. Between us, Alicia and I can fill you in on the size of the guest lists and the brides' themes, and point out any items of particular interest."

"That works for me," Tara agreed, setting aside her plan to spend the morning in the library. The opportunity to talk with Alicia and Jenny was too good to pass up. She didn't add that she'd be keeping a sharp look-out for problems. Or that, from what Regina had told her, there were bound to be plenty.

"We have fourteen weddings scheduled here this week." Alicia took a plate from the buffet and served herself as she spoke. "They range from a small affair at the gazebo for family and a few guests one evening to the Garrison wedding on Saturday. That bride has chosen a tropical theme you might enjoy. Then, there's the Smith wedding in the Green Room next Wednesday. Jason and Evelyn will perform as Captain Thaddeus and Mary for over three hundred guests."

Tara stole a quick glance at Jason, her stomach giving a happy shimmy when she imagined him dressed as the seafaring captain. His height alone gave him a commanding presence. Decked out in all the trappings of his famous ancestor, he'd make an imposing figure.

"Don't forget Bessie Glover's ceremony."

Tara threw a net over thoughts that had swerved off-course. Regina hadn't sent her here to daydream about handsome sailors. She'd been sent to dig up dirt on Heart's Landing. With a renewed determination to uncover all she could about what went on behind the scenes in the Captain's Cottage, Tara fixed her focus on Jenny.

"Her nieces will be the flower girls, and they're just adorable."

Nieces. Flower girls. Right.

Over a breakfast casserole her father would have been proud to serve in his Savannah restaurant, she listened while Alicia and Jenny provided insights into a dozen or so ceremonies. The more the women talked, the more impressed Tara grew at the planning that had gone into each event. Alicia, especially, seemed so prepared that Tara found herself questioning how Regina's wedding could have gone awry. As she chose three of the ceremonies to attend, she eyed the older woman over her coffee cup. She couldn't help but wonder if there was another side to Regina's story, and considered asking about it. When Jason casually shifted away from the table, though, she put her questions on hold for the time being.

"Whenever you're ready, I'll take you into town, introduce you to some of the key members of our business community," he offered.

Spending time with Jason sounded a whole lot better than discussing her boss's ill-fated wedding plans. She closed her notebook and smiled at the tall man beside her. "I'd like that. I want to visit a few of the shops and get a feel for what makes Heart's Landing such a popular place."

"We're all set then? Meet here in..." Jason waited for her answer.

"Five minutes?" She said, filling in the blank. "I just need to grab my camera and drop my laptop off in my room." She glanced down, surprised to see that while they'd talked, she'd cleaned her plate.

"Terrific." Jason grabbed his phone. "I'll wait for you in the foyer. If you'll excuse me, I'll let everyone know we're on our way." Their eyes met as he stood. For a long second, he lingered, his phone in his hand. Just when Tara was going to ask if he needed something else, he pressed the device to his ear and strode from the room.

Ten minutes later, Jason escorted her to a serviceable town car parked under the porte cochere. "We'll start with a visit to one of my favorite places in Heart's Landing, Forget Me Knot Florist on Bridal Carriage. For over forty years, the shop has been a mainstay for brides who want only the best."

Tara bit back a smile. Jason didn't know it, but their first stop was sure to point out one of Heart's Landing's flaws. It'd be difficult for any florist, no matter how long they'd been around, to compete with New York's flower district. At least once a week, she rose early and roamed up and down the aisles, choosing an exotic orchid for a friend's birthday one time, assembling a bouquet of freshly picked wildflowers to brighten her cubicle at work another. So far from the hustle and bustle of the big city, she doubted Heart's Landing could even offer half as many choices.

Her conviction suffered a minor setback a few minutes later, however, when she stepped beneath a rose-colored awning. She whipped out her camera, unable to pass up the chance to capture one of the prettiest table settings she'd ever seen. In the display window, floral swags created curtains around an elegant centerpiece that dripped orchids on satin ribbons from a stunning arrangement of ivory roses, hydrangeas, and wispy baby's breath. From an open doorway came the heady scent of flowers and greenery.

Tara took a deep breath. Somewhere in the mix, she caught the sweet, sweet smell of hyacinth. The flowers grew everywhere in Savannah, and a wave of homesickness swept over her. How many Saturday after noons had she and her mom spent on their knees in the flower beds around their home? Back then, she'd complained about the late-summer sun that had beaten down on her while she'd worked fresh compost into the soil, dug holes, and planted bulbs pointy side up. But it had been worth every bit of effort when the hyacinths bloomed in the spring. Now, with Jason trailing in her wake, she followed their scent, wandering an aisle crowded with beautiful arrangements until she reached the counter where her favorite flower bloomed in clay pots.

"I'm Mildred Morey. Welcome to Forget Me Knot Florist." Her silvery hair shining, a woman wearing a green apron over a rounded middle stepped forward. "It's such an honor to welcome you to Heart's Landing."

Tara wrenched her gaze from the flowers that reminded her so much of home. "You have a beautiful shop, Ms. Morey."

"All my friends call me Mildred. I hope you will, too." A pleased smile played about the owner's lips. "As for Forget Me Knot, we do our best to give every bride her dream wedding. Flowers play a huge role in her special day."

Tara whipped out her notebook. She refused to let herself get so taken in by the cuteness of the shop that she forgot what she'd come here to accomplish. She glanced over a list of questions Regina had provided. "If I was planning a wedding, what could I expect you to do for me?"

Mildred maintained a steady smile while she spoke. "We handle everything, from the initial design work to the final delivery and cleanup. Our brides trust us to take care of every detail while they relax and enjoy their special day."

The answer was exactly what she'd expect from a top-notch florist, but her next question was sure to uncover Forget Me Knot's weak spot. "And if a bride wants something really exotic?" She waited for Mildred to prove her right.

"I think the best way to answer that question is to show you our workroom." Mildred led the way between swinging doors to an area where dozens of varieties of flowers crowded immense glass-fronted coolers. "We like to say that this is where the magic happens."

Long wooden work tables filled a space the size of a small gym. Beyond them, colorful ribbons spilled from large reels along the back wall. Vases in every shape and size lined sturdy-looking shelves. At one of the tables, a young man and woman wrapped satin tape around the base of boutonnieres that featured Birds of Paradise. Farther down, another pair of workers skillfully assembled lilies, waxy leaves, and frangipani into low centerpieces. The back room smelled like Hawaii and, for a second, Tara could almost see palm trees and women in grass skirts.

"You asked about exotic flowers." Mildred plucked a stem from a cluster of bright red blossoms. "The Garrison wedding is a good example. It has a tropical theme."

Tara nodded. The ceremony was one of three she'd chosen to attend. "This is all pretty amazing," she admitted, "but what if a bride chooses flowers that are out of season? Or impossibly costly?"

Mildred's lips thinned. "I never encourage false expectations. If she has her heart set on heirloom roses, and my suppliers can't get them, or they're out of her budget, I let her know up front. We can usually find a substitute. Once in a while, though, the bride will go somewhere else. In which case, I wish her the best. The important thing, no matter what, is her happiness."

A heaviness draped itself across Tara's shoulders. Discovering the town's Achilles heel might be more difficult than she'd anticipated. She tapped her pen against her notebook. "What was your biggest challenge this year?"

"That'd be Jennifer Longely's wedding." Merriment danced in Mildred's eyes while the florist smothered a laugh. "The one she came here to plan. Not the one she ended up having."

Behind her, Jason coughed. Tara's head swiveled. Both Mildred and Jason wore the same amused grins. Her curiosity aroused, she asked, "What set that wedding apart?"

"It started off as a small affair, but the bride kept changing her mind. As it turned out, there was nothing simple about that wedding at all."

"Ooooh, that sounds interesting." Tara cupped her chin. "Tell me more."

"For that, you'll need to talk to Jennifer." Mildred's kind eyes crinkled. "It's her story to tell."

"And where would I find her?" Tara leaned forward, eager to find a chink in the town's united front.

"She's Alicia Thorne's assistant. You met her this morning at the Captain's Cottage. She's Jennifer Bell now."

Tara scribbled a note. "Right. She married the owner of I Do Cakes."

"None other." Jason checked his watch. "In fact, we're headed there next. Are you ready?"

"I think so." She turned to Mildred. "I probably shouldn't say this, but your shop has definitely exceeded my expectations. I love the flower district in New York. I wasn't sure anything could compare with that. But this is pretty special."

As she headed for the door, Tara's lips thinned. The current top wedding destination in the country had a stellar reputation and, from what she'd seen so far, the town deserved it. But with her job and her parents' respect at stake, she couldn't fail in her assignment. She'd find a fatal flaw if she had to turn over every rock in Heart's Landing. She supposed it was too much to ask, but she crossed her fingers and hoped, for her own sake, that something would go terribly wrong before the day was out.

If anything, though, I Do Cakes was even more impressive than the flower shop. She breathed in air thick with the tantalizing scents of sugar and yeast. A pair of glassed-in displays beckoned her to try an array of cakes, cookies, and sweets, each more enticing than the next. Through an archway, tables and chairs tempted shoppers to linger over coffee and pastries in a charming room where large picture windows overlooked the tree-lined street.

Despite the hearty breakfast she'd eaten a scant two hours earlier, Tara's stomach rumbled. She pressed a hand to her midsection as a dark-haired man wearing the traditional chef's whites topped off by a toque blanche emerged into the front of the shop through swinging doors.

"Nick." Beside her, Jason extended his hand in greeting. "I'd like you to meet Tara Stewart, from *Weddings Today*. Tara, this is Nick Bell."

"On behalf of our staff and all of Heart's Landing, welcome to I Do Cakes," the baker said.

So, this was the man Jennifer Longley had married. Tara raised an eyebrow. Mildred and Jason had dropped a few not-so-subtle hints that, like Regina's, Nick's wedding hadn't gone according to plan. Hoping to ferret out the details, she put out her first feeler. "I understand congratulations are in order. I hear your wedding was quite 'interesting.'" She framed the last word in air quotes.

"There's never been one like it in the history of Heart's Landing," Nick said with a mysterious smile.

That sounded promising. "I'd love to hear more about it," she prompted, hoping for a juicy tidbit about a wedding gone wrong. "I understand there were quite a few problems leading up to the big day."

"I prefer to think of them as opportunities." Nick grinned. "By overcoming each of those challenges, Jenny and I fell deeper and deeper in love."

"And the ceremony itself?"

Nick's eyes glazed over. "It couldn't have been more perfect. The whole town turned out, including a few unexpected guests."

Hoping to hear about gate-crashers of the worst sort, Tara leaned forward. "Oh?"

"As it turned out, I was marrying into Hollywood royalty—who knew? My wife's cousin and her new husband put in a surprise appearance. They created quite a stir. Me, though? I only had eyes for Jenny. She was the most beautiful bride I'd ever seen. And, in my work, I've seen quite a few." The baker and Jason shared an amused glance.

Seeing the stars in Nick's eyes, Tara admitted defeat. Her line of questioning was getting her nowhere. The baker either deserved an award for his acting skills, or he harbored no dark secrets about his wedding. Maybe she'd have better luck with Jenny. She'd make a point of pressing for details the next time they ran into each other. For now, she'd let the matter drop. "Well, congratulations again. I wish you both much happiness."

"A Heart's Landing love for the ages, that's what we have." Nick nodded. "You've met my wife?"

"This morning at the Captain's Cottage. She sorted through all the details of the weddings scheduled there this week. She was very helpful."

"That's my Jenny. I didn't know what true happiness was until we found each other." Tilting his head, Nick cast a speculative glance in her direction. "Are you married? Or is there someone special in your life?"

She laughed. *Newlyweds.* They were so wrapped up in wedded bliss, they thought everyone else should be, too. "I'm afraid I haven't met my Mr. Right, Nick. Right now, I'm too busy to even look for him."

The baker's lips pursed. "Don't give up. You never know when you'll run into him."

She was trying to come up with a dry response when Jason's quiet laughter caught her attention. She eyed her host for the day. Mirth tugged at his lips. "What am I missing?" she asked.

"Sorry. That's a little inside joke." Jason aimed a thumb toward the entrance. "Nick and Jenny met when they literally ran into each other right out there on the sidewalk."

"Okay, okay!" Nick threw his hands in the air. "I'm sure Tara has a very busy schedule. She doesn't need to waste her valuable time hearing all about Jenny and me," he grumbled good-naturedly.

Recognizing her cue, she asked, "So, what do you have for me today, Nick?"

The baker squared his shoulders. He pointed to the display cases. "As you can see, we offer our customers quite the selection of baked goods. Everything is prepared from scratch and baked fresh daily on the premises. Of course, cakes are our specialty, and we provide a full range of services to ensure that each of our brides has the perfect cake for their special day."

Somewhere in the back of the shop, a motor hummed to life. The air sweetened until Tara bet she'd taste sugar if she stuck out her tongue. "If your cakes are half as good as they smell, your customers must be pleased."

"We rarely get complaints." Nick beamed.

She liked the way he said it, as if he were merely acknowledging a fact and not bragging.

"Of course, the best way to prove that is to see for yourself. I have samples of our most popular flavors for you to try. Why don't you and Jason take a seat, and we'll have a taste testing." He pointed toward a trio of alcoves along one wall. Each had been outfitted with banquettes and tables.

"That sounds great," she said, looking forward to finding out firsthand if the bakery's goods were as tasty as the aroma in the air.

Once they were seated on the comfortable cushions, Nick folded his arms across his chest. "I want you to pretend you're the bride, Tara, and Jason is your fiancé. We'll start from there and walk through the same process our clients experience when they arrive at I Do Cakes."

She aimed a doubtful expression at Jason. "Oh, I don't know about that. I'd need to know a lot more about you before I agree to be your wife. Where will we live? Do you want children? How many?" She couldn't prevent the teasing lift in her voice.

The laugh lines around Jason's mouth deepened. Without missing a beat, he rattled off a series of answers. "At the Captain's Cottage. Yes. More than one but less than thirteen."

His willingness to play along eased the tension that had raced across her shoulders the minute Nick had suggested they pretend to be a couple. If Jason was game, so was she. Purely in the name of research, of course. "I'm in," she said.

"Me, too." Jason's grin widened.

"Good." Nick pulled an order sheet from a drawer on his side of the banquette. "The first bit of information I need from every bride and groom is the number of guests they plan on having at the wedding. That number determines how large a cake they'll need. So?"

Tara studied the tabletop. Outside of family, she could count the number of friends she'd invite on her fingers and have a digit or two left over. "Maybe twenty-five?" she ventured.

Beside her, Jason gave his head an emphatic shake. "That'll never do. I grew up in

Heart's Landing. Practically everyone in town will expect an invitation to my wedding. I'd say three hundred."

"Oh, no," she protested. She'd faint dead away if she had to walk down the aisle in front of that many people. Just the thought of it made her heart race. "I'm thinking more like a hundred guests. Max."

Jason's brows knitted. "I might be able to shave off fifty, but I'm warning you, my great-aunt Matilda might never forgive me if I don't invite her to our wedding."

"I'll take my chances." Not that it was much of a risk. She knew full well he didn't have a great aunt. He and his cousin Evelyn were the last of their line.

"I'll give you that, but I know a lot of people. They'll all want to be there."

"You have that many friends?" She couldn't imagine it, but he sat there, nodding like it was the most normal thing in the world. "I can go as high as one-fifty."

"Ouch! You wound me." Jason pressed a hand to his heart. "Two hundred, and that's as low as I'll go."

Though Jason, with his good looks and charming demeanor, would make a handsome groom, this was just a game. She could afford to give in on the number of guests.

"And there you have it, the first rule in a successful marriage—the art of compromise." Nick smiled broadly. "Okay. We need a cake to serve two hundred guests. Plus attendants and vendors, you're looking at two twenty-five. For that size, we have loads of options, depending on your theme. Did you have something particular in mind?"

Tara relaxed. This was fun, especially since it wasn't the real thing. "I always imagined a summer wedding on the veranda of the Captain's Cottage. I'd have armloads of purple and white hyacinths."

She glanced at Jason to see what he thought, but the man who pretended to be her fiancé only stared at her with a shocked look on his face.

"What?"

"I'm sorry, but we can't fit that many guests on the veranda. We'll have to hold the ceremony in one of the ballrooms. I'd suggest the Green Room. It has the biggest dance floor. Your flowers will look stunning in there." The tiny crows' feet at the corners of his eyes crinkled.

"Tara?" Nick tilted his head to one side while he waited for her answer.

"I suppose we could serve cocktails on the veranda," she ventured, surprised at how difficult it was to let go of her dream, even in a game.

"The roses will be in bloom." Jason's shoe tapped out a warning beat. "The scent will clash with your hyacinths. To say nothing of the colors."

"It sounds like you have another tough choice to make." Nick leaned back in his chair. He held out his hands like a set of scales. "Color?" One hand dipped. "Or venue." He lifted the other one. "Which will it be?"

She'd thought she knew what went into planning a wedding. She should have, considering where she worked. But when it came to arranging her own special day—even a pretend one—each decision impacted a hundred others. She tapped her finger to her chin. Jason was right. Red roses and grape hyacinths didn't go together. "What if we erected a tent on the grounds and served cocktails there between the ceremony and the reception? Maybe, under the weeping willows?" She'd spotted them when Charlie turned onto the driveway.

"Perfect!" Jason declared.

That wasn't the term she'd use, but the exercise had certainly opened her eyes. Planning a wedding involved a much larger cast than she'd ever imagined. The decision she and Jason made about their pretend head count would affect not just the baker, but everyone from the caterer to the person who arranged the chairs at the reception.

"Now you're getting somewhere." Nick

pulled a pad of paper and a pencil from the drawer. "Normally, this is where I'd hand you my portfolio and have you page through pictures of my best work. But in the interest of time, let's assume you want a simple design." He quickly sketched a towering cake with flowers cascading down one side. "Would something like this do?"

Tara smiled. "It's lovely."

"That brings us to the part our brides—and grooms—enjoy the most. The actual taste test." Nick snapped his fingers. As if by magic, the swinging doors popped open, and a parade of apron-clad staff members emerged. Each carried a miniature cake on a silver platter. One by one, Nick's helpers placed their wares on the table and disappeared into the back of the store.

"What we have here," Nick said when every inch of the table had been covered, "are some of our most popular flavors. Let's start with a staple—almond with white buttercream icing. This particular one has a raspberry filling." He cut two slivers and plated them.

Tara eyed her portion. Nestled between the off-white layers, the red center practically glowed. She forked a small bite. The frosting melted in her mouth but not before it awakened all her taste buds. A divine almond flavor tickled the tip of her tongue.

The filling complimented it perfectly. "That's yummy," she declared. "I can see why so many of your customers choose it."

"It's a nice, safe choice," Jason declared after sampling a bite. "Personally, I think I'd like something a little more out of the ordinary."

He was teasing, right? Tara shot a quick glance at the man seated on the banquette. The laughter in Jason's eyes contradicted his serious attitude.

"How about coffee-infused layers separated by a chocolate rum filling and topped with a vanilla bean frosting?" Nick asked. He sliced into the next sample.

Tara hadn't been sure he could improve on the first cake, but her next bite exceeded all her expectations. As a quick burst of intense chocolate faded, rum and coffee lingered on her tongue. She ran her fork through the icing and licked the tines. Sugar crystals melted in her mouth. *More, please!* She swallowed. "I've never tasted anything quite like this, Nick. Is it your own recipe?"

"This particular combination was my dad's favorite. He opened I Do Cakes over a decade ago. I've been running the place for a couple of years."

Though she tried to resist, Tara helped herself to a second bite that turned out to be as delicious as the first. She rubbed her hands together. "What's next?"

Over the next hour, she and Jason worked their way from one end of the table to the other. Though she'd been certain any number of bakeries in New York would out-shine I Do Cakes, she couldn't recall a single one that offered a buttercream frosting as luscious as Nick's. Fillings that ranged from sweet to savory tempted her to linger over each bite. And that wasn't all. She'd walked into the shop convinced that no one could make a pecan cake better than her mom's. Nick's, though, packed so much dense flavor into each light and airy layer, she couldn't imagine how he'd done it.

"There you have it," the baker an-nounced after she and Jason narrowed their choices to their absolute favorites. "Working together, you've created the perfect, one-of-a-kind cake for your wedding."

Tara felt her cheeks heat. She should never have participated in the taste test. One bite of that first sample had robbed her of the ability to write a single, negative word about I Do Cakes. Not that she'd found any-thing to complain about. The shop had been absolute perfection, from the moment she'd stepped across the threshold and heard the cheery bell over the door.

At this rate, she'd return to New York

singing the praises of Heart's Landing. Which wouldn't get her the promotion she deserved. It would only get her fired. Something that wouldn't earn her parents' respect at all. She clenched her teeth. With only one more store to visit this morning, her chances of finding anything wrong were diminishing quickly. She gulped. At their next stop, she'd have to be more careful about remaining impartial. Judgmental, even.

On the sidewalk outside I Do Cakes, Jason inclined his head to hers. "The Memory Box is a block down and left on Honeymoon Avenue. Do you mind walking?"

Despite a renewed determination to remain cool and distant, she couldn't get snippy with him. He didn't deserve it. She patted her tummy. "After all that sugar, a walk sounds like a very good idea."

With Jason in the lead, they made their way down the shady sidewalk, past store windows filled with tempting displays of items ranging from chocolates to dressy dresses. At Bow Tie Pasta, the tantalizing odor of onions and garlic floated in the air. Tara inhaled deeply. "That smell reminds me of the dinner you ordered last night. Did it come from here?"

"It did. Wait till you go there in person. It's a great place to hold a rehearsal dinner."

"Humph." She reached for her newfound

determination. She'd be the judge of that. "I don't eat out much, but when I do, there's the perfect little place less than a block from my apartment. Red-and-white checkered tablecloths. Chianti bottles for candle holders."

A memory of the creamy goodness of the Bow Tie's alfredo sauce tickled her tongue. At dinner, she'd savored every bite of her lasagna. Her shoulders rounded in defeat. Who was she kidding? "Honestly, I always thought the atmosphere at Anthony's was authentic, but the food doesn't compare with what we had last night."

"Not every restaurant can find that perfect balance of service, atmosphere, and taste," Jason said with far more understanding than she'd expected. "Not in Boston. Or even in New York. But you like it in the city?"

"I love it," she said, thinking of all her favorite places. "Taking the Staten Island Ferry past the Statue of Liberty. Stopping for dim sum in Chinatown. Walking through Rockefeller Center. Times Square—though it should be old hat by now, I still get a thrill every time I see myself on the big monitors." She could stand in front of the cameras for fifteen minutes at a time while she waved to the crowds with one hand and kept a firm grip on her purse strap with the other.

"I sense a *but* in there somewhere."

How did he know what she was thinking before she did? Yes, there was a "but," as in, *but* with all the hours she was putting in at work these days, she didn't get to enjoy much of living in the city. Could she admit that to Jason? Something in the tilt of his head, the interest that flickered in his gray eyes urged her to confide in him.

"It's, um, more—much more—than I anticipated. More crowded. More hectic. More expensive. Especially that. I'm still living in the fifth-floor walk-up I moved into when I first arrived. My whole apartment could fit inside my parents' bedroom closet. There's no air conditioning, and the heat is a joke. Before I moved to New York, I'd built up a nice nest egg. I've had to dip into it just to make ends meet. I'm not sure how much longer I can live there if I don't get this promotion I'm up for."

"Well, I'll keep my fingers crossed that you get it. You love what you do, don't you?"

That part she didn't have to hide. "From the first time I saw a copy of *Weddings Today*, I've dreamed of covering celebrity weddings and helping brides make the right choices. It's just that, well, there have been too many days when going on a coffee run for the senior editors was the most important contribution I made to the magazine." She clamped her mouth shut. She absolutely would not tell him she'd been doing exactly that as recently as last week.

"It's tough starting out. Especially in a creative field. It'll be worth the sacrifices you're making now, though, when you get that big promotion."

"I wasn't sure I'd make it until Regina gave me this assignment. This could change everything for me." *And Heart's Landing.*

"Everyone here is going to help you with that," Jason said. "Ever since my great-grandmother glided down the circular staircase of the Captain's Cottage to marry into the Rockefeller clan in a wedding that turned the socialites of the day misty-eyed, our town has been a premier wedding destination. Today, we're doing everything we can to maintain that position. You're not going to find one thing to mark us down on, and when you turn in your report at the end of your stay, your bosses will agree that you've done a great job."

If he only knew. The problem with his plan was that in order to please her boss, she'd have to dig up some dirt on Heart's Landing or destroy the myth the town was built on. Both were tasks she looked forward to less and less with each step she took on the tree-lined sidewalk. If her career was the only thing at stake, she might have a different perspective. But having her own byline would go a long way toward making her parents see that she'd chosen the right career, and that made whatever she had to do worthwhile. She simply couldn't let herself get attached to the town.

Or Jason. Especially not him. Firming her shoulders, along with her resolve, she was determined to reach her goal.

Soon, Jason's footsteps slowed to a stop beside another intriguing window display. On the other side of the glass, a lacy blue garter dangled from a mannequin's hand over an intricately carved wooden box. Wedding invitations, reply cards, church programs, and a bouquet of dried flowers spilled from the box to puddle in artful disarray on a low table.

"Helen's store specializes in storage boxes for wedding memorabilia," Jason explained, "though I suppose you could use them for other purposes, too. Want to take a look inside?"

"I've always loved pretty containers," she answered with a sigh. She'd begun collecting any that caught her eye when she was still in grade school. Her favorites were stacked in the closet of her old bedroom in her parents' house.

"Then you're sure to like these. They're one-of-a-kind creations." Ever the gentleman, Jason held the door for her.

Where bakery products had crowded the shelves of Nick's display case and flowers had been everywhere she looked at Forget Me Knot, here only a handful of boxes had been artfully arranged on display stands. Recessed spotlights highlighted intricate carvings that covered the sides and lids. On one, a bride and groom toasted each other with champagne flutes. Another featured a horse-drawn carriage.

Jason's long strides led the way to the counter where a young woman stood. He made the standard introductions, and Tara shook hands with Helen Berger, the co-owner of The Memory Box.

"I must say, I've never seen anything quite like these." Tara ran one finger along the edge of a box lined with velvet. The workmanship was every bit as good as some of the pieces she'd seen on display in New York art studios. "These are exquisite. I want to buy one, and I'm not even getting married."

"B-brides do buy m-most of our boxes," Helen admitted with a charming stutter. "We have a wide variety of patterns you can choose from, or we'll help you design something perfect, j-just for you." She walked over to one that featured a chubby-cheeked baby. "S-see?"

Tara's midsection tightened. For an instant, she pictured herself cuddling a

141

baby with Jason's gray eyes and dark hair. She blinked the image away. All that talk of weddings back at I Do Cakes had addled her mind. Much as she wanted a family of her own, she hadn't even started looking for her Mr. Right. Whoever he turned out to be, it wouldn't be Jason. Her current assignment would see to that.

She wrenched her gaze away from the carving. She needed to focus on the task at hand if she had any hope of getting ahead at *Weddings Today*. "Where do you get all these?" she asked, hoping Helen would admit she stocked cheap imports.

"My brother starts with oak or black walnut and hand-carves each exterior panel. Once he's satisfied, he and my dad stain the pieces and treat them to several layers of protective polyurethane. After that, they assemble the units. Mom adds the lining. She also handles our website."

"A family business." She could relate to that. Her sisters were very much involved in her dad's restaurant. "And you run this wonderful shop." Tara gestured to the attractive displays, the muted wall colors.

"Yes." Helen smiled. While they chatted, her slight stutter had eased until it was barely noticeable.

"How's business?" She glanced around

at the empty shop. No brides or grooms browsed the aisles. Why was that?

"Excellent. For custom designs, we have a three-month waiting list. While most of our orders come through our website, we get a fair amount of walk-in customers. The weekends are usually pretty busy."

Tara's fingers itched to trace the carved drawings. To keep them busy, she flipped open her notebook. While Jason stood in the corner quietly talking on his cell phone, she asked the first question on her list. "What do you do when someone isn't happy with their purchase?"

Helen bit her lip. "We take precautions to make sure that doesn't happen. Every customer approves a series of drawings before Brett, my brother, carves the first notch. He sends them photographs of the work in progress. It's rare for someone to be unhappy with the final product, b-but, I won't lie to you—it d-does happen. On those occasions, we give them their choice of a full refund or having us start from scratch with a new design."

Tara had never heard of such a generous return policy for a custom item. With a sigh, she closed her notebook and slipped it into her purse. She wouldn't waste any more time looking for problems in The Memory Box. The store, like everything else she'd seen in Heart's Landing, was utterly delightful.

She smothered a groan. It was beginning to look like her only hope of getting a promotion lay in uncovering some terrible truth about Captain Thaddeus.

Chapter Seven

STEPPING FROM THE SHOP INTO the bright, midday sun, Jason dropped his sunglasses into place. "The mayor sends his apologies. When I spoke with him on the phone this morning, he sounded a little stuffy. He said his allergies were kicking up. It sounds a little more serious than that. He has a fever." He studied Tara to gauge her reaction.

"It's just you and me for lunch, then?" She stared up at him, her shoulders softening while the faintest trace of a smile played across her lips.

When Tara wasn't disappointed or angry at the change of plans, he took it as a good sign. "If that's all right with you," he said, breathing easier.

"Actually…" Her footsteps slowed.

"Yes?" He braced himself for bad news.

"After gorging myself on that wonderful cake, I don't think I could eat another bite. I'd just as soon skip lunch and return to the Captain's Cottage."

"That's fine with me." Though the owner of the White Dove Deli would be disappointed, he'd make sure Tara had another chance to visit the sidewalk cafe.

As they retraced their steps to the car, Tara stopped several times to take pictures. The little breaks gave him a chance to think about how things had gone so far, and he was surprised that he hadn't minded showing her around as much as he'd thought he would. She wasn't the jaded New Yorker he'd been told to expect. Instead, she came across as a down-home girl trying to make it in the big city. Bright and witty, she was probably good at her job. She had to be, or she'd never have landed this assignment. He wished her luck. He wanted her to succeed at it as much as she did. Maybe more.

Yet he couldn't help the feeling that something about Tara's overall reaction this morning had been a little off. There'd been a few times when it had seemed as though proving that Heart's Landing deserved its stellar reputation was the last thing she wanted. Which was ridiculous, right? If Tara had come to Rhode Island intent on making sure the town lost its number one rating to another competitor, wouldn't she constantly complain, build a huge mountain out of every tiny molehill? That was what he'd do. And he wasn't alone.

When he'd managed one of the smaller convention centers in Boston, he'd sometimes dealt with performers who were less than impressed with the venue. There'd been eye rolls—lots of them. Bored sighs. An occasional yawn or two. The kind of reaction he'd expected from Tara if she intended to grade them harshly. But on the whole, her responses had been enthusiastic. That, as much as anything, had convinced him she was exactly what she claimed to be—their best chance at retaining the title of America's Top Wedding Destination.

"So, what'll you do this afternoon?" he asked when they'd reached the car. "Is there anything I can help you with?"

"No, thanks. I need to type up my notes from this morning. I want to do that while it's all fresh in my mind. Then, I might read in the library some more, as long as I won't be in anyone's way. I want to dig into Captain Thaddeus's logs and journals." She brushed a hand through her hair.

"I have to say, that's not something I hear very often." By the late 1800s, travel between America and Europe had become almost routine. The logs were filled with pages and pages of mundane reports and chart headings.

"Okay, I'll admit it." Her blue eyes crinkled as her lips curved into a teasing grin. "I don't study every entry. In the journal I read last night, the *Mary S* was at sea for thirty days straight. Nothing much happened until the ship ran into a storm on the tenth day out. From what I could gather, things got a bit rough, but the crew handled themselves well. On the fifteenth day, they ran across a pod of blue whales. The captain filled four pages describing the encounter. That was fascinating. Another storm struck just before they reached land. The rest, I might have skimmed."

"Some of that might be worth a second look," Jason advised. "A daily accounting of rations might seem a bit repetitive, but knowing how many pints of rum were distributed at evensong lets you know how many sick they had on board. They didn't have penicillin in those days. If a ship with a sick crew tried to make port, they'd be forced to ride at anchor until everyone on board recovered."

"Thanks." A bright understanding lit Tara's eyes. "That gives me more insight."

On the short drive back to the Cottage, they talked more about Captain Thaddeus and his crew. All too soon, though, Jason pulled to the curb in front of the mansion. Watching Tara head up the steps and through the front entrance, he felt the strangest stirring in his chest.

Was he attracted to Tara Stewart?

He brushed the idea away like one of pesky black flies that regularly made nuisances of themselves in the spring. Tara might be smart and witty, she might share his interest in history, but getting involved with the person who held the fate of Heart's Landing in her hands was a very bad idea. Besides, in a few days, she'd return to New York. Forming anything more than a casual friendship with someone who lived two hundred miles away was the last thing he wanted. He'd already done that with Clarissa and had the hole in his heart to prove that long-distance relationships didn't work out. He shook his head. He'd talk to the review committee before tonight's cocktail party. He'd done his part by filling in for Greg today. It was time for someone else to take over.

That evening, while the waitstaff bustled about putting the finishing touches for the cocktail party on table settings, he joined the other committee members in a niche outside the Green Room.

"Well, Jason, how'd the first day with

Ms. Stewart go?" Mildred had stepped into her role of Deputy Mayor after they received word that Greg wouldn't be able to attend the evening's festivities.

Jason squared his shoulders. He couldn't lie to his friends. The stakes were too important. "So far, things haven't gone according to plan at all."

Mildred and Helen drew in shocked gasps. When she recovered, the florist asked, "What do you mean? She hasn't found anything to complain about, has she?"

"No, but think about it." Jason ticked items off on his fingers. "We were prepared for Regina Charm's arrival, which was supposed to happen this afternoon. Instead, Tara showed up. Unannounced and a day early. Our plans for this morning suffered another jolt when Greg couldn't get away from Tux and Tails."

"B-but we've adjusted," Helen pointed out. "We d-didn't abandon her to roam around town on her own. She's b-been happy with what she's seen so far?"

"The morning did go smoothly," he allowed. Better than he'd hoped. "But Greg was supposed to be her escort for her entire stay. Now, he's sick with a cold, and from what his wife says, it's a doozy. He's probably out of commission for a week or more."

"That doesn't leave us much choice."

Mildred propped her fists on her ample hips. "You'll have to take his place."

"Me?" Jason scanned the group, hoping everyone else considered the idea as ridiculous as he did. But not a single eyebrow twitched. Not one of the other three on the committee moved a muscle.

"Yes, you." A keen intelligence lay beneath Mildred's sweet, grandmotherly presence. She pinned him with a steely glint. "You two looked like you were getting along just fine when you were in the shop this morning."

That much was true. He had to admit, Tara's reaction when they'd arrived at Forget Me Knot had warmed his heart. One glimpse of the display window, and her doubtful attitude had given way to an infectious enthusiasm. Her love of hyacinths especially had been so endearing that he'd had Mildred send a bouquet of the purple blossoms to her room.

Nick canted his head. "She didn't object to picking out a cake for a pretend wedding. In fact, I think she actually enjoyed herself."

Jason was pretty sure she had, too. He'd noted the slight stiffening of her posture when Nick had shown them into the alcove. Whatever misgivings Tara had harbored, though, they'd melted the moment she'd sampled the first cake. By the time they'd finished with the last one, the three of them had been chatting like old friends.

"Sh-she had nice things to say about The Memory Box."

"We got lucky there," he said, giving Helen a warm smile. "She has a thing for storage containers—who knew?" Despite Evelyn's best efforts, she'd been unable to dig up much information about Tara. "She really appreciated that yours is a family business. Her mom and dad own a restaurant in Georgia. Her sisters work there, too."

"Have you spoken to her this afternoon?" Nick leaned forward. "What's she been up to since you got back to the Cottage?"

His own work had kept him busy for several hours, but he'd kept tabs on Tara's comings and goings. "On the way back here, she said she wanted to write up her notes. After an hour or so, she came downstairs and went to the library. She stayed in there until it was time to get ready for the party."

"The library?" Mildred's brows rose at a sharp angle. "That's an odd choice."

Careful not to leave a mark, Jason scuffed one toe along the hardwood floor. "Before she arrived, we received a request from *Weddings Today* to make all of Captain Thaddeus's journals and logs available. She and I have talked about him a little bit. I think she's a history buff."

"Well, that's right up your alley." Relief softened Nick's features. "Gives you something else to discuss while you show her around town."

"I couldn't agree more." Mildred had her own list of reasons why Jason should fill in for Greg. She toted them out. "You were on hand to greet her when she arrived. You gave her the grand tour of the Captain's Cottage yesterday. Your first outing this morning went well. You both share a love of history. There's no one better suited to point out the historical aspects of Heart's Landing while she visits all the spots she wants to see while she's here. For someone else to take over doesn't make sense. You're the perfect choice."

He was far from perfect, but he was the right man for the job. "I'll fill in for Greg. At least, until he's up and around again."

Voices in the hall signaled the arrival of the first guests for the cocktail party. Jason nodded at the others. They needed to wrap this up before Tara put in an appearance.

"What do you think of her so far?" Mildred's face wrinkled as if she was dealing with a thorny problem. "Is she here with our best interests at heart?"

Jason stopped to think about that for a moment. If there was one thing he was certain of, it was that Tara Stewart was a little bit in love with Heart's Landing. Besides, according to what she'd said this morning, she was up for a big promotion at *Weddings Today* and needed to do an excellent job with this assignment. That could only work in their favor. It followed that he needed to do everything in his power to help her achieve her goal.

"Yes," he said, putting all his assurance into it, "I think she's on our side."

Tara inhaled the fragrance of the hyacinths she'd discovered in her room when she'd returned to the Captain's Cottage. The familiar smell eased some of the tension that had sunk its claws into her shoulders after she and Jason had toured Heart's Landing this morning. One thing was sure, she had her work cut out for her. She hadn't spotted any evidence to support Regina's claim that the town had grown complacent. The three shops she'd visited couldn't have been more perfect. She supposed someone could complain about the three-month waiting list at The Memory Box, but wasn't that actually a good sign that their stock was in high demand?

Her time in the library hadn't been any more fruitful. She'd spent hours poring through the ship's logs without finding a thing that might tarnish Thaddeus's reputation, much less disprove his love for Mary. In nearly every entry, the captain had described his progress on the stone heart he'd planned to give her at the end of his current journey. Only a man in love with his wife would do that.

Standing at the window overlooking the Cottage's gardens, she bit her lower lip. She'd read enough about tall ships to know that a real captain's quarters looked nothing like those on TV and in the movies. In all likelihood, Thaddeus had bent over a work table in a cramped, dimly lit cabin. The air would thicken as his dark hair worked loose from its leather binding to frame his face. With the floor constantly shifting beneath him, he'd tap the chisel with the mallet, again and again, until at last he was satisfied. Only then would he take a long pull from the tankard that waited at the end of his desk.

She must have pictured that scene in her mind a dozen times while she studied the logs this afternoon. But whenever the good captain looked up from his task, she saw Jason's face in the flickering light from an oil lamp.

What was that all about?

She sank onto the edge of her bed. She

wasn't attracted to Jason. She couldn't be. Okay, she'd admit he checked all the boxes for tall, dark, and handsome. He was well educated and an excellent tour guide. But she had a job to do while she was in Heart's Landing, and falling for the owner of the Captain's Cottage was definitely not on her agenda.

She shook her head, determined to dislodge the idea before it could take root. There was nothing going on between her and Jason. The attention he'd paid her, the interest he'd taken in her—that was all simply part of being a good host. As for the shiver of emotion she felt in her chest, well, she was smack dab in the middle of a town devoted to love and happy-ever-afters. It should come as no surprise that being here stirred thoughts of finding her own Mr. Right. She simply refused to make anything more out of it than that. Especially when doing so might jeopardize the very thing she'd come to Heart's Landing to accomplish.

The soft murmur of people gathering on the floor below reminded her that it was time for the cocktail party. Maybe she'd stumble across some hint of trouble there. She crossed her fingers. Her first twenty-four hours in Heart's Landing had flown by. The rest of her visit would pass just as quickly. With so much to accomplish and so little time to do it, she'd have to keep her eyes and ears open.

Grateful that the superb housekeeping staff had steamed and aired her clothes while she was out, she thumbed through the hangers. In honor of the flowers that had been delivered to her room, she chose a purple frock that always gave her an extra boost of self-confidence. A light dusting of powder and a quick swipe of her lipstick, and she was ready to go.

At the top of the stairs, she paused the moment she caught a glimpse of the Green Room through an open doorway. She hadn't expected much of a turnout. Apparently, she'd been wrong about that. Musicians tuned their instruments on the small stage erected in one corner of the room. People in business attire stood five or six deep around tall tables that had been draped in white linens and topped with black accent pieces. The rest of the crowd moved about the room, stopping here to talk, there to exchange a greeting.

Butterflies swarmed through her chest. The fluttering wings sent a rush of nervous energy through her. Even though it had only been a game, she'd meant it this morning at I Do Cakes when she'd said she wanted a small wedding. She'd never been good with crowds or public speaking. At least, she hadn't since the fourth grade, when she'd forgotten her lines in the holiday play and had been so embarrassed she'd run from the stage. Now, though, it looked and sounded as if the entire population of Heart's Landing had turned out for the party. And every person there would be looking at her.

It was a good thing no one knew the real reason she was here. If they did, she suspected the mood in the room below wouldn't be nearly so festive. Her grip on the banister tightened. Prying her fingers loose, she pressed damp palms to her skirt. A thousand reasons why she should head downstairs floated through her thoughts, but she remained rooted to the spot. How was she supposed to face all those people, knowing what she knew and what they didn't?

She didn't know how long she might have stood there, unable to move, if she hadn't spotted Jason at the edge of the crowd. An instant later, their eyes met. Almost as if he'd been waiting for her, he broke away from his group of friends. His footsteps sure and even, he strode to the newel post at the base of the stairs. With a flourish that brought a smile to her lips, he came to a halt and bowed deeply. When he straightened, his grin settled her nerves. She still wasn't quite sure how she made it down the stairs, but a few seconds later, she stood on the bottom step, face-to-face with the man who might have been her Mr. Right if circumstances had thrown them together anywhere but in Heart's Landing.

"You look especially lovely tonight," he said, his voice deep.

"Thanks." Jason's appreciative glance made her doubly glad she'd chosen her favorite dress. "Thanks for the flowers, too. They're perfect."

"My pleasure. Shall we?" He tilted his head toward the room behind him.

"Do we have to?" She scanned the faces in the crowded room. "I have to confess, I prefer smaller groups."

"You said something about that at the bakery this morning." His smile deepened.

"You were paying attention." At the time, she'd thought he'd seen her protest as part of the game, but he'd taken her words to heart. The realization ignited a warm glow in her chest.

"The first rule of being a groom—listen to your fiancée," he quipped with a grin.

Recognizing the line as a take-off on Nick's patter earlier that day, she let her smile widen a smidge. "Do you think anyone would notice if I just hung out right here for the rest of the evening?"

"What? And miss all the food and

drinks? I have it on good authority that the sausage balls are not to be missed."

"I could eat a bite or two. It's been a while since that cake tasting this morning." Beyond Jason, black-suited waiters offered trays of champagne and goodies to guests.

"Aw, they're just friends and family who want to welcome you to Heart's Landing. You'll be fine."

"I don't know." She shifted her weight from one foot to another while she fought the urge to bolt up the stairs to her room. "I don't have to give a speech or anything, do I?" The thought turned her stomach positively mutinous.

"Nope. This is all fun and no business. No speeches, no toasts, no long-winded introductions." He stopped himself. "Well, there's always a toast, but you won't have to give it. Come on." He backed away a step. "You'll enjoy this. I promise."

Looking into his gray eyes, she trusted him enough to let go of her grip on the banister. And he was right. For the next hour, with Jason lending her his quiet strength, they worked their way from one end of the ballroom to the other. They were halfway across when a pleasant, middle-aged couple introduced themselves as the owners of the pretty bed and breakfast Chuck had pointed out on Union street.

"Come by any morning while you're here. We have the best blueberry waffles anywhere in the state," Mark invited.

"We'd love to have you join us for breakfast," Marybeth added.

"I'll be sure to visit soon," Tara replied. She'd already put the inn on her list of places to visit. The owners were so warm and friendly that she made the stop a high priority.

A little farther on, Ames, the owner of Chantilly Veils, suggested she should drop by for a fitting. "You have such gorgeous bone structure, you'll look absolutely stunning in one of my creations," he gushed.

Ames' enthusiasm was contagious, and Tara soon found herself deep in conversation about Guipure versus Duchesse lace.

"Oh, honey. You simply must see a piece that arrived this week. It's edged in such an exquisite lace. It's simply to die for."

They set a date for later in the week before Ames waved to another friend and moved on. When he was gone, Tara glanced at Jason. "Is he always that kind-hearted?"

"I've never been in for a fitting myself," Jason said with warmth in his eyes, "but I've heard more than one bride praise him. Apparently, he has quite the knack for finding the perfect veil to match any dress."

At the buffet line, Chef Janet Hubbard

introduced herself. "I own Food Fit For A Queen. We provide catering services for weddings and special events throughout the area."

"Janet trained at Le Cordon Bleu in Paris," Jason pointed out. "We're very fortunate she chose to make Heart's Landing her home."

"Impressive." *If it's true.* Having grown up in a family that boasted not one, but two chefs, Tara knew a thing or two about the prestigious school. Some cooks claimed to have trained there but hadn't actually completed any of the programs. She lobbed a question guaranteed to separate a pretender from the real deal. "Which specialty did you choose, patisserie or cuisine?"

A knowing smile graced Janet's lips. "Both. I received the Grand Diplome before studying under Chef Walburg at Mikeline's."

Tara whistled softly. The Parisian five-star restaurant was known for its new take on traditional dishes and impeccable service. Jason hadn't been kidding when he said Heart's Landing was lucky to have Janet. "What made you decide to open up a catering business? And why here?"

"I learned early on that I didn't enjoy working the front of the house nearly as much as I wanted to be in the kitchen. Catering allows me to focus on what I love—the food—without having to worry about the decor and atmosphere. As for why I came here, that's a story for another day." She gestured toward the buffet line. "Everything we're serving tonight is on our regular menu. I hope you enjoy it."

"You saved some of those sausage balls for me, didn't you?" Jason cast a worried glance down the long row of tables.

"You brought your appetite, did you?" The tall, angular woman who wore a snug, white jacket chuckled. "There might be one or two left." She turned to Tara. "Be sure to try the roast. The Dijon caper sauce is my own recipe. It's quite popular. The horseradish is pretty good, too."

Jason nudged Tara's shoulder. "Janet's being modest. It's the best you'll ever eat."

The compliment was high praise coming from a man who'd regularly wined and dined clients in some of Boston's best restaurants. With a slight nod to the chef, Tara moved through the line. The waitstaff manning the chafing dishes and trays efficiently filled her plate with a variety of tasty-looking dishes. At the end of the row, she spooned generous helpings of both the chef's special sauces onto the paper-thin slices of beef a burly fellow cut from a spit.

"Oh, my goodness," she whispered moments later as she and Jason stood at nearby tabletop. "You were right about the biscuits. They're fantastic." Cheesy goodness and sausage filled each round bite. Not to be outdone, the tender beef practically melted in her mouth. She contemplated a skewer of roasted vegetables. Carrots weren't her favorite, but the shiny glaze on these tempted her to try a bite. She was glad when she did. Perfectly done to a nice crunch, the veggies burst with flavor. "I'd love to know what she put on these to make them taste this good."

"It's a balsamic demi-glace." Jason popped a mushroom cap in his mouth. He chewed and swallowed. "It's part of my job to know my way around Fit For A Queen's menu. We use them for most of our catering needs."

"You're very good at what you do." She nodded, taking another bite of carrot. After spending the day with Jason, his in-depth knowledge of the Cottage's suppliers didn't surprise her in the least. His attention to detail was impressive. Which, she had to admit, made it all the harder to keep the real purpose of her visit a secret.

Just then, the band struck up a spirited number that saved her from embarrassing herself any more than she already had. She tapped her foot to the lively beat as couples poured onto the dance floor.

"C'mon," Jason said, pushing away his empty plate. "Let's join them."

"Why not?" Where was the harm? She could enjoy herself and still maintain her professional dignity. After all, she and some of her coworkers spent the occasional Friday night dancing at The Scribe. No one there gave that a second thought.

Arm-in-arm, they joined the others on the floor as the band kicked off the next number. Music had always soothed her and, for the first time since arriving in Heart's Landing, she felt at ease. The first tune led to a second just as peppy. When that song ended and the band shifted to a waltz, it seemed the most normal thing in the world to step into Jason's arms. Considering their height difference, she was surprised when her head fit perfectly onto the smooth plane beneath his collar bone. His movements were so fluid and graceful that she gave herself over to the music and the comfort of having his arms wrapped around her. Her feet moved in step with his as if they'd been dancing together for years instead of only a few minutes. Her eyes drifted shut.

A hush descended as they swayed together. Cocooned in Jason's arms, she focused on the thud-thud of his heartbeat. Strong and steady, it was a sound she could go on hearing forever. The fresh, clean scent of laundry soap rose from his shirt. It mixed with his spicy cologne to form an intoxicating fragrance she thought she might always associate with him.

Plates rattled at the buffet line. Jason missed a step. Her eyes sprang open. Around them, the dance floor had cleared while the musicians took a break. Shocked that she'd momentarily lost track of where she was, of who she was, of what she'd come to Heart's Landing to accomplish, she backed away from Jason.

"I'm sorry," she said, her face heating. "We shouldn't have... I shouldn't have..." She gave up. "I need to go."

Resisting the urge to run, she calmly, deliberately made her way out of the room. At the foot of the stairs, she stopped long enough to cast a quick glance over her shoulder. Jason had disappeared into the crowd. It was just as well. She had no idea what to say to him.

In the safety of her room a few minutes later, she leaned against the door.

Sure, Jason was an amazing dance partner. An amazing man. But she had no business dancing with him, much less getting caught up in the moment and losing sight of the reason she was in Heart's Landing. She was here for one purpose—to destroy the very foundation of his home. That was something she couldn't afford to forget, not even for a second. She'd lose her job unless she carried out Regina's instructions to the letter. With no money to pay for rent, she'd lose her apartment next. And if that happened, she'd have no hope at all of ever convincing her family that pursuing her dreams had been a good decision.

Chapter Eight

JASON PUNCHED THE END CALL button and dropped the phone on his desk. He stretched his arms above his head. "I think I've spoken with everyone in town this morning." Everyone, that was, except for the one person he wanted to hear from. Elbows bent, he threaded his fingers together behind his neck. "They all wanted to say how much they enjoyed the party."

Seated in the visitor's chair where, between phone calls, she'd brought him up to speed with events around the Cottage, Evelyn asked, "Who was it this time?"

"Jimmy." The young man who'd recently been promoted to assistant manager at I Do Cakes took his job seriously. Maybe too seriously. "He wanted to make sure we were pleased with the petit fours and éclairs.

When I told him they were great, he asked if there was anything else we needed. There wasn't, was there?"

"You didn't happen to mention the extra sweet rolls for tomorrow's breakfast, did you?"

Jason blinked. He vaguely recalled Evelyn saying something about placing a larger order for the morning after the Garrison wedding. It wasn't like him to forget something that important. Freeing his hands, he rocked forward. "I'll call him right back."

"Never mind. I'll handle it." Though Evelyn gave him a questioning look, she accompanied it with a nonchalant wave of her hand. "I have to swing by the bakery later today. Now, as I was saying, this week's paychecks are right here, ready to be signed." She tapped a folder on the corner of his desk. "I triple-checked the hours against the time clock. There weren't any discrepancies."

"Paychecks. Right." Verifying the staff hours was normally his job. This week, though, Evelyn had offered to take that task—and many others—off his hands so he could focus on the *Weddings Today* review. Speaking of which, he hoped he hadn't ruined things by dancing with Tara last night. He'd half expected her to call or text after she'd practically run out of the ballroom, but he'd looked for a message from her a dozen times this morning. So far, nada. Should he check in on her? He picked up his cell phone. Thinking better of the idea, he set it back on his desk.

"That last rainstorm washed away some of the gazebo's foundation. I have the grounds crew working on repairs. It'll cost us some overtime, but it'll be worth it. They promised to complete the job by the weekend."

"Why the rush? We don't have a ceremony scheduled in the gardens this week." Jason ran a hand through his hair. Speaking of gardens, he hadn't taken Tara on a tour of the grounds around the Cottage yet. Should he?

"The Smith couple wants to have their wedding photographs taken there. Are you even listening to me?" Evelyn stared at him.

Seeing the concern etched on his cousin's face, Jason swallowed. He'd better pull it together. Ever since the party last night, his thoughts had been drifting toward Tara far too often. "Sorry. I've been, um, distracted."

"It wouldn't have anything to do with a certain blonde journalist, would it?" Evelyn leaned forward, a playful eagerness shining in her eyes. "Do you two have something going on besides the review?"

"Don't be ridiculous." Jason stiffened.

"I'm simply doing what everyone asked me to do, showing her around town and making sure she sees the best of Heart's Landing."

"I don't know about that." Evelyn tsked. "I saw you on the dance floor. You two looked like a pair of lovebirds."

"Was that before or after she stalked off and left me standing there by myself?"

"Ouch! What'd you do?"

"Nothing." He held up his palms. "I swear." One minute, he and Tara had been moving about the dance floor in time with the music. The next, she'd sprung from his arms like a Jack-in-the-box. He had no idea what he'd done wrong. The worst part was that dancing with her had awakened a dormant longing. For the first time, he'd caught himself wanting what other grooms came to Heart's Landing to celebrate...with her. But when she'd abandoned him in front of the roomful of people, he'd come face-to-face with the facts. He had no business even thinking those kinds of thoughts about her. Not now, and not later, either.

The phone rang, and he held up one finger. "It's Greg. I've got to get this."

He greeted the mayor with a sigh of relief. The call had put a stop to Evelyn's prying questions.

But the moment he finished bringing the ailing man up to speed, his cousin picked up the conversation right where she'd left off. "Just be careful." She leaned back in her chair. "I like Tara, but you're coming off a breakup. I wouldn't want to see either of you get hurt by rushing into something."

"You have nothing to worry about." Tara would be headed back to New York before long. After that, they'd probably never see each other again. "I'm not going to make the same mistake I made with Clarissa and get involved in another long-distance relationship," he said with far more assurance than he felt.

His answer, though, apparently satisfied Evelyn. She relaxed into her chair. "So, what are your plans for today?"

"She wanted the morning to herself. I'm taking her into town after lunch. We have places to go and people to see." There'd be plenty of time to chat while they were out. With luck, Tara would tell him why she'd run off like she had last night. "By the way, Ames invited her to stop by for a fitting sometime this week."

"His veils are spectacular." Her perpetual grin widening, Evelyn fanned herself. "I wish I could afford to have him design one for me."

"Hmmm." She'd set her sights on a

headpiece from Chantilly Veils, had she? "That sounds like the kind of thing one cousin might give another as a wedding gift," he suggested.

Disbelief widened Evelyn's eyes. "You'd do that?"

"As much as you do around here, I figure I owe you that much. But maybe you should concentrate on finding the right guy first." Whoever he was, he'd have to measure up. His cousin deserved the best.

"If I'd known there was a veil at stake, I'd have started looking earlier." Evelyn sobered. "When the time's right, don't think I won't hold you to it. And don't forget. You need to have Tara back here by five for the Garrison wedding."

"Right." He checked his watch. The morning was still young. He pushed away from his desk. "Are we all caught up?"

Smiling, Evelyn shook her head. "You still need to sign the paychecks, or you're going to have some very unhappy employees."

"Right." He reached for the folder. With all that was on his mind and on the schedule, he'd be lost without Evelyn to keep tabs on him this week. Still, he hated to see her work so hard. Last night, she'd dropped in on the party only long enough to fix a plate. According to at least one source, she'd taken her food back to the office to eat. "As long as I'm sticking around for a while, why don't you take the morning off? I'll cover the phones and such."

"Can't. I have a meeting with vendors at ten." Her features brightened. "But I could practice our songs for Wednesday night till then. I'd love to run through the whole routine."

"That sounds like a good idea." Clicking his pen, he flipped the folder open and took the first check off the stack.

"Okay. I'll be in the conservatory if anyone needs me."

"We won't." Shooing Evelyn out of his office, Jason couldn't help but feel that by the time the contest was over, he'd owe his cousin far more than a wedding veil.

In the meantime, he'd make the morning do double duty by mulling over exactly what had gone wrong last night. One thing for sure, he should never have asked Tara to dance with him. Holding her in his arms had only led to problems. The kind neither of them could afford.

The heart wants what the heart wants.

The saying was one he'd heard his dad repeat often enough. He'd begun to wonder if his heart wanted Tara, but his mind knew better. This time, for a lot of reasons, he had to side with his mind.

Tara sipped coffee while she watched the little circle on her screen spin. What was taking so long? Yesterday, her reports to Regina had gone in a flash. Today though, long seconds had passed since she hit "send," and her laptop was still deciding whether or not it wanted to follow her instructions. Worse, it kept shutting itself off in the middle of the task, forcing her to log in and start over.

What to do. What to do.

She could sit here and simply wait for the device to do its thing. Or, she could practice her apology to Jason. Not that she needed to. She'd been over what she intended to say a thousand times during what had turned into a sleepless night.

She drummed her fingers on the table as the screen timed out for the third time. Phooey. Changing the settings went against the company's security protocols, but enough was enough. Once the computer booted up again, she brought up the control panel. With a few keystrokes, she modified several of the power options. By the time she finished, the laptop no longer shut itself off mid-task or required her password every time she stopped typing to think for more than five seconds.

Satisfied that the machine would attempt to send her reports until it succeeded, she pushed away from the table. At the buffet, she doctored a second cup of coffee. A tempting aroma rose from a breakfast dish that featured layers of fruit and thick slices of bread in an egg-y custard. Her mouth watered. Though she'd told herself that she'd eaten enough for three days at the party last night, she couldn't resist taking a plate from the warmer and dishing up a small helping. One glance at her computer put a smile on her face when she returned to her table. The circle had disappeared, the email sent.

Her mom liked to say that snow and adolescence were the only things that went away if you ignored them, but Tara had a few new candidates to add to that list. Patience—and the occasional reboot—solved most computer problems. Snarled traffic in Midtown would unknot itself, given enough time. And her attraction to Jason would fade, too, if she simply pretended it didn't exist.

Yes. That was exactly what she'd do. She'd ignore the way her tongue got all tied up in knots whenever she saw his tall form striding toward her. She'd banish him from the dreams that had kept her tossing and turning through the long night. And she absolutely would not think about how good it had felt when he'd held her. Because she couldn't afford to develop feelings for the man. Not now. Not when she'd finally been given her one big chance to succeed at *Weddings Today*.

Her decision made, she concentrated on her breakfast, which tasted every bit as good as it smelled. Snatches of piano music drifted into the room while she ate. The notes stirred a familiar itch to run her fingers over the ivories, press her feet on the pedals. She'd inherited an upright from her grandmother, but her apartment was far too small to accommodate it. Even if she could figure out how to lug it up five flights of stairs.

Her laptop chimed. A quick glance assured her that her reports had reached their destination. Finished with breakfast, she powered the computer off, tucked it under one arm, and headed down the hall in search of the source of the music.

It didn't take long to find it. In a salon she'd barely looked inside during Jason's tour of the house, Evelyn sat at a grand piano. Light poured through the mullioned windows, setting her red hair aflame while she sang along as she played a rollicking song about life on the high seas. Tara didn't recognize the melody but tapped her toe along with the music. When the young woman struck the final chords, she applauded.

"I didn't know anyone was there." Evelyn's ever-ready smile widened. "Did you want to play? I can leave." She started to stand.

"Don't be silly." Tara waved the woman back onto the bench. "I enjoyed listening to you. Was that one of the numbers you and Jason perform together?" She wandered closer.

"Yes. It's part of the set we'll sing at the Smith reception on Wednesday." Evelyn slid a few pages of sheet music across the lid's glossy, black surface. "I've been so busy this week I've hardly had a chance to practice. Everyone wants to get married in June. I don't know why. Me, I'm going to get married in the Fall. The colors are so lovely that time of year." She plinked an ivory key. The clear tone of a middle-C rang through the room. "I thought I'd get in an hour or two before things get hectic again."

"That's probably because I'm here, right?" She didn't expect an answer to the question and studied the sheet music. The chords seemed simple enough, the words straightforward.

"Not really." Evelyn grinned. "We were already slammed to begin with. Don't tell

Jason, but I actually enjoy filling in for him when he's busy. It gives me a better sense of what it takes to run this place."

Tara handed the sheets back to Evelyn. "Do you ever see yourself doing that? Taking charge of the Captain's Cottage?"

"Full-time? Not on your life. Too much responsibility for me—I'll leave that to my cousin. Keeping track of the weddings that take place here at the Cottage, making sure there's adequate turnover time between events—that alone is hugely complicated. Then, there's working with the vendors, maintaining the website, handling all the publicity, supervising the maintenance and housekeeping crews. People depend on him for their jobs. Brides count on him to provide the perfect venue. I don't know how he does it all, but he never complains, never loses his cool." She paused to take a breath.

"He must really love what he does." Her chest ached when she thought of how her assignment might impact Jason. Unable to meet Evelyn's eyes, she studied the view on the other side of the window.

"He does. We all do. Working here, work-ing anywhere in Heart's Landing, it's more than a job. It's a calling. We're dedicated to seeing that every bride who walks through our front doors has the best experience of her life. You know that saying, 'It takes a village?'"

Tara nodded.

"Well, it might take a village to raise a child, but it takes an entire town to pull off one perfect wedding after another. I do my small part by keeping the books and making sure that when the cook wants to bake a red velvet cake or the housekeeper says it's time to polish the silver, we have whatever they need on hand."

"You must be really organized." It would require a staggering number of items to maintain a house the size of the Captain's Cottage for a single day. Evelyn performed the task day in and day out. But she might not have a job much longer. She, along with everyone else in town, would face some major adjustments once *Weddings Today* awarded some other city the title of America's Top Wedding Destination.

"It's my secret power." Evelyn's dark eyes twinkled. "We all have them."

"Oh yeah?" Curious, she asked, "What's Jason's?"

A teasing glint lit Evelyn's eyes. "I'll never tell. You'll have to figure that one out for yourself."

Tara trailed a finger over the line of keys. She might enjoy doing just that, except the man with the swashbuckling good looks was going to be so furious when he learned the truth behind her presence in Heart's Landing that he'd never speak to her again. Plus, she'd already sworn to keep her involvement with Jason to a minimum.

"And yours? What's your secret power?" Evelyn tipped her head to one side.

"That depends on who you ask." As a child, her mother had called her stubborn. The few men she'd dated had complained that she put work above their relationship, while Regina praised her dedication. She liked to think of herself as determined—once she figured out what she wanted, she went after it with all her heart.

"Stick around—we'll figure it out together."

"If only I could," she said turning wistful. She'd been in Heart's Landing less than two full days, but the place had gotten under her skin. She loved the quaint shops, enjoyed seeing brides and grooms wandering up and down Bridal Carriage Drive, felt perfectly at home here in the Captain's Cottage. But her job, her future, waited for her in New York.

As if she'd expected the answer, Evelyn patted the bench beside her. "Here, join me," she said, scooting over to make room. "I could use a partner."

"Thanks, but I'll pass." Tara eyed the space Evelyn had cleared and shook her head. Standing in the choir loft where her voice blended in with twenty others was one thing. The idea of singing in the salon with someone as accomplished as Evelyn made her nervous, and that was without stopping to consider who might overhear them.

"Come on. It's just the two of us. These old sea shanties are easy-peasy."

Okay, she was tempted. She glanced over her shoulder at the empty doorway. "I'm rusty," she said at last. "Don't say I didn't warn you."

Sliding onto the bench, she listened as Evelyn played through the first number. When the other woman started over at the top, Tara joined in, hitting the first note at the top of the bar, just as she'd learned to do in countless choir practices. The timing was trickier than she'd anticipated, and she faltered a bit on the first run-through. By the second, though, she matched her partner note for note.

"That was great," Evelyn said when they finished. "Want to try another one?"

Tara shrugged. Why not? From what she could tell, their voices worked well together. As for someone peeking in on them, no one had wandered past the open door. Chances were, this far away from the main entrance, no one would.

Over the next hour, they worked their

way through all the songs in Evelyn's set. For some of the easier numbers, Tara plunked out the harmony on the keyboard, a move that drew a nod of approval from her new friend. The ballad at the end was a crooked tune with an odd set of beats that made it trickier than the rest. It took three tries to get it right, but Tara kept at it until she had it down pat.

"Excellent!" Evelyn exclaimed while the last notes faded. "If you lived here, you could fill in for me once in a while."

"Oh, I don't think so," Tara protested. Though she wouldn't mind spending more time in Heart's Landing, there was another, bigger problem. "I don't like speaking in public. I can't imagine singing a solo in front of a big group."

"It's all in the way you think of it." Evelyn ran the scale on the piano. "If I focus on my feelings, my fears, I get stage fright, too. But if I concentrate on the bride and the groom, see the songs or the skit as a gift to them, then walking up on the stage or singing along with Jason isn't half as bad."

"That's such a sweet thought." Tara bet the crowds loved her for it. As for her, though, just thinking about performing for strangers loosed the butterflies in her stomach.

"Speaking of Jason, look who just

stopped by." Evelyn lifted her chin. "I guess our time is up."

As Evelyn began gathering up the sheet music, Tara glanced toward the door. Her thoughts stuttered the moment she caught sight of Jason's long, lean form propped against the frame. She swallowed. How long had he been standing there?

He cleared his throat. "I hate to break this up, but Tara, we need to get started if we're going to get you back here for the Garrison wedding this evening."

"Good grief!" When she was in middle and high school, she could practice for hours without being aware of the passage of time. Once she'd started college, though, her studies had taken precedence. After that, between her job and her tiny apartment, singing in the church choir had been her only musical outlet. Today, for the first time in ages, the music had swept her away again.

She jumped to her feet. "Let me just run my stuff up to my room, and I'll meet you at the entrance." She turned to Evelyn before dashing off. "Thanks so much for letting me join you. I hope I didn't waste all your practice time."

"Nonsense." Evelyn waved the thought away. "I enjoyed it. Let's get together again, soon."

Tara's smile firmed. "I'd like that," she said, surprised by how much she looked forward to it already.

In her room a few minutes later, she tucked her laptop into her briefcase and dashed into the bathroom to dress for spending another day with Jason. She took a minute to draw in a steadying breath.

She could do this. The ride into town offered the perfect opportunity to deliver the apology she owed him. Of course, she couldn't admit the truth to him. Couldn't tell him that the sound of his heart beat had calmed her, that she'd never felt safer than she did in his arms, that she'd wanted the moment to last forever. She especially couldn't tell him that thinking those thoughts, having those feelings, jeopardized the very reason she'd come to Heart's Landing in the first place. So, no. She wouldn't tell him the whole truth and nothing but the truth. Instead, she'd stick to the apology she'd practiced. The one that said "I'm sorry" without delving into the tricky matter of feelings.

After that, well, for the rest of her stay in Heart's Landing, she'd make sure she kept her distance from him. She'd learned her lesson. It was one she wouldn't repeat. From here on out, she'd simply be a journalist going about her job with Jason as her guide.

For the rest of her stay, she'd ignore his strength, his kindness, and his bright intelligence, just like she'd ignore how handsome he was. Instead, she'd concentrate on what she'd been sent here to accomplish. No matter how much she wanted to stand in the protective circle of his arms. Or how cold she felt outside it.

Chapter Nine

AT THE ENTRANCE TO THE music salon, Jason looked his cousin up and down, trying to figure out what she was up to. "You two sang well together," he said tentatively. "What prompted that?"

As if it had been the most normal thing in the world for her to make friends with the woman in charge of determining their future, Evelyn shrugged. "She heard me playing and stopped by. One thing led to another. She's talented."

"She's not bad." He refused to say more than that. He certainly wouldn't admit that he could listen to Tara's sweet voice for hours and not grow tired of it. Nor would he confess how much hearing her sing the ballad that closed out their routine had moved him.

"I'll call you next time we practice to-gether. Maybe you can join us." Evelyn's eyes sparkled.

Jason swallowed. He'd seen that specu-lative gleam on more than one occasion. It always meant trouble. Usually for him. "I don't know what you're thinking, but what-ever it is, don't do it," he cautioned.

"I'm not planning anything." Evelyn held up three fingers. "Scout's honor." She slid the lid closed over the piano keys.

Though she sounded sincere, he knew for a fact that his cousin had never joined a Brownie troop, much less been in the Girl Scouts. "Evelyn…" he said using his sternest voice.

"All right, already. I won't push it." The sheet music clutched to her chest, she covered the short distance between them. "I guess, now that you're heading out, I'd bet-ter get back to work."

Jason stepped out of the doorway to let her pass. He tapped his phone's ear piece. "I'll be available if you need me." They parted at the main corridor, Evelyn disappearing around the corner that led to her office. He shook his head. Assurances to the contrary, he was pretty certain his cousin had some-thing up her sleeve. That was all he needed. *Not*. Not when he already had his own prob-lem to deal with.

At the front door, he shoved his hands into his pants pockets and concentrated on the apology he intended to give Tara. Though he still wasn't quite sure where he'd gone wrong last night, he couldn't afford the slightest chance that tension between them might harm Heart's Landing's chances. Not that he thought she'd give the town a bad mark over a single mistake. He hadn't known her long, but his gut told him she wasn't the kind to hold grudges. No, her openness and honesty were two of the qualities he admired most about her.

Promptness, however, was not one of her virtues. A full quarter of an hour slipped past before he finally heard motion in the upstairs hallway. A single glance up the stairs told him it had been worth the wait. Tara had exchanged her sweats for a loose-fitting top in the perfect shade of brown that highlighted the gold in her hair. Beneath it, a pair of skinny jeans hugged her long legs all the way to slim ankles where the hem brushed the tops of low-heeled shoes. His pulse shifted into overdrive.

"You look..." He swallowed, his mouth dry. Words that normally rolled off his tongue stuck in the roof of his mouth. How had he failed to notice how pretty she was until now? "Nice," he finished, hurrying to tuck an unwanted surge of emotions behind a thick barrier.

"Thanks." She plucked at the hem of her shirt. "Sorry I took so long. I tried to check in with my boss, but her phone went straight to voicemail." Expelling a breath, she fidgeted with the hair that spilled over her shoulders.

The random motions told him she was nervous about something. He had a sinking feeling he was the cause. Though the car keys jingled softly, he kept his hand in his pocket. He didn't want to leave before they cleared the air between them. "Can we talk for a sec?" he asked as she headed for the door.

"Now? Here?" Tara gave the foyer a cautious look.

"There's no time like the present." He drew in his own steadying breath. "I wanted to say—"

"I'm so sorry about—" Tara spoke at the same time.

Silence filled the space between them as their words ground to a halt. From somewhere in the interior of the building, a door slammed.

He grinned. "Ladies first," he said, glad for a reprieve, however temporary.

"No. I interrupted you. Go ahead."

He showed her his empty palms. "Whatever I did to upset you last night, I'm sorry. I hope you won't let it impact your opinion of Heart's Landing."

"You?" Tara's eyes widened. "You didn't do anything wrong. I'm the one who owes the apology," she argued. "I shouldn't have danced with you. Don't get me wrong—I enjoyed it very much—but it was unprofessional of me. I don't want to give you the wrong impression. I'm here to do my job and nothing else."

So, she'd liked dancing with him, had she? Her admission sent warmth surging through his chest. In a perfect world, he'd tell her he'd enjoyed those moments on the dance floor just as much as she had. He could have held her close for the rest of the night. The brush of her soft breath against his neck had weakened all his defenses. He'd grown intoxicated on the floral scent of her perfume while they'd whirled around the dance floor. But this wasn't a perfect world, and he couldn't so much as whisper a word of how he'd felt. She'd made her position perfectly clear. Besides, his own reasons for steering clear of her were just as valid.

"Look," he said, his voice soft with the need to shoulder the blame. "I'm just as much at fault. In a few days, you'll return to New York, while I'll stay right here in Heart's Landing. Our paths may never cross again.

It doesn't need to be any more complicated than that."

"Right," she said on a long sigh. "So, we're agreed. We'll keep things strictly professional between us."

"Agreed," he said, despite an ache to hold her close again.

"And we're okay? No hard feelings?" The tip of her tongue darted across her lips.

"Definitely." Even as he agreed with her, he wrenched his eyes away. Watching her moisten her lips had delivered a kick straight to his gut. That was definitely on the wrong side of a line he couldn't cross if he had any hope of maintaining his distance. Stuffing his feelings behind what he hoped was an impenetrable wall, he managed a grin. "Ready?"

"Ready. Where to first?"

He let his gaze fall to her feet. Judging from the cute little bows on her shoes, she was going to love their first stop. "Have you heard of The Glass Slipper?"

"Oh! I was hoping you were about to say that." Tara pressed one hand to her heart. She couldn't think of anything she'd rather do than spend the morning in a shoe store...

unless it was making another circuit of the dance floor with Jason.

"Well, you're in luck, 'cause that's where we're headed."

She didn't think twice when he held the door for her. But that had been a mistake, she quickly realized when she caught the now-familiar scent of Jason's aftershave. The smell immediately plunged her into the memory of being held in his arms. She brushed aside a sudden longing, determined to stick to the decision that was best for both of them.

In the car, she rambled on about the weather, then kicked herself for bringing up such a mindless topic. But finding something to talk about that didn't skate too close to her feelings was difficult in a town where happy couples walked arm-in-arm beneath shade trees. For a while, she thought they'd never reach their destination before she stuck her foot in her mouth. When Jason turned onto Union Street, her shoulders softened with relief that they'd arrived without another misstep.

"I think I'm going to like it here." The Glass Slipper drew her attention like a strong magnet. "Have you ever seen such perfect signage?" Etched into the window, the name of the shop and the outline of a strappy high-heel sparkled like cut diamonds. Lights mounted beneath the pink awning bathed the entire entrance in a welcoming, rose-colored hue.

"Can't say I've given it much thought."

She was already out of the car and snapping pictures when a tiny slip of a woman who wore her hair in a towering French twist swung the entrance door wide. "Welcome to The Glass Slipper," she called. "I'm Opal Burnette. I'm delighted to have you make this one of your stops in Heart's Landing."

Jason faded into the background as Opal ushered them into the store's hushed atmosphere. Tara had no sooner crossed the threshold when a younger version of their hostess stepped from behind a curtained area.

"This is my daughter and fellow shoe aficionado, Laura," Opal said with an effusive gesture. "Together, we help brides put their best foot forward, whether they're walking down the aisle or just living their lives. Laura, this is Tara Stewart."

"The pleasure is all mine." Tara's gaze bounced between the two women who looked more like sisters than mother and daughter. "I've wanted to come here ever since I saw an advertisement for the store in *Weddings Today*." Wearing a happy grin, she turned in a slow circle and soaked up the surroundings.

White walls and carpet gave the main

showroom a clean, modern air. Centered in front of a low table, a tufted red velvet couch interjected just the right touch of whimsy. Atop built-in cabinets, wide-screen televisions featured a fashion show of brides striding down a runway, their skirts lifted to show of one exquisite pair of shoes after another. Tiny spotlights shone into individual niches built into the wall. Each held a pair of perfectly drool-worthy heels.

"We focus on wedding apparel in the front room," Opal offered. She motioned toward a second space off to the side. "Over there, you'll find footwear ranging from beach sandals to towering stilettos that cry out to be worn on a night on the town. Feel free to look around as much as you'd like."

Knowing she could spend hours in the store, she looked for Jason. She found him leaning against a wall like it needed his support. "This might take a while," she warned.

"Take as much time as you need," he said, peeling himself upright. "I'll be just outside. I have a couple of calls to make."

She and Opal traded amused glances as he pulled his phone from his back pocket while, with three long strides, he made his escape. The door had barely swung shut behind him when a pair of heels adorned with ornate silver tips caught Tara's attention. The scroll work on the shoes looked familiar, and she darted toward them. "Are those Sophie Olsens? I didn't know she'd launched a new line." The shoe she lifted from the display threatened to slip from her hand when it weighed more than she expected.

Like she was divulging a secret, Opal leaned in close. "Sophie is a close friend. We're carrying a few of her styles to help her test the market." Her gaze shifted to the shoes. "Those feature four-inch heels, hand-beaded teardrop crystals, two sets of cross ankle straps, and extra padding for comfort. The tips are sterling silver. And, of course, her signature scrollwork, which you no doubt noticed." In a stage-whisper, she added, "Retail on each pair is $1295."

Whew! Air rushed between Tara's lips. The pricey shoes were so far out of her budget, they might as well be on the moon. Afraid she might drop one she held and lose a couple of the expensive gems in the carpet, she gingerly handed the heel to Opal. "Have you sold many?"

"Laura keeps track of our inventory. Honey?"

Beneath a bee-hive of dark brown hair styled like her mother's, Laura pursed red lips. "We've handled three sales so far this month."

Pretty good for a pair with such a hefty price tag. "Do you mind if I mention them in my write-up?" When Opal agreed, she snapped a picture of the shoes in their little nest. So far, no one at *Weddings Today* had mentioned Sophie's new venture. Getting the scoop on the story was quite the feather in her cap.

"If you have any questions, don't hesitate to ask."

"Actually, if you wouldn't mind, I'd love to hear more about you and Laura and The Glass Slipper." Tara opened the notebook she carried with her everywhere she went. Flipping past the list of questions she'd asked of other vendors, she turned to a blank page. "How long have you been in business? What made you decide to specialize in bridal footwear?" She stood at the ready, pen in hand.

A half hour later, she had enough information to write an entire article on her new favorite store in Heart's Landing. After taking a few minutes to window shop and snap pictures of several elegant pairs of shoes, she thanked Opal and Laura for their time and rejoined Jason on the sidewalk.

"All done," she announced. The interview had lasted longer than she'd expected. She tapped her notebook. "I have everything I need. The store's a beauty, and the owners are sweethearts."

"You liked the shoes, I take it?" Jason pocketed his cell phone.

"They have an amazing selection. I'd definitely come to The Glass Slipper to shop for my wedding." Her words faltered. "Not that I have any plans to get married anytime soon. I'm focused on building my career right now."

Who was she trying to convince—him or herself? Either way, it didn't matter. She and Jason had already agreed that they didn't have a future together. With a renewed determination to maintain a professional relationship and nothing more with the man whose company she enjoyed far more than she should, Tara squared her shoulders. "According to my itinerary, the rest of the afternoon is free time."

Jason nodded. "We left a few gaps in the schedule in case you wanted to wander about on your own."

"If it's okay, I'd like to spend the time in the library."

Jason spread his hands wide. "With all this at your disposal, you're going to spend the day reading?"

"What can I say? I'm fascinated by the captain's journals and logs." She certainly couldn't admit that the clock was ticking on her secret assignment. Or that she could use a little time away from the man who made her pulse race. She held her breath until, with a dismissive shrug, Jason finally started toward the car.

Once he was behind the wheel, he slowly drove through town. On Bridal Carriage Way, he pointed out the Perfectly Flawless Day Spa. "Evelyn swears by their mani/pedi. She goes there at least twice a month."

Further on, they passed the Honeymoon Travel Agency. A young couple stood on the sidewalk studying the window posters that featured white-sand beaches and swaying palm trees.

"Do you like to travel?" Jason asked.

"I haven't done much. When I was a kid, we took day trips to the beach, but we didn't go on long vacations. It's too hard to get away when you run a restaurant." Tara crossed one leg over the other. Once she landed her next promotion, there'd be a lot more travel in her future.

"I hear you. Running a small business makes taking time off difficult. I'm lucky to have Evelyn as a backup, but I still haven't spent more than a handful of days away from the Cottage since I took it over." He drummed his fingers against the wheel.

"Where would you go if you could?"

"Europe, definitely."

"Let me guess. The Eiffel Tower and Big Ben. Maybe the Trevi Fountain," she suggested, rattling off some of the more popular tourist spots.

"Nope. I'd want to see all the great cathedrals. The Duomo, St. Peter's Basilica, Westminster Abbey, St. Stephen's in Vienna. The list goes on and on."

"You're kidding." Now, that was interesting. They were on the top of her list, too. She leaned closer. "What do you like about them? Their history? The architecture?"

"All of that. I'm a bit of a history buff. How about you?"

"Promise not to laugh?" He'd probably think her reason was silly. That was why she'd never told another soul. "The weddings. I'm a little nuts about royal weddings."

"No!" Jason's face morphed into a look of absolute horror, but the laughter in his eyes saved her from total embarrassment.

"Yes, I'm afraid it's true." Her cheeks warmed. "I taped Meghan and Prince Harry's wedding. I must have watched it a hundred times."

"I see." He pulled at his chin. "Tell me, are you harboring any other deep, dark secrets?"

Ouch! That hit a little close to home. Afraid he'd read her thoughts, she turned to stare out the window. "Everyone has secrets," she whispered.

Chapter Ten

*J*ASON SWORE THE TEMPERATURE IN the car had just dropped ten degrees. He hadn't meant to pry but, judging from the silence that filled the air, he'd touched a nerve. At the next corner, he pointed out a stone heart mounted on one of the few original buildings left in Heart's Landing and was pleased when Tara warmed enough to ask questions. He enjoyed sharing what he knew about his famous ancestor, and they spent the rest of the ride to the Cottage talking about Thaddeus and Mary, the momentary freeze all but forgotten.

Once he'd parked the car, he left Tara in the library to continue her research and headed for his office. He'd taken less than a half dozen steps, however, when someone called his name.

"Jason! Yoo-hoo! Jason!" The bottom of a white apron flapping against a pair of churning legs, the head chef for the Captain's Cottage hurried toward him with a picnic basket. "We have an emergency, Jason."

His stomach dropped. Images of flames leaping from the kitchen's massive oven shot through his head. He banished the thought. Connie was upset, but not *that* upset. Had she discovered melted ice cream dripping from the freezer? Whatever the problem, he reached for his cell phone, ready to call in the cavalry. "What's wrong, Connie?"

"It's the strawberries." Plump cheeks rosy with exertion, the cook skidded to an abrupt stop. "They slid off the cart when Amos was bringing them up from the cooler. An entire flat, ruined."

Jason sucked in a deep breath and let it out in slow dribbles. Deliberately, he rolled the tension out of shoulders that had gone rock-solid in an instant. "I'm pretty sure we can resolve this without declaring a national emergency."

"But it's the *strawberries*, Jason," Connie protested. "We're completely out. You know how many orders we fill for strawberries and cream every night? It's our most requested item. What am I going to tell our brides and grooms when they ask for them?"

Jason flexed his fingers. "Have you contacted our suppliers? Checked the grocery store?" Someone in Heart's Landing had to have a few on hand.

"I've tried everywhere." Connie's bottom lip quivered. Damp white curls escaped the bandana she wore instead of a chef's toque. "Our only option is the U-Pick place north of town, and I can't spare someone to go get them. Essie has the day off. Fiona is up to her elbows in cookie dough." Each afternoon, the kitchen staff replenished the tea and coffee station and put out immense trays of house-made cookies. They were always a big hit. "Can you go?"

He looked down the corridor toward his office. An afternoon of sunshine and fresh air held a definite appeal over the paperwork that awaited him. "I suppose."

"Oh, good! Look, here." The cook thrust the picnic basket in his direction. "I packed a lunch for you. All your favorites." Connie's eyes filled with a conspiratorial glint. "There's more than enough for two."

Jason blinked. His eyes widening, he studied the woman who'd run the kitchen of the Captain's Cottage his entire life. Connie had given his hand a good-natured tap whenever he'd tried to grab a second fistful of cookies from the counter after school. When he'd been sick with a cold or the flu, she'd brought him chicken soup and milky tea with lots of sugar. She was more than an employee. She was family. But in all the time they'd known each other, she'd never once tried to play the matchmaker. Until now.

"You think I should ask Tara to come along?" he asked, bemused.

"I wouldn't presume to choose your company for you, Mr. Jason." Connie dried her hands on her apron. "You just make sure you come back with that basket full of strawberries."

He slanted a smile at her retreating figure. "Yes, ma'am."

It took less cajoling than he'd expected to convince Tara to join him. "Thanks for coming with me," he said as he pulled off the highway at the sign to The Right Berry Farm a short while later. "I hated to take you away from your research."

"Oh, I didn't mind. I probably shouldn't admit this, but the captain's logs make me sleepy." Tara crossed one slim leg over the other. "Besides, Manhattan's not known for its berry patches. I'm looking forward to spending some time in a garden. My folks grow a lot of their own vegetables for the restaurant. I miss that."

"Spent a few hours picking beans, did you?" He shot her a quick grin while he parked the car between two mini-vans.

"Planting, watering, weeding, picking—my sisters and I did it all. We grew everything from beans and tomatoes to strawberries and melons. And herbs, of course." She examined her fingertips. "I'd like to have a garden of my own one day. Not a huge one like theirs, but enough to have something fresh-picked for dinner once in a while." Slowly, she lowered one hand to the door handle. "That's probably not going to happen in New York, though."

"I hear you. When I lived in Boston, I was constantly on the go and couldn't keep a houseplant alive. Rhode Island is so green in the summer. I love that about living here. You ever think of moving out of the city?"

For a long minute, Tara stared out the car window at the orchards, corn fields, and gardens that covered the gently rolling hills. She gave her head an emphatic shake. "*Weddings Today* has their headquarters in New York. Almost all the magazine's staff lives there. If I get this next promotion, I'll be able to move to a slightly bigger apartment, but that's about as good as it's going to get for the foreseeable future."

Jason's eyes narrowed. Tara had paused a bit too long before insisting that her ties to the city were permanent. Wondering what that was all about, he set the brake. He'd circle back to the topic later. "We'd better get started. Connie will have my head if I come back empty-handed."

Car doors thumped shut, and they stepped out into the warm summer air. In front of them, pavers formed a path that led to a low-slung farmhouse. Vines climbed the support columns and clung to the eaves above the porch. Nestled among the leaves, bronze hedgehogs perched on cement stands. The sun felt good on his shoulders as he guided Tara up the walkway to a shady spot where rocking chairs beckoned guests to sit and enjoy the view. The rustic building housed products by local artisans. He skirted it, instead steering them around to the back. He and Tara took wicker baskets from conveniently placed stacks and followed signs for the strawberry patch. They didn't stop until they were a dozen rows past the nearest clump of children who ate as much as they picked under the watchful eyes of young mothers.

"Now, this reminds me of home." Tara flung her arms wide, her T-shirt stretching across her chest.

"You miss it? Savannah?" It had been tough enough for him to move away from all that was familiar, but at least he'd known his stay in Boston was temporary. It must have taken a lot of courage and determination to move to a strange city on her own, but he wasn't surprised that she'd succeeded. He'd already decided that Tara was an amazing woman. Especially right now when she stood in the sunshine wearing shorts and a T-shirt above a well-broken-in pair of running shoes. He busied himself with their baskets, refusing to give in to an urge to wrap his arms around her in a move that wasn't nearly as platonic as he told himself it should be.

"I do, but..." Her hands dropped to her sides.

"But?"

"My folks weren't exactly thrilled when I chose a career in journalism over the family business. Though they'd never admit it, I've always felt like they're waiting for me to get this 'writing thing' out of my system and come back to work for them."

"Doing what? You said one of your sisters is a chef, and the other runs the front of the house." He searched for names and gave himself a pat on the back when he recalled them. "Lulu and Maggie, right? Where would you fit in?"

Tara held up empty palms. "I keep asking the same question. I guess they'd put me to work waiting tables. There's nothing wrong with that, but it's not exactly my dream job." Her shoulders slumped. "Plus, I'd always be the little sister who couldn't make a go of it in the big city. That's one of the reasons this promotion is so important. It's my chance to finally prove I was right to follow my dreams."

"Well, I'll keep my fingers crossed for you. If there's anything I can do to help, let me know."

"You've done so much already." Tara's hand brushed his forearm. "I'm not sure how I'll ever repay you."

Her touch sent warmth coursing up his arm and across his chest. Deliberately, he studied the field. "You can start by picking some berries." To give his hands something to do besides reach for Tara, he twirled his empty basket by the handle. "We're looking for the biggest, ripest ones we can find."

"Of course. Only the best for Heart's Landing's newlyweds." Tara slanted a grin up at him. "I saw a sign for hand-churned ice cream. Last one to finish pays?"

Oh, so she was competitive, was she? Deciding that was another trait he liked about her, he raised the stakes. "Double dips. The Rights use an old family recipe. It's the best ever."

"You're on. Let's find a good spot."

Hand on one hip, Tara cast a critical eye at the low, green plants that stretched a hundred yards or more into the distance. A few ripe berries poked out from beneath the closest leaves. Declaring their immediate area picked over, she started moving at a good clip. Layers of straw mulch crackled under their feet until they reached the middle of the field. At last, Tara hunched down beside a plant laden with large, luscious berries. Deftly, she plucked one and held it up for him to examine. "These are nice."

Seeing her kneeling on the ground, her long legs tucked gracefully beneath her, her ponytail curling softly over one shoulder, the sun gently kissing the top of her head, Jason felt his heart lurch. *Steady now.* Tara might be smart and kind and make him smile more than he had in a long time, but Heart's Landing was only a temporary stop on her road to success. Falling for her wasn't just a bad idea, it was a terrible one. Still…

"Jason? What do you think? Ready to pick?"

Tara stared up at him, a puzzled frown on her lips.

He cleared his throat. "Yep." He swiped the berry from her outstretched fingertips and popped it into his mouth.

"Hey!" she protested.

"I had to make sure it tasted as good as it looked." He grinned around the sharp-sweet flavor of fruit at the height of perfection.

Following his lead, Tara helped herself

as well. "Mmmm." She smiled, her eyes closed. "I could eat these all day, but we have work to do. Ready. Set. Pick." Gathering berries in both hands, she began filling her basket.

Unable to banish the saucy tilt of Tara's head from his mind, he kneeled beside her, grasped a plump strawberry, and gave it a tug. Their hands in motion, they worked their way down the row while fat bumblebees lumbered through the still air like overloaded cargo planes. The noisy shouts and laughter of children faded in the distance.

The sun warmed Jason's shoulders and back while he drank in the good smells of rich earth, green plants, and ripened fruit. Almost before he knew it, their baskets couldn't hold another berry. It was time to leave. He stood and extended a hand to Tara. She grasped it, unfolded her long legs and rose with a grace he only wished he was capable of. In an instant, they were face-to-face, their bodies mere inches apart. His breath stalled.

"What?" she asked, her voice suddenly hoarse.

Falling for someone who lived so far away was not on the agenda, even if she stirred a yearning in his heart he couldn't explain. He straightened and took a step back. "Nothing. You look relaxed and happy. That's all."

"I miss working in a garden more than I thought I did." Like a cloud drifting in front of the sun, a shadow passed over her face. She hefted her basket. "Well, I guess we're done here. We should probably get back."

"Hungry?" Suddenly, he didn't want the day to end. "Connie packed a picnic lunch."

"I could eat a bite or two. And don't forget, you owe me an ice cream."

"Me?" Jason gave her a look filled with mock indignation. "I filled my basket first."

"Not a chance."

The easy banter chased away the tension between them, and they headed for the main building to weigh and pay for their purchases. Tara was telling him a story about her office-mate when they reached a bench at the end of one of the rows. Amid the backpacks and diaper bags piled atop the seat, a young woman sat wiping red smears off a grinning toddler's face. The little tyke beamed a strawberry smile at them as they passed. If he hadn't been paying attention, he'd have missed it when Tara's face nearly melted.

Jason swallowed. *Someday*. "Do you ever see yourself having a family, children?"

Tara gave the child a wistful glance. "One day. Sure." She shrugged. "Not for a while yet. And of course, I'd have to meet the right man and fall in love. How about you? You think you might ever change your mind about having a family?"

A baby to swaddle and push through town in a carriage? A child he'd teach to throw a ball, to take on piggy-back rides or play hide-and-seek with? Someone he could pass his legacy on to, who'd carry on the Heart name? His eyebrows slammed together. "Who said I didn't want children?"

"You did. That first day when you took me on the tour of the Captain's Cottage, you said you didn't think kids and a family were in the cards for you," Tara murmured, her voice soft.

"Oh, that." He took a deep breath. "Clarissa and I had just called it quits the day before. I was a bit sour on, well, everything." His feet stirred up a grasshopper that went shooting off into the distance.

"This is probably none of my business, but were you two together long?"

"A few years. We met at a fundraiser in Boston when we were both starting out. She had just landed her first client at Handon's Ad Agency. I'd recently taken over as the manager of a great little venue in South Boston. We had a lot in common and, for a long time, I convinced myself that she was the one."

"What happened, if you don't mind my asking?" Tara pulled the elastic band free from her hair and swept the thick, blond strands into a new ponytail while they walked.

Did he mind? No. Like the print on some of the old photographs in the attic, his feelings for Clarissa had faded. "She realized it before I did, but we simply weren't headed in the same direction. Things were never quite the same after my dad died. I had moved back to Heart's Landing to help out while he was sick. After he passed, I was busy learning the ropes at the Captain's Cottage. When she begged to help entertain Regina Charm, I thought maybe she was hearing wedding bells. As it turned out, she only saw an opportunity for a potential client. She has her heart set on a vice presidency and all that comes with it—the brownstone in Back Bay, rubbing elbows with the rich and famous, nannies, and private schools. She never understood how I could give all that up for what I have here."

Tara tucked a few loose strands behind one ear. "This is what makes you happy. Anyone who loves you should understand that. I've only been here a few days, but I get it."

Neatly Jason turned the tables on her. "And your job, does it make you happy?"

"Not yet." Tara's mouth turned down at the corners. "It will, though. Soon. My days of doing the legwork for the senior editors will end once I get this next promotion."

They reached the entrance to the old farmhouse that had been converted into a store. Jason held the door for her. "I hope that works out for you. I really do. In my experience, a promotion just means more of the same." He shrugged. "I could be wrong. That might just be the way it worked out for me. As for Heart's Landing, yeah. I can't imagine living anywhere else."

"It is a beautiful town. I'll admit, in the short time I've been here, I've fallen a little bit in love with it."

He wanted to ask if she'd ever consider moving here, where she saw herself in five years or ten, if her plans for the future could ever include someone like him. But he held his tongue. In less than a week, Tara would return to New York and the future she'd planned for herself, while the life he loved was here in Heart's Landing. He had no business falling for her, no matter how perfect she seemed. The problem was, he thought he'd already fallen. And the more he learned about her, the deeper he fell.

He grew silent, unable to think of anything to say to that.

Tara stared into a cooler filled with locally produced cheeses while Jason stood in line at the checkout counter. Her thoughts in turmoil, she couldn't get the conversation with him out of her mind. He'd shared more than she'd expected. But then, everything about Jason was more than she'd expected. Just being in the same room with him made her pulse race. Her mouth had gone so dry when she'd watched the firm muscles in his calves flex as he'd squatted over the low plants that she'd had to look in a different direction. Hearing the low timbre of his voice created images of the two of them curled up beside each other on a porch swing.

If that were all, she'd chalk her reaction up to hormones and rest assured that she'd be back to normal as soon as she returned to New York. But in one of her first assignments at *Weddings Today* she'd learned enough about venues to know that Jason had given up quite a lucrative career to take over the reins at the Captain's Cottage. His roots ran deep in Heart's Landing, and she respected that. He'd discovered what was most important in his life and committed himself to it. All of which made him one of the most interesting men she'd ever met.

The sound of the bell on the old-fashioned cash register at the checkout counter rang. Deciding she wasn't in the mood for cheese, she turned her back on the display just as a freckle-faced teen handed Jason his change.

"Thank you for visiting The Right Berry Farm today. I do hope you'll visit again soon."

If Jason noticed the flirty smile that danced across the cashier's lips, he showed no sign of it. Another factor in his favor. No matter what else was going on, he made the person he was with feel like the center of his universe. For the time being, at least, Tara was that person. As his eyes met hers, she found it hard not to fan herself.

Balancing a large cardboard box piled high with strawberries, he led the way to the parking area. There, he placed the box in the trunk, exchanging it for a heavy picnic basket. Tara chose a table under a towering maple, and soon they were feasting on thick pastrami sandwiches, dill pickles, and house-made chips.

"Ah, that's a slice of heaven right there," Jason said, holding half his sandwich in a two-fisted grip. He took a bite and chewed, a blissful look on his face.

Tara bit off a corner. The sweet-and-sour taste of the sauerkraut complimented the lean, salty pastrami perfectly. "What's in the sauce?" she asked when new flavors and textures rolled across her tongue.

"Connie's special blend of cheese and mustard. Don't bother asking her for the recipe. She won't even give it to me."

A dribble escaped Jason's mouth and ran down his chin. She pointed to it out to him. Sheepish, he swiped it with a napkin and missed. She pointed again, and this time he mopped successfully. "I feel like I've monopolized the conversation this afternoon. The stage is yours. What else is there to Tara Stewart?"

"You pretty much know all there is to know about me." Except for the most important thing, that she was here to knock Heart's Landing off its pedestal. She bit into a crisp potato chip. "I work, go home to my apartment, get up the next day, and do it again. I'd like to say I go out on the weekends, take in the sights or a play on Broadway. The truth is, I'm usually too busy keeping body and soul together."

"I can hardly believe you're not seeing someone. No one special in your life?"

"Not for a while now." Heat rose in her cheeks. The ghostly remnants of her longest relationship still lingered two years later. Though she didn't talk about it often, she felt a need to confide in Jason. "To be honest, I haven't been serious about anyone since I called it quits with my boyfriend the summer after college graduation."

"A bad breakup?" Jason leaned across the table, concern written in his eyes.

"Eh." She tilted her head. "I'd just been offered the position at *Weddings Today*. We went out to dinner that night to celebrate. He saw someone he knew at the bar and went over to have a word. Left his phone on the table. It buzzed. Some girl had texted him about their date the night before. I thumbed through his messages and discovered she wasn't the only one—he'd been cheating all along."

"I'm sorry that happened to you. You didn't deserve it."

So much sympathy welled in Jason's eyes that it momentarily took the wind out of her sails. His honest reaction stirred the need to tell him the part she'd never revealed to anyone else. Did she trust him enough to share her deepest hurt? One look at the warmth in his gray eyes, and her reluctance faded.

"I broke it off with him that night. Lulu and Maggie helped me drown my sorrows in cheesecake." She shuddered. That was a mistake she'd *never* make again. "But I didn't tell them the rest of it. It was too em-barrassing to admit that he turned to other women 'cause I wasn't enough for him. The whole thing has made me a little gun shy. I've gone out on a few dates since then, but I always call it off before things get serious. I can't stop thinking I'll never be good enough for any man."

"He's the one who didn't measure up," Jason said, his words freighted with the kind of reassurance she hadn't known she was looking for. "Any man who was lucky enough to have you in his life and let you go, well, he should have his head—and his heart—examined."

Jason's gaze bore into her own. Tender and compassionate, his eyes held depths waiting to be discovered. Long seconds ticked past before she glanced away. When she did, she felt certain she'd never doubt herself again. At some point while she'd been pouring out her soul, Jason had reached across the table and enfolded her fingers in his. The intimacy of that simple gesture ignited a warmth in her chest she couldn't deny.

She drew in a shaky breath. Getting involved with Jason would be so easy...and so wrong. She had to put a stop to it before it was too late. Summoning a breezy attitude, she exclaimed, "Whoa! That got deep. I think you'd better buy me that ice cream before I turn into a weeping ball of mush."

While every fiber of her being screamed

that she was making a big mistake, she withdrew her fingers and began gathering up the remains of their picnic. A beat or two later, Jason stood and helped her load the leftovers into the basket. When they were finished, he wiped the last of the crumbs from his hands. "Now, how about dessert?" he asked.

"I thought you'd never ask," she answered, choosing to ignore what had transpired under the tree.

Once they had their cones, they raced to finish before the delicious ice cream melted. It wasn't until she was in the car on the way back to the Captain's Cottage that Tara had a chance to think about what had happened.

What had possessed her?

She'd known better. She and Jason were attracted to one another, but they'd already decided that was as far as it would ever go. So why had she agreed to abandon her research and pick strawberries with him? She could let herself think she'd spent the afternoon with him in order to learn more about Heart's Landing for her article. Or that she'd doubted the lengths people here went to in order to assure the brides' and grooms' happiness so much that she had to see Jason get his hands and knees dirty before she could believe it. She could tell herself that, but she'd be lying.

Though she was loath to admit the

truth, she couldn't deny that she'd developed more than a little crush on the handsome owner of the Captain's Cottage. From the moment she'd stared up at him in his office the first day she'd arrived in Heart's Landing, she'd been entranced by his cool, unruffled manner, his startling gray eyes, his take-charge attitude. She'd been sure that, given time and exposure, her instant infatuation would fade. That as she found out more about what made Jason tick, she'd learn he wasn't anyone's Prince Charming, and certainly not hers.

So far, things weren't working out the way she'd thought they would. For one thing, he listened—really listened—to her. She'd only mentioned her sisters' names once, yet he'd committed them to memory. She couldn't think of a single friend who'd done the same. Even after sharing an office for a couple of years, Van often forgot which of her sisters was the cook. But Jason remembered. He understood how difficult it had been for her to leave home and move to a huge city where she hadn't known another living soul. Plus, he'd offered to do anything he could to help her land her next big promotion.

Which was another reason that, as much as she might wish he were, Jason could never be her Mr. Right. Because, in order to achieve her goal, she'd have to ruin the reputation of his famous ancestor. A fact she needed to remember, no matter how tempted she was to lose herself in Jason's eyes or lean into his outstretched arms.

There was only one little problem. No matter how many times she told herself otherwise, she had the strangest sensation that she'd fallen head over heels for the one man she could never have.

"Will I see you at the Garrison wedding this evening?" she asked when they'd reached the foyer.

"I might pop in for a minute, but I won't be able to stay." Regret shown in his eyes. "Saturdays are our busiest days of the week. With three weddings on the schedule, I'll be on the go most of the night. See you tomorrow?"

No matter how much she tried to stop them, her lips tugged down at the edges. "Breakfast, maybe? I'll be busy after that. I've made appointments to check out some of the hotels in town after church, and then I have a conference call with my boss."

It was just as well. They'd spent practically every waking moment together since her arrival in Heart's Landing. A day apart would do them both some good, give them some much-needed perspective on an attraction that couldn't lead to anything.

Chapter Eleven

"*H*AGGARD," JASON MUTTERED, STARING AT his reflection in the mirror the next morning. He rubbed his hand over his chin. The description fit. He looked and felt like something the cat had dragged in.

He supposed he could blame the Garrison wedding. The reception had stretched until well past midnight. Only, he'd never had problems rolling out of bed on the mornings when other parties had lasted into the wee hours.

Maybe it had been all the paperwork. Even with Evelyn's help, reports and requests had piled up on his desk. Last night, while he'd waited for the festivities to wind down, he'd done his level best to catch up on it.

That was, when he wasn't lingering by the door, hoping for a glimpse of the woman he'd vowed to treat purely as a business associate. Sheer force of will had been the only thing that had kept him from wandering into the ballroom and offering to take Tara for another spin around the dance floor.

He checked his reflection in the mirror one last time. The black Polo shirt he wore over a pair of jeans made him at least look presentable. He ran a comb through his hair and double-timed it down the stairs, more determined than ever to protect his heart and his town.

The chatter that drifted from the dining room mingled with the soft clinking of silverware, the occasional scrape of a fork across a plate. Jason lifted an eyebrow in surprise that anyone from the wedding party had rolled out of bed after such a late night. Or that, unlike him, they sounded no worse for wear. He detoured to the doorway, where Evelyn's insistence on increasing their bakery order finally made sense. Though the bride and groom were conspicuously absent, both sets of parents, as well as assorted relatives from both sides, had gathered for an early breakfast. With a reminder to thank his cousin for keeping him out of hot water, he made his way through the room, shaking hands and offering congratulations.

Having done his duty as host, he carried on to the corner table Tara had made her own. The urge to lean down and brush a light kiss on her cheek whispered through him. He resisted, barely. Firming his resolve, he turned to the one topic everyone in the Cottage was discussing.

"How was the Garrison wedding? Did you enjoy it?"

Tara rested her fork on the side of her plate. "It was beautiful in a different sort of way. The bridesmaids wore sarongs and leis. The groomsmen had on white suits with Panama hats. They brought in instructors to teach us all the hula."

Jason's breath hitched. Deliberately, he stared out at the front lawn of the Captain's Cottage while he tried to erase an unbidden image from his mind. It was no use. Asking about the wedding hadn't been a smart move, after all.

"The food was amazing, even though there weren't any sausage balls."

He couldn't ignore the comment any more than he could overlook the teasing glint in Tara's eyes. "How about the cake? Were there coffee-infused layers separated by a chocolate rum filling and topped with a vanilla bean frosting?" The combination had been her favorite out of all the ones they'd tried at I Do Cakes.

"No, but this was every bit as good. Coconut and mango. Positively dreamy." She licked her lips. "Oh, and I caught the bouquet."

"Congratulations," he said, despite the feeling that he'd just taken one on the chin.

So much for his idea that talking about the wedding would steer the conversation away from dangerous territory. He was looking for an escape route when Evelyn appeared in the doorway. She beckoned, pointing at her watch.

"I have to run." He and his cousin caught the early service at the church each Sunday and had brunch afterward with friends in town.

"Sure. See you around." And with that Tara picked up her fork and returned to her breakfast as if she hadn't just rocked his world.

Telling himself that spending the day apart was a good thing, Jason headed out the door with his cousin. But a short while later, Tara lingered at the edges of his thoughts while he listened to the Sunday sermon. Though their paths didn't cross while he ate lunch with friends and looked over the repairs to the gazebo, her sweet smile was constantly on his mind. As a result, Sunday afternoon and evening dragged by. Listening to the ticking of the clock in his room that night, he counted the passing hours and wondered if Monday would ever arrive.

But at last, it did, and he trotted down the stairs with a fresh spring in his step. Soon, he and Tara were in the car once more, headed to one of his favorite haunts. He rounded the sharp curve at Boutonniere Drive where Bridal Carriage turned into Boston Neck Road. A quarter of a mile farther, he pulled onto a wide dirt apron in front of a two-story barn.

"Here we are," he announced.

"A farm?" Tara's eyebrows rose.

"Not exactly. C'mon." He popped the latch on his seat belt and sprang from the car. Rounding the front of the vehicle, he held her door for her. "This is Your Ride Awaits." He pointed to a discreet sign on the barn door.

"I should've known." Tara tapped one finger to her nose. "Horses." She swept the empty barnyard. "Where is everyone?"

Jason shrugged. "Probably out on calls. But the owner said we could make ourselves at home. Want to look around?"

He took the spark of interest in Tara's eyes as a positive sign. Resisting the urge to take her hand, he crossed to the entrance of the barn, where a pair of enormous wooden doors had been propped open. Stepping from the bright sunlight into the cool, darkened interior, Jason led the way. Halfway down the wide corridor that ran between rows of stalls, he stopped in front of the pen that housed his favorite.

"This is Lady," he said when a large white horse stuck her head over the railing. "She's retired from the carriage business, so she gets to spend her days here or in the paddock out back."

Blowing softly, Lady nudged Jason's shoulder.

"Just a minute, old girl." He stroked her long cheek. "Would you mind giving her some attention while I scour up a treat for her?"

Tara smiled broadly. "I'd love to." She moved closer. Without a moment's hesitation, she ran her fingers through the mare's silky mane.

"You've spent some time around horses, have you?"

"I know my way around a muck rake, if that's what you mean. In college, I was assigned to the stables as part of the work study program. I never quite figured out what that had to do with my Journalism studies, but I enjoyed it."

While she treated Lady to a good scratch, he aimed for the snack bins at the end of the aisle. He returned with a couple of carrots, which he broke into quarters and handed to Tara. Holding a piece in the palm of her hand, she offered it to Lady. The horse nipped it gently. Tara's answering giggle warmed his chest.

"Their lips are always velvety soft," she said in a breathy gasp.

Tara looked so cute, standing there with her hand outstretched as she offered the horse a second piece, that Jason had to give himself a stern reminder that she was off-limits. He settled for brushing shoulders with her while they listened in companionable silence as Lady's powerful jaws made quick work of the carrots.

On their way out of the barn minutes later, Tara glanced around. "We aren't far from the center of town, are we? You'd think this would be farther out."

"It was," he acknowledged. "Heart's Landing grew up around the barn and stables. The town is filled with businesses that have been handed down from one generation to another. Your Ride Awaits is one of the oldest. It's been here nearly as long as the Captain's Cottage. Tom Denton—he's the current owner—he makes a big production out of getting brides to the church in style. When he's not busy with that, he takes people on carriage rides."

"I've heard the carriage business can be

hard on horses." Tara's lips tugged hard at the corners. Her arms folded into a protective stance across her chest. "There were some instances in New York—"

"That doesn't happen here," he said, interrupting before she could finish. "We have one of the best large-animal veterinary clinics in the state, just over that hill there." He pointed to a small rise behind the barn. "Doc Cooper, he keeps a close eye on things, and he flat-out won't tolerate neglect. Not that he needs to worry about Your Ride Awaits. Tom cares more about his horses than he does some of his family members."

Tara's arms relaxed. "Well, Lady certainly did look healthy. Her coat is soft. There wasn't a single tangle in her mane."

"That's what I'm talking about. She might be past her prime, but she gets excellent care, plenty to eat, and regular exercise."

He'd barely finished when, with a jangle of metal, two high-stepping black horses rounded the curve and pranced into sight. Silver trim on the gleaming white carriage caught and reflected the sun's rays. Seated on a high bench and resplendent in top hat and tails, the driver steered his team into the barnyard. He circled the parking area and pulled to a halt with a creaking of leather and wood.

"Your ride awaits, madam." The driver doffed his hat.

Jason risked a quick glance at Tara. She stood entranced, her lips slightly parted, her eyes wide. After a little bit, she turned to face him. "What's this all about?"

"Tom and I—this is Tom, by the way—we thought you'd like to take a carriage ride through Heart's Landing. See the town from the perspective of a bride on her way to her ceremony."

An excited grin stole across Tara's face. "I'd like that very much!"

Tom set the brake and smoothly climbed down from his perch. "Allow me," he intoned. The step he lowered from beneath the carriage snapped into place. Extending a hand, he assisted her onto the leather cushions.

But when Tom bent to fold the step back into place, Tara leaned forward. Her pointed gaze landed on Jason. "You aren't coming?"

"I'll drive and meet you at Bow Tie Pasta." The more time he spent with Tara, the more difficult it became to maintain his distance. A task that would be impossible if he joined her in the buggy's tight space.

"Well, then…" Tara gave the cushions a wistful look. "If you're not riding in the carriage, I'm not either."

He'd spent enough time with Tara these last few days that he recognized the futility of arguing with her once she'd made up her mind. Oddly enough, he liked that quality in her. "Do you mind dropping us off at the restaurant?" he asked Tom.

"It'd be my pleasure," the livery owner answered with a knowing grin. "Guess she's got your number," he whispered as the carriage sank beneath Jason's weight.

She had his number, all right. And here he'd been doing so well with the whole keep-your-distance thing. But how was he supposed to remain detached and separate from Tara in a carriage built for two?

Now what have I done?

She should've done the smart thing and just gone along with Jason's plan, but she hadn't been able to resist asking him to join her on the ride. And when he'd refused, she'd known that he'd insist on coming with her rather than let her miss out on the experience. He was caring and generous like that. But what was she going to do now? No matter how much she wanted to, she couldn't very well rest her head on his shoulder or enjoy the feel of his arms around her. She'd simply have to make the best of the awkward situation.

While the coach dipped and swayed under Jason's weight, she scooted over as far as she could, but there was only so much room in the cozy carriage. There certainly wasn't enough for her to avoid the press of Jason's thigh against hers when he sank onto the plush cushion beside her. Her shoulder brushed against his arm no matter how far she leaned in the opposite direction. Even with the top down, there was no escaping the pleasant smell of his aftershave mixed with the masculine scent that was his alone.

Nor did she want to. And that was a problem.

The carriage dipped again as Tom took his seat on the high bench in front of them. With a quiet "Cluck cluck" to the horses and a gentle slap of the reins, he headed in the general direction of town. Springs creaked and wheels turned beneath the coach. Unable to face Jason, to let him read the thoughts that most certainly played across her face, Tara pretended the passing landscape demanded her full attention.

She might as well admit the truth, to herself if to no one else. Her feelings for Jason ran far deeper than they should considering the short time she'd known him. His very presence inspired trust. She wasn't the only one who saw that in him, either. The people of Heart's Landing could've chosen anyone else to fill in as her escort when the mayor had fallen ill, but he'd been their first pick. He might not think she'd noticed, but she'd seen how everyone relied on his leadership and strength. Nor could she help but admire how he'd returned home when his father got sick, or that, after his passing, Jason had thrown himself into the family business. He'd earned her respect for the way he'd dedicated himself to preserving the Captain's Cottage as a place where brides and grooms started their new lives together. The more she knew about him, the more certain she felt that there was something between them, something more than just the usual friendship that sprang up between two people who'd spent as much time together as they had over the past few days.

Unless she was seriously mistaken— and she didn't think she was—her feelings weren't at all one-sided, either. Jason had shared his thoughts, his plans for the future with her. He'd sought her company when he didn't have to. When he was around, they were always laughing, telling jokes. On more than one occasion, she'd caught him admiring her when he didn't think she was looking. He could have treated her like a business associate, but when they'd danced together, he'd leaned in closer than friends did. As if that wasn't enough to send warmth flooding through her whenever she thought of him, Jason had encouraged her to pursue her dreams and hopes.

Which brought her to the main reason why snuggled next to him was the last place in the world she should be right now. Because, in order to achieve her dreams, she'd have to destroy the very thing he valued the most—the legacy he'd inherited. She had no doubt there was something amiss in the legend of Captain Thaddeus. Over the years, there'd been too much speculation, too many hints, that the facts of his story wouldn't hold up under close scrutiny. The proof she needed existed in the ship's logs and journals—she just had to find it. But when she did, it would destroy even the faintest hope she and Jason had for any kind of relationship.

If only they'd met under different circumstances. Or in a different time altogether. Then maybe things would've turned out differently for them. But as things stood, they had no hope for a future. So, why had she asked him to ride with her?

Because she couldn't resist him any more than she could resist breathing.

Beside her, the man who was foremost in her thoughts cleared his throat. "You're awfully quiet," he said when they'd ridden in silence through half of Heart's Landing. "Is everything all right? Tom can turn the buggy around and take us back to the barn if you'd rather."

"No. This is great." She summoned a smile for the gentle sway of the carriage, the clop-clop of the horses' hooves on the pavement, the happy couples who walked hand-in-hand on the city sidewalks. One day, she hoped to have that kind of relationship with someone. But not with Jason. Not when her main purpose in coming to Heart's Landing was to challenge his long-held beliefs about his ancestor. She shivered at a sudden chill.

Ever attentive, Jason asked, "Are you cold? I didn't think to bring a blanket. I should have." Without waiting, he stretched his arm around her shoulders and snuggled her closer.

And heaven help her, she leaned into him. It didn't matter that she told herself it was the wrong thing to do. As she soaked up the warmth of Jason's chest, she couldn't retreat from the firm press of his fingers on her arm. Even though she knew she should move away, should hug her side of the carriage, she remained exactly where she was all the way through town.

Long before she was ready for him to, Tom signaled the team to a halt in front of a canopy cover that stretched to the curb from the doorway of Bow Tie Pasta. While the horses snorted and tossed their heads, she reluctantly straightened. The time had come to put a stop to whatever was happening between her and Jason before one—or both—of them got hurt. She'd indulged herself for as long as she could. She had to say "enough."

Her lips parted, the words on the tip of her tongue. Before she could speak, however, Tom dismounted and held the door to the carriage open.

"Text me when you're finished, and I'll come back to pick you up," he told Jason. Tom doffed his tall hat. He extended a hand and helped Tara disembark. "Ma'am. I hope you enjoyed the ride."

"Very much," she said. Feeling the loss of Jason's arm around her and knowing that she needed to tell him it could never happen again, she added a silent "too much."

But holding what was sure to be an awkward conversation on a public sidewalk didn't feel right. Besides, she'd hardly had a chance to recover her balance after stepping down from the carriage before, with his hand at her elbow, Jason guided her up the covered walkway to the entrance of the most popular restaurant in Heart's Landing. Once inside, she was too entranced by exposed brick walls, cherry-wood trim, and curved windows overlooking lush plantings to broach the subject that should've been first on her mind.

Within minutes, the maitre d' ushered them to a center table. A veritable phalanx of waitstaff stood at attention nearby. They sprang into action the moment she took her seat, and soon she found herself paging through a menu the size of a novel while a tuxedoed waiter reviewed the day's specials. Next, the sommelier stepped forward with his recommendations, followed by the ritual tasting and approval of their selection. Shortly after the wine steward poured their first glasses of an outstanding pinot, another waiter appeared bearing a basket of bread and rolls, along with a trio of flavorful dipping oils.

If she thought she'd have a moment for a quiet discussion with Jason once they'd placed their orders, she was proven wrong again. Word that they'd be dining at Bow Tie Pasta must have spread. Either that or practically every business owner in Heart's Landing had developed a sudden urge for Italian food. In groups of two or three, they stopped by her table to chat. Between interruptions and bites of excellent pasta, the lunch hour sped by. Almost before she knew it, Jason had texted Tom and arranged their return trip to Your Ride Awaits.

But she couldn't get in the carriage

again. Not and keep her wits about her. She was too weak, her attraction to Jason too strong. Once she climbed the steps into the buggy, she knew, she just knew, she'd cuddle against him again. And that wouldn't be fair. She wouldn't, she couldn't mislead him like that. It was time to pull the plug. She had one final chance to clear the air between them before it was too late. A few words were all it would take to destroy any misconceptions either of them might harbor. She just had to say them.

Except, she couldn't. She couldn't end things between them. Not now. Not yet.

On the sidewalk outside the restaurant, she took the coward's way out. "I think I'd like to stretch my legs a bit," she said, putting several steps between them before her new resolve weakened.

"You don't want to wait for Tom?" Confusion and something that looked an awful lot like disappointment clouded Jason's features.

"No. If you don't mind, I'll walk back." She needed time away from the man who made her pulse race. Needed to gather her thoughts and figure out what to do next. "I'll probably work in my room for a while. I'll see you tomorrow."

"About that." Jason stuck his hands in his pockets. "If we get an early start, we can check out the widow's walk first thing in the morning. After that, though, the weatherman says we're going to have quite a bit of rain. Tomorrow might be a good day to work indoors. I was thinking I could help you in the library. If you still want my help, that is."

Great. Jason had given her exactly what she didn't want—a chance to back away gracefully. She should take it, should tell him she was fine, thank you very much, but she'd prefer to finish her evaluation of Heart's Landing without him at her side. Only, there were problems. Seeing the widow's walk firsthand was a must if she was going to complete her assignment. As was ferreting out the truth behind the myth of Captain Thaddeus. And who better to help her than the man who'd spent his childhood reading the ship's logs and journals? Yet, as much as her head told her that enlisting Jason's help was the smart career move, her heart warned that spending more time with him wasn't the wisest choice.

"I'd love to have your help," she answered, throwing caution to the wind and taking her chances.

Chapter Twelve

*J*ASON GRABBED THE KEY RING from the post just inside his office. A thrill of anticipation raced through him. In just a few minutes, he'd meet Tara in the lobby. He'd planned to keep his distance from her, but yesterday's events had changed things, hadn't they?

What he'd intended as a sightseeing trip for one had turned into much more than that when she'd insisted on having him join her in the carriage. The moment he sat beside her, he'd felt her pulse race, heard the sharp intake of her breath. Her shivers had given him the perfect excuse to wrap his arm around her. Not that he'd needed one. Or had done anything wrong by pulling her close when the breeze had raised goose bumps on her arms. He'd wanted nothing more than to do it again on the return trip and see where their attraction led them.

Common sense told him that acting on his growing feelings for Tara was the worst thing he could do. Not only did she hold the fate of Heart's Landing in her hands, but in a matter of days, she'd return to New York. He had no business even thinking of getting involved with yet another woman who put a different zip code in her return address.

But, no matter how he fought it, he couldn't deny that he was attracted to her. She drew him to her like no woman he'd ever known before. And, on the off chance that she felt the same way, didn't they deserve to give things between them a chance?

The question had plagued him all night. Rather than sleeping, he'd remained on edge, unable to get her out of his mind. Somewhere around four this morning, he'd finally come to the realization that he had to face the truth. Despite his efforts to the contrary, he was falling for Tara. And that was a bad thing, a very bad thing. By doing so, he was putting his heart in jeopardy. Worse still, he'd be putting the fate of Heart's Landing on the line. Neither was a risk he could afford.

There was only one course of action open to him. He'd have to be stronger. Have to bury his feelings for her. Have to hide them so deep, they'd never trouble him again. His course set, he squared his shoulders and slipped the key ring into his pocket. It'd be better if he could avoid her altogether, but he'd promised to escort her during her stay. He couldn't break his promise. Not with all of Heart's Landing counting on him. But today, while he and Tara visited the widow's walk and later, when they worked in the library, "cool" and "detached" would be his watch words. No matter what.

Minutes later, he cleared his throat in the lobby and stared over Tara's head. One look at her eager face had nearly been his undoing, but he was stronger than that. He wouldn't give in to temptation.

"I checked the weather," he announced. "The skies should remain clear for the next hour or so. That'll give us plenty of time before the rain starts."

Tara lifted the camera she carried like other women carried purses. "Lead on," she said with the grin that warmed his heart despite his best efforts to remain aloof and distant.

Side by side, they headed for the stairs. Once in the attic, he wasted no time cutting through the storage area and opening the door to the widow's walk. There, safety overtook chivalry and he stepped onto the deck first, using his shoulders to block the

243

door while he gave the exposed roof a quick study.

No water pooled on the slate tiles. He'd personally checked the railing around the widow's walk before he'd retired last night. It appeared as sturdy today as it had then. A bank of low clouds hugged the horizon, but only a few white wisps dotted the blue sky overhead. Satisfied that all was as it should be, he stepped aside and let Tara pass.

His chest clenched at her soft gasp. Had she tripped? He reached to steady her, only to have her slip beyond his grasp.

"Well, I'll be..." She stared at square tiles closest to the railing. Cracked and broken, they outlined the circular track Mary had followed while she'd watched for Captain Thaddeus's ship from the widow's walk. "When people said she'd worn a path in the slate, I expected scratches and scrapes, at most a faint indentation. Not this."

Dredging up what he knew about the tiles, Jason chuckled. "Slate is one of the toughest, most durable materials known to man. It's practically impervious to wind and rain. But for all that, it's surprisingly fragile. Especially when struck repeatedly by hard-soled shoes, like the ones Mary wore."

Tara lifted her camera. "I owe you an apology," she murmured as she snapped pictures of the broken pieces.

"How so?" She'd done nothing wrong. Quite the contrary. After his last girlfriend, Tara's honesty and forthrightness was a refreshing change of pace.

"To tell the truth, I never bought into the story that Mary stood watch for her husband's ship. Not until now." She pointed toward the circle of broken tiles. "If I hadn't seen this with my own eyes, I'm not sure I'd have believed it. It's hard to argue when the evidence is right in front of you." She toed a loose shard. It fell back into place with a soft chinking sound. "Why didn't anyone ever replace them?"

Jason shrugged. Of all his ancestors, only Thaddeus had made his living on the sea. Once he'd retired, the widow's walk had fallen into disuse. Decades had come and gone while the isolated spot remained undisturbed. "My dad would tell you that they're part of the history of the house. They give it its character. While that's true, there's another, more practical reason."

"What's that?"

A gust of wind whipped a strand of hair onto his face. He tucked it behind his ear. "We can't get our hands on the same color slate. The tiles you're standing on came from a quarry north of Philly. They were hand-shaped before being shipped here in horse-drawn carts over a hundred years ago. That mine has long since played out and closed."

"Which explains all these broken pieces."

"For now. As durable as slate is, it doesn't last forever." He gestured toward the pitched roof behind them. Here and there, empty squares dotted the surface. In other spots, whole sections had been smashed. "I've started getting bids for a new roof. It's a horrifically expensive undertaking." One he wouldn't be able to afford if Heart's Landing lost its title as America's Top Wedding Destination.

"Watch your step," he cautioned as Tara moved to the railing overlooking the ocean. Though the slate looked dry, appearances could be deceiving.

Tara nimbly picked her way to the rail. "Is this where Mary stood to watch for Thaddeus's ship?"

"In all likelihood, yes." Tara had chosen a spot that provided the best view. "In her day and age, wives with sea-faring husbands kept one eye on the horizon and one eye on their children."

The pages of Tara's notebook ruffled in a gusty wind. In fits and starts, the breeze tugged strands of hair from her ponytail and sent them streaming out behind her in twisting ribbons. He longed to capture them in his hands, but a renewed promise to keep his emotional distance stilled his fingers. To avoid temptation, he forced his focus on the birds that wheeled and turned above the waves. He pointed out a porpoise that broke the surface of the water. Below them, bikers and the occasional jogger moved along the path that followed the curve of the land.

"Do you spend a lot of time out here?" Tara asked after they'd lingered at the railing for a while.

"Not as much as I'd like, but I make a point of it when the fog rolls in. On mornings when it's thick as clam chowder, the railing disappears, and it's just you and the mists. They deaden the sound of the ocean." He liked days like that, when the damp fog wrapped him in a blanket. "A passing ship blew its fog horn one time, and I swore it was right on top of me."

"I'd like to see that. If I lived at the Cottage, this would be one of my favorite spots."

"It could use a little sprucing up." Other than the occasional coat of fresh paint, the secluded area remained exactly as it had been in Mary's day. The wooden railing and the slate tiles were a history unto themselves, but they didn't create much atmosphere. Nothing prevented him from hauling a couple of lounge chairs out onto the deck, though. He could install a cabinet and stock it with snacks and beverages. Maybe add one of those round tables with a wide umbrella to protect Tara from the sun's rays.

He stopped himself. His thoughts had veered toward a cliff, something they'd started doing whenever a certain blonde was near.

Standing beside him, she mopped her face with one hand. "I can almost feel the salt spray on my face."

He pointed to a dark bank of clouds that had moved closer. "It's probably time to go in." He turned toward the door. Tiles that had been bone dry only moments before now bore a wet sheen. "Careful," he warned, just as Tara skidded on a damp spot.

One second she was standing upright. The next, her foot went out from under her. Without giving it a second's thought, he reached for her. Once he had her, though, he couldn't let go. His arms pulled her close to his chest as if they had a will of their own. Tara's breath hitched so hard and so fast, he felt it. His own heart responded with a pounding beat.

As gently as if she were a skittish colt, he held her at arm's length. His gaze rose from her lips to search her eyes for permission to do the one thing he'd sworn he wouldn't do—kiss her. Soft and pliant in his grasp, Tara stared up at him while her breath came in quick gasps. When her eyes filled with the same yearning he felt, he bent low, intending only to place a single chaste kiss on her lips. If that led to more, well...

"Hey! Everything okay up there?"

He froze at the sound of a familiar voice.

As if someone had doused her with a bucket of cold water, Tara flinched.

"We shouldn't. We can't," she whispered.

Not sure what he'd been thinking but certain he'd been on the verge of making a huge mistake, he let his hands fall. Like two people who'd wandered too close to a hot oven, he and Tara took a few hasty steps away from one another.

He gazed over the railing at the path below. An audible groan worked its way up from his chest when he spotted his cousin, one hand cupped over her eyes, staring up at them. He should have expected nothing less. Evelyn had always had impeccable timing. No matter what he was up to, whenever he stood on the cusp of making an important decision, she put in an appearance.

"We're fine," he called down. As fine as two people who'd almost made a huge mistake could be.

"The rain's due to start any minute." Evelyn's warning floated on the fitful wind. "Things might get rough."

He lifted a hand. He'd gotten the message, loud and clear, and it had nothing to do with the weather. He turned, hoping Tara would understand, but only air filled the space where she'd been standing seconds earlier. A flash of color at the door told him she'd headed inside without him. Three long strides took him to the opening. He ducked into the attic.

He spied her across the room near the bookcase. Even in the dim light, he could see the tension that radiated in the set of her shoulders, her carriage. Knowing he owed her another apology, he closed the space between them. "About what just happened—" he began, determined to dive right in.

"Nothing happened." Tara spun to face him. "I slipped. You caught me. The story ends right there."

"But..." He longed to tell her that it was more than that, or it could have been.

"Nothing happened," she repeated, her voice firm and uncompromising. "I admit I'm attracted to you. I have been from the first moment I saw you. I think you feel the same." At his nod, she continued. "But neither of us can afford to let our feelings get in the way of the jobs we have to do. There's too much at stake. My career is on the line."

"Heart's Landing's reputation hangs in the balance," he said dutifully.

She sighed and gazed over his shoulder as if looking into the distant future. "My job hinges on this assignment. I can't risk it all on what might just be a passing temptation. Nothing is going to happen between us now."

He swallowed. Tara had just said all the things he'd been saying to himself ever since she'd arrived in Heart's Landing. He should be relieved, but when he checked his gut, he couldn't ignore the frisson of happiness that had passed through him when she'd admitted she was drawn to him as much as he was to her.

"You're right," he agreed, surprised when he sounded far calmer than his racing pulse made him feel. "We'll put this, whatever it is, on the shelf for now. To be examined later, if we want." But make no mistake, when later came, he'd be the first to unwrap that box.

Tara turned toward the bookcase. Running her fingers over the spines, she browsed through a stack of books. "What are these?" she asked, unearthing a couple from the bottom of the pile. Dust filled the air when she blew softly on the cover. "These are Mary's diaries, aren't they?"

He squinted at the unfamiliar script and the initials embossed in the leather cover before he nodded.

"Would it be all right if I took these to my room to read?"

He should refuse her request. He should at least read through them first. As much as he loved history, he'd never done more than page through the first few entries in his great-great-great-grandmother's journals. Plus, he'd made it a policy that the books and journals had to remain in the attic or in the library. But Tara was special. Though she'd come to Heart's Landing to evaluate the town, he'd seen the way she reacted to every business they'd visited. He'd heard her quiet murmurs of approval when she'd tasted one of Nick's cakes at the bakery. Her eyes had practically glowed when she'd smelled the flowers in Forget Me Knot. He could trust her to have Heart's Landing's best interests at heart. Not that he had anything to worry about. From the little he'd seen, Mary's diaries were nothing more than daily reports on her children with a few reci-pes tucked in for good measure.

"Why not?" He shrugged and offered to carry the books downstairs for her.

Outside, water dripped steadily from the eaves. Rain pelted the library's thick glass windows. In the distance, branches of the weeping willows bent and swayed in time with gusts of wind. Opposite Tara, Jason leaned on the table using his arms as props for his wide shoulders. The ship's logs stood in neat stacks between them.

"Okay, what's the goal here?" he asked, pen at the ready.

She pulled her lower lip inward, then let it slide slowly between her front teeth. Jason's presence in the library had its plusses and minuses. He probably knew more about Captain Thaddeus than anyone and, with his dark hair, rugged physique, and piercing gaze, she couldn't think of anyone's company she'd rather share on a rainy afternoon. On the other hand, there was the little matter of lying to the man she thought she might be falling in love with.

Well, not exactly lying. But she'd definitely kept the true purpose for her presence in Heart's Landing a secret. With her job—her entire career—on the line, she didn't have much choice, did she? She could carry out her assignment for *Weddings Today*, destroy Captain Thaddeus's reputation, and earn the promotion she'd worked so hard to get. Or she could fail to find the proof she needed, get herself fired, and have to crawl back home to Savannah. At the thought of admitting that her parents had been right to question her career choice, she cringed. She'd be lucky if they gave her a job bussing tables in the family restaurant.

Either choice spelled disaster. Choosing Door Number One meant destroying any faith Jason might have in her and what little hope they had of ever having a future together. But Door Number Two wasn't much better. If she opted for that one, she'd end up in Savannah, at the other end of the country from a man who didn't believe in long-distance relationships. So, no. She couldn't miss out on her one big opportunity at *Weddings Today*. Not for a love as impossible as hers and Jason's.

Straightening, she gave him the answer she'd prepared. "All the previous articles on Heart's Landing have focused on the services the town provides for the brides and grooms who choose to hold their weddings here. Mine will include that, of course, but I also want to give our readers a sense of history. I want them to know how Heart's Landing came into being and why it's become America's Top Wedding Destination. To do that, I have to learn all there is to know about Captain Thaddeus's and Mary's love for one another."

"You think you'll find what you're looking for in his ship's logs?" Jason's eyebrows rose in what could only be described as a skeptical glance.

"I've only read about half of the journals, but I ran across several mentions of the stone hearts Thaddeus carved for Mary.

At least, I think I did." Between the stilted prose, the ornate penmanship, and the fact that the logs were written on a rolling ship, she'd had trouble deciphering some of the passages.

"You don't need to plow through all these to get what you're after." Jason gestured toward the log books. "The pageant on Saturday will tell you everything you need to know."

"That's only a reenactment. Someone else's interpretation." She prided herself on doing her own research. "I want to share his experiences through his eyes. I need to know what it was like to spend days on end sailing beneath clear skies in order to appreciate how horrible it must have been when huge waves broke over the sides of the ship. Understanding the sheer monotony of a normal day will make me more aware of the terror that must have filled the crew when the captain ordered them to sail straight into a hurricane."

Jason nodded slowly. "I get it. I do. When I was fifteen, I took one of the Cottage's Beetle Cats out on my own. I was young and stupid and didn't pay attention to the weather until it was too late. The storm caught me just off the point. It tossed that little sailboat around for a couple of hours like it was a piece of driftwood."

She tried to imagine what it must've been like for him, alone on the ocean, buffeted by the wind and rain, lightning striking all around. Her hand trembled. She couldn't imagine a world without him in it. "Do you still sail?"

"I do." He nodded. "But I'm more careful. A lot more." He stared at the stacks of journals and ledgers. "How can I help?"

She tapped a pencil against the desk. She was walking a perilous tightrope by working with Jason. He'd never forgive her if she succeeded at what she'd set out to do. He'd never forgive himself if he helped her. "Don't you have something else you need to do?" she suggested. "This can't be the only thing on your agenda today."

"I promised to take you up to the widow's walk and help you with your research. I always keep my promises. So, where do I start?" He slid gracefully onto the chair next to her.

Well, she'd tried to talk him out of it. With about as much success as she'd had when she'd tried to talk herself out of falling for him. She inhaled slowly. "You probably know these logs better than anyone. Could you help me go through them and earmark the references Captain Thaddeus made to his wife's birthday?"

She'd given up on disproving the legend

of the stone hearts. In numerous entries, Captain Thaddeus had mentioned working on them. She knew for a fact they existed. She'd personally seen them mounted on buildings throughout the town.

That left the hurricane. Legend had it that one fall the captain had braved howling winds and high seas in order to reach port in time for his wife's birthday. Official weather reports dating back that far were sketchy, at best. According to those still in existence, only one strong October storm had come as far north as Rhode Island during the late 1800s. So far, she'd been unable to find an account of it in any of the *Mary Shelby*'s log books. But she'd have to if she was going to debunk the myth that the captain had loved his wife so much that he'd risked his life, his ship, and his crew for her.

"Glad to help." Jason took the first journal from the stack and began paging through it. Five pages in, he marked a spot with a scrap of paper.

An hour passed. Then, two. Occasionally, she'd interrupt to ask for Jason's help in deciphering a word or phrase. Sometimes, he'd read an excerpt from a particularly exciting passage aloud. Together, they spent the afternoon poring over the remaining ship's logs. Four hours later, she was no closer to finding what she needed than she had been at the start.

Only one of the journals remained on the table. She reached for it. According to the first entry, the captain started the book in 1897. This account offered little change from the minutia of daily life onboard the *Mary Shelby* recounted in all the other journals. Following Jason's advice to pay attention to every detail, she scanned the bills of lading, inventories, and nightly distributions of the crew's rum. Captain Thaddeus's report of making port in New York where the crew off-loaded cargo and took on fresh supplies varied little from previous accounts. The only difference being that, at some point, the Captain had acquired a new pen. The finer point made his handwriting even more difficult to decipher, and she squinted as she continued reading after the ship weighed anchor on October 10th, bound for Heart's Landing.

She'd nearly reached the end of the journal when she stumbled across a passage about a storm. Her breath caught. Her grip on the aged leather tightened. This had to be the event she'd been searching for. Sticking her finger in the log book to hold her place, she tapped Jason on the shoulder. "Listen to this." She read the section aloud.

We encountered a squall at eight

bells of the morning watch. The crew reefed the sails without delay. While rain fell in thick sheets, I kept nose of the Mary S headed into the wind. By the afternoon watch, we were past the worst of it. The crew having comported themselves well, we suffered no loss of life nor cargo. God willing, the Mary S shall drop anchor in Heart's Landing on the morrow.

She let the cover fall closed. "Well, that was a bit of a letdown. Not much of a hurricane, was it?"

Jason studied her, amusement shining in his dark eyes. "What did you expect?"

From the man who'd taken four pages to tell about the visit of a pod of whales? Who'd described the gleaming scales of flying fish in such detail she could see them if she closed her eyes? "After all the hype, a more detailed accounting at the very least. Where are the monstrous waves crashing over the deck? The blinding rain? The howling winds?"

"Thaddeus was a ship's captain, not a dime novelist. His reports are a bit dry and to the point."

She tugged on the end of her ponytail. The strands slipped through her fingers. As far as swashbuckling tales of terror on the high seas went, the account left a lot to be desired. Growing up in Savannah, she was no stranger to hurricanes. They were massive storms that stretched out from a central eye in a series of rings. While the winds around the eye could topple buildings and uproot trees, the feeder bands on the outer edges were often little more than summer squalls. According to the legend, Captain Thaddeus had sailed his ship straight through a hurricane to reach port. But from his report, it sounded like the *Mary S* had only encountered one of the weaker bands.

Was that enough to undermine the captain's reputation? She shook her head. No one could deny that Thaddeus had sailed through rough weather. Quibbling over whether or not he'd faced the worst of the storm would make *Weddings Today* look small-minded and mean. Her heart sank lower as she thumbed through the journal. As much as she wanted to save her job, it was time to throw in the towel. Despite all the nights she'd spent paging through the ship's logs, and despite Jason's help, she'd found no proof, no evidence that would destroy the legend of Captain Thaddeus.

Quite the contrary. In every reference, the good captain professed his love for Mary. He had chosen stone for the hearts he carved for her so they'd last for generations, like his love for her. He'd sailed his ship through a hurricane—or at least the outer edges of one—to reach port for his wife's birthday.

Regina had demanded that she destroy the legend, and she'd done her best to carry out the editor's wishes. She'd failed because her boss had been wrong. Thaddeus and Mary's love for one another had indeed been strong enough to form the foundation of Heart's Landing.

Tara's breath came in easy gulps. Her heart skipped to the happy beat of one of the tunes she'd practiced with Evelyn. A smile tugged at her lips. There was another plus to proving that Thaddeus's legend was true. It freed her to think about Jason in a new light. True, they'd face other hurdles. She did, after all, live in New York, not Rhode Island. But now that she was no longer focused on destroying the myth behind Heart's Landing—and Jason's livelihood, as well—she was free to explore her feelings for him.

Before she could do that, though, she needed to talk with Regina. According to tonight's schedule, she and Jason were having dinner with several of the town's dignitaries at A Cut Above Steakhouse. She checked her watch. If she hurried, she had just enough time to contact her boss before dinner.

Chapter Thirteen

"TARA. I'VE LOOKED OVER ALL your reports. I appreciate your efforts to keep me informed." Regina's precise tones didn't offer the slightest hint of whether she'd actually liked what she'd read or not.

In her room at the Captain's Cottage, Tara nodded, caught herself, and added a hasty, "Yes, ma'am." She'd done all that she'd been asked and more, transferring her notes on each day's events into a full account before she turned in for the night. First thing the next morning, she'd emailed a summary to Regina while she sipped her first cup of coffee in the dining room.

"I'm disappointed with the rosy picture you've painted of Heart's Landing. The weddings you've attended, there haven't been any mistakes? No problems?" Regina's voice turned hopeful.

"No wedding goes off without some kind of hitch," Tara conceded. Rain had nearly spoiled an outdoor wedding earlier in the week, but the staff at the Captain's Cottage had been quick to react. The tent they'd erected moments before the ceremony had kept the wedding party and guests perfectly dry. When the father of the bride raised a water goblet instead of a wine glass for the traditional first toast at another wedding, Alicia had deftly exchanged stemware before the second round of well-wishes. Mildred Morey had plucked a wilted Bird of Paradise from the bridal bouquet and replaced it with a fresh one just before the Garrison bride had walked down the aisle.

Tara glanced at the bouquet she'd caught. She drew in a breath of floral-scented air for strength. "The only problems I'm aware of have been so minor or so quickly corrected, dwelling on them would make us look petty and biased."

"Well," Regina huffed. "I guess the town cleaned up its act after they botched my wedding. I warned you it wouldn't be easy to pull Heart's Landing off its pedestal. That's why I told you to focus on Captain Thaddeus. If you're calling, that means you must've found something to discredit him. What is it?"

She could practically see Regina leaning into the phone, twirling her eyeglasses in anticipation of some juicy tidbit. She gulped. "Nothing. Everything I've learned about Thaddeus Heart indicates that he was what the legend says—a man with an unconditional love for his wife."

"There has to be something. Piracy. Smuggling. Mistreatment of the passengers or crew."

Shocked by the implication, Tara sucked in a breath. "No," she said firmly. "None of that. I've gone over the cargo manifests and the bills of lading with a fine-toothed comb. He was as upright and moral as they come."

"You can't expect me to believe that all the rumors floating around about him are false." Regina's shrill, nasal tone raised the hairs on the back of Tara's neck. "If you haven't found anything negative about Captain Thaddeus, you haven't tried hard enough, dug deep enough."

To say the woman was less than happy with the results of her research was a vast understatement. Nevertheless, Tara refused to smear a good man's name without proof. "I've read every one of the captain's journals and the *Mary Shelby*'s log books twice. Some of them, three times. Without exception, he professes a steadfast love for his wife."

"The storm, then. What about that? He couldn't have sailed through a hurricane to make port for her birthday."

"It looks like he did. According to the weather reports, the year everyone says Captain Thaddeus braved a hurricane, one roared up the East Coast in October." She read the passage she'd copied from the last log book. "I know it doesn't sound like much of a blow. I suppose we could accuse people of embellishing the story."

"There's more to it than that, Tara. I feel it in my gut. You need to keep digging."

"I've just about run out of options."

"This isn't the kind of defeatist attitude I expected to hear from you."

Regina's voice was so taut, Tara could practically hear the editor's teeth grind together.

"I know. I'm sorry. But if there's validity to the rumors about Captain Thaddeus, the proof is not in his journals or in the ship's logs."

"Well. I guess that's it, then."

Tara held her breath while Regina drummed her nails against her desk. She braced herself when the drumming stopped.

"Finish out the week there as planned. I'll expect your report on my desk first thing

Monday morning. Two pages, max." Regina paused for effect. "Payroll will have your final check ready the day we announce this year's winner."

"You're firing me?" Tara gulped. Her worst fears had come true.

"We had a deal, you and I. You were supposed to give me the proof necessary to knock Heart's Landing out of the running for America's Top Wedding Destination. In return, I'd hand you that promotion you've been after. I warned there'd be consequences if you failed."

"Wait—wait a second." Tara swung a searching glance through her room. Her desperate gaze landed on the thin volumes on her desk. The answer to her dilemma might be sitting in her very room, and she hadn't even had time to thumb through them. "There's one more avenue I haven't explored. I stumbled across Mary Heart's diaries in the attic this morning. They could contain the proof we're looking for."

"For your sake, I hope so, Tara."

"I—" she started, intending to reassure her boss, but she was speaking to dead air. Regina, having said her piece, had ended the call.

Tara drew in a thready breath. *Fired.* Regina actually planned to let her go. She'd expected it might come to that when she'd taken this assignment. But anticipating an event and actually experiencing it were two entirely different things. Tears she was powerless to stop rolled down her cheeks.

What was she going to do if Regina followed through with her threat? With her savings nearly depleted, she might be able to hang on to her apartment for another month, two tops. She could land a job as a barista or a waitress while she looked for a position with another magazine, but what was the point? No one in the industry would hire her, not after she'd been fired by *Weddings Today*.

She might as well admit defeat and get it over with. Her dream of becoming a world-famous journalist had crashed and burned on Rhode Island's rocky shores. As soon as she returned to the city, she'd pack up her belongings, rent a car, and head south. Back to Savannah. Back to her childhood bed in her parents' house. Back to a job in her parents' restaurant. Sadly, she shook her head. They'd be so disappointed.

And where would that leave things with Jason? New York had merely been a four-hour drive from Heart's Landing, but Savannah was a thousand miles away. She couldn't ask him to give them a chance if she moved back home. For a man who'd already been hurt by one long-distance relationship, the risk of more heartache was simply too great.

Her cell phone chirped a reminder of tonight's dinner with the town's dignitaries. She was supposed to meet Jason downstairs in less than half an hour. She didn't feel much like going, but that was beside the point, wasn't it? She'd agreed to evaluate Heart's Landing for *Weddings Today*. As long as she still worked for the magazine, she'd keep her word. Brushing the tears from her cheeks, she spun toward the closet. As she did, her gaze landed once more on the stack of Mary Heart's diaries lying on the desk where Jason had left them. She clutched her fingers into a two-handed fist and pressed it against the underside of her chin.

According to Jason, every child in Heart's Landing could recite the story of Captain Thaddeus, but how many knew Mary's side of things? Had she shared the same deep, abiding commitment to her marriage? Had the captain's wife actually lashed herself to the railing while she'd watched for her husband's ship?

There was only one way to find out.

She'd have to read all of the diaries from cover to cover. But her time in Heart's Landing was rapidly coming to a close, and she didn't have a minute to waste. She traced the initials engraved in the leather cover on the top of the stack. Tonight, as soon as she returned from dinner, she'd get started. She crossed her fingers. Her only hope of salvaging her career, her dreams, lay in disproving the "love for the ages" that had formed the foundation of Heart's Landing.

"Jason, can we talk?" Evelyn whispered from the doorway.

Laughter tugged at Jason's lips. He looked up from the calendar of upcoming weddings that would be held at the Captain's Cottage. "I don't know. Can we? Or does the cat have your tongue?"

Across the room, his cousin's fingers spanned her neck. "Laryngitis," she croaked, her voice barely a whisper.

"You've got to be kidding me." Even as he said the words, Jason's grin collapsed. He glanced at the calendar. The Smith wedding, one of the largest events of the season, would take place that night. Already, the Cottage hummed with activity as caterers, decorators, and florists prepped the ballroom. The couple had gone all in on their nautical theme, from engraved invitations that featured the image of a swashbuckling sailor right down to a ship-shaped head table. And the highlight of the evening was an appearance by none other than Captain Thaddeus and his wife, who'd entertain the bride and groom's three-hundred-plus guests with sea shanties and love ballads. Something that couldn't happen if "Mary" squeaked like a mouse every time she opened her mouth.

Evelyn gave her head a vigorous shake. Crossing to his desk, she sank into one of the guest chairs. "I wish," she hissed.

"Have you gargled? Taken something for it? Tea and honey? Throat lozenges?" He leaned forward to catch Evelyn's whispers.

"Doc says there's a virus going around. I'm not supposed to talk for three days. I could do permanent damage to my vocal chords."

That was that, then. He'd have to find someone to take Evelyn's place. He reached for his cell phone.

"Clarissa?" Evelyn whispered.

Jason made a face. "No." His ex-girlfriend hadn't just backed out at the last minute. She'd reneged on all their practice sessions. He doubted she knew the melodies, much less the words to the songs. "I'll call Lydia Thomas." The mayor's daughter had filled in for Evelyn once before.

But his cousin shook her head. "She has the same thing. Caught it from her dad."

Jason groaned. Lydia had been his last hope. His thoughts shifting, he considered alternatives. Performing solo wasn't ideal, but he could usually do it in a pinch. In this case, though, that wasn't an option. The couple had specifically requested a ballad at the end of the performance. The love song had been written as a duet. He couldn't handle it on his own.

His heart sank.

On the other side of his desk, his cousin tried and failed to speak. Her lips pressed tightly together, she snagged a pad and a pen. After scribbling something on the paper, she held it up for him to see.

Ask Tara.

His heart hauled his thoughts back to the night he'd held her in his arms on the dance floor. He swallowed dryly. "You think she'd do it?"

Evelyn's head bobbed. She wrote another note.

She knows the music, the songs.

Jason closed his eyes. With his hands tented, he tapped his forefingers to his lips. The day Tara had joined Evelyn in the music conservatory, he'd been so intrigued by her voice that he'd lingered in the hallway far longer than anyone had suspected. He had no doubt that with just a little more practice, Tara could handle the music. After all, she sang in her church choir each week. The Captain's songs weren't nearly as challenging as some hymns. His pulse rate steadied. He couldn't wait for her to experience the joy their performance brought to the bride and groom, their families and friends.

"Okay." He opened his eyes. "I'll ask her. You'll accompany us on the piano?" Thank goodness laryngitis hadn't affected Evelyn's fingers. If it had, they'd really be in trouble.

When his cousin nodded, he rose. After dinner last night, Tara had told him she needed to spend the morning working in her room. He'd head there. "I'd better talk to her right away."

He knocked on her door a few minutes later. Tara opened it looking adorable in sweat pants and a loose T-shirt, her hair piled in a messy top knot.

"Hey." Warmth bloomed in his chest and spread through his midsection. "Busy?"

She brushed a wayward hank of hair from her face. "Yeah, but I could use a break. What's up?"

"I need to ask a favor. It's a pretty big one," he warned.

"As much as you've done for me these last few days, I'd have to be an ogre to turn you down." A soft smile broke across her face. "Whatever it is, if I can, I'd be happy to help out."

"Evelyn and I were scheduled to appear as Captain Thaddeus and Mary at a wedding tonight, but she's developed laryngitis. The woman who fills in for her is sick, too. I'd really appreciate it if you could take her place."

"Me?" Tara's blue eyes widened. "You're sure you can't find anyone else?"

"Positive." Her hesitation took him by surprise. He was pretty sure he'd stated his case clearly. "I'd hate to disappoint them if we had to cancel. You know how much Heart's Landing prides itself on delivering the perfect wedding for every bride."

Tara stroked the soft skin under her chin, a motion he'd noticed her make whenever she felt stressed. "As long as there won't be too many people there, I guess I could handle it."

His weight shifted from one foot to another. He wished he could offer her the reassurance she wanted, but the truth was, tonight's wedding was a big one. "Well, we've handled much larger weddings at the Captain's Cottage, but this one isn't as small as some of the others you've attended this week," he hedged.

Tara's sharp understanding quickly put the pieces together. "Tell me this isn't for the Smith wedding. Doesn't that have, like, a huge guest list?"

"It'll be fun. You'll see. I'll be there, right beside you, every step of the way. So will

Evelyn. She might not be able to talk or sing, but she can still play the piano."

"I don't know. I..." Tara's complexion paled.

Afraid she was about to turn him down, he rushed ahead. "Tell you what. Let's meet downstairs in an hour. I need the practice anyway, so why don't you run through the songs with me? Meanwhile, Evelyn will continue looking for someone else to play the part." If all else failed, he'd skip the love song, handle the vocals by himself, and re-fund his fee. The solution was far from ideal, but he'd make it work if he had to.

"I guess it wouldn't hurt to practice." She wrung her hands together.

"Great! Meet you in the conservatory in one hour. You'll be awesome. You'll see." Shoving every ounce of confidence he had—and some he didn't possess—into the state-ment, he turned smartly on one heel and left her standing in the doorway, afraid that if he pressed her any more, she'd turn him down flat.

Chapter Fourteen

TARA STOOD STOCK STILL IN the dressing room while the urge to run and hide swept over her in waves. How had she gotten herself into this mess? One minute, she'd agreed to run through the songs for tonight's program with Jason while his cousin looked for someone to play Mary's part. The next, she was moments away from going on stage wearing a dress straight out of the 1800s. Behind her, Evelyn tugged the gown's corset strings so tight, Tara feared she'd faint dead away from lack of air. She started to object but stifled her complaints. Being unable to breathe had its advantages. No one could expect her to sing if she was passed out cold on the floor. As an added plus, it would save her the embarrassment of fainting dead away in front of the crowd gathered in the Green Room.

Unfortunately, Evelyn must have read her thoughts. Jason's cousin pressed her forefinger and thumb together in the sign for okay. She loosened the strings enough for Tara to inhale, and tied them off.

"There." Evelyn's hoarse voice whispered over her shoulder. "You look stunning."

Studying her image in the mirror, Tara had to agree. Thanks to Evelyn's deft hand, stage makeup highlighted her cheeks, her eyes, and darkened her lips. Her hair had been swept into a fancy updo. A few curls cascaded to her shoulders where they brushed the top of a dark blue ball gown designed to showcase an hourglass figure. She fanned her fingers above the sweetheart neckline. "Don't you think it's a bit too low?"

"Psh." Evelyn not-so-gently tugged Tara's hand to the side. "It's perfect."

Someone raised a toast in the ballroom next door. Classes clinked.

"It's show time," Evelyn declared. "Ready?"

Tara's heart thudded so hard she thought her chest might explode. She back-pedaled a step. She would have retreated farther, but her feet tangled in the hem of her dress. She clutched a nearby door post and hung on for dear life. "I don't think I ca—"

"It's too late to back out now." Evelyn's voice firmed. "You can't disappoint the bride and the groom. Or Jason. He's counting on you."

Tears stung the corners of Tara's eyes. "I-I don't want to go out there and make a fool of myself."

"Oh, honey, you won't." Sympathy dripped from Evelyn's every word. "Just don't look at the audience. Watch Jason. He'll be right beside you every minute." The redhead backed away as another round of clinking glassware drifted from the other room. "That's my cue," she said, her voice as clear as a bell. Her eyes cut to one side, and she cleared her throat. "Remember," she croaked, "Jason will sing one song, then you come in. Follow his lead."

With an impish grin, Jason's cousin dashed out the door before Tara had a chance to point out that Evelyn's laryngitis seemed to come and go at will. She laughed shortly at the realization that she'd been played. From the room next door came a soft creaking. Evelyn had taken her seat on the piano bench. Tara stiffened when the scrape of silverware against china stilled. Conversation and laughter died. The opening bars of the first number filtered through the Green Room.

Her heart in her throat, Tara made her way to the spot where she was supposed to stand until Jason signaled her. She stared as he entered the ball room from the opposite side. The hours they'd spent practicing hadn't prepared her for seeing him dressed as Captain Thaddeus. Her breath caught as her gaze rose from a pair of pointed shoes. She inched past the white breeches and stockings that outlined the muscles of his calves and long legs. Gold braid sparkled from a sharply cut jacket that made his shoulders look wide enough to carry the weight of the world. She knew the moment he'd spotted her by the appreciation that flared in his dark eyes. He tipped the feathered hat he wore at a jaunty angle. With a rakish grin, he launched into the first of a series of sea shanties.

She couldn't tear her gaze away from him. And when he beckoned her forward, her doubts and her fears fell away. Her focus unwavering, she closed the distance between them, joining him in the second song just as they'd practiced. She'd expected stage fright to rear its ugly head. Instead, with her eyes trained on Jason, her confidence grew with every line until, midway through the next number, she risked a glance at their audience. Hearty smiles and clapping hands gave her just the boost she needed. She shot Jason a grin as they finished out the rousing set with a flourish.

But the ballad, with its complicated runs and crooked beats came next. Like smoke from a smoldering fire, fear sifted through her chest. It filled the nooks and crannies. It fogged her brain. When Evelyn played through the opening bars of the song, Tara opened her mouth. She shut it immediately. She couldn't remember the words. Her lower lip quivered. Certain everyone was staring at her and that she was poised on the brink of ruining the bride and groom's special day, she turned toward Jason.

And there he stood. Offering her his hand, letting her lean on him like he'd promised. Her feet ate up the distance between them. She reached for him. The touch of his fingers on hers steadied her. She barely had time to catch her breath when he launched into the ballad. As he sang, the room around her ceased to exist. The fear that had nearly paralyzed her simply vanished.

She leaned into the song, matching him note for note, bar for bar. Halfway through the story of a love so strong it could withstand every challenge thrown in its path, her voice thickened. Her heart echoed the words. She stared into Jason's eyes and knew for once and for all that she loved him. She had from the moment they'd met.

As the song drew to its conclusion, Jason reached for her, and she stepped into his embrace. For a long moment, they clung together like two souls who'd been buffeted by the winds of chance and emerged on the other side of the storm, whole and in love. With his arm around her waist, he dipped her low, his hat shielding them from view. She knew he intended to kiss her. Without a doubt, she wanted him to. He leaned in, his lips nearly grazing hers.

Applause thundered through the room. Jason rolled his eyes. "To be continued," he murmured and pulled her upright.

Flushed and happy, she remained at his side. Her hand in his, they took their bows until, at last, the clapping came to an end. This was it, the moment she'd been waiting for, the moment when they'd pick up that kissing business right where they'd left off.

Jason lifted Tara's hand in his as they bowed deeply to deafening applause. His heart swelled nearly to bursting with pride for the woman who stood beside him. He'd known she didn't like large crowds. That was one reason he'd been so reluctant to ask her to join him on stage. When she'd frozen, his heart had very nearly stopped. But his faith in her had kept him from rushing to her rescue. He was glad now that he'd waited. She'd conquered her stage fright to finish the show. More than that, she'd overcome her fears and given the performance of a lifetime. He couldn't be happier for her.

He hadn't been able to believe his eyes the moment he'd seen Tara standing in the wings, waiting for her cue to step on stage. He'd always appreciated her poise and her beauty, but she'd never looked lovelier than she did tonight. More than mere physical attraction drew him to her, however. The trust he saw in her blue eyes stirred all his protective instincts. He longed to be her knight in shining armor, to slay her dragons—whatever and wherever they might be. The faith she had in him made him want to be a better man than he'd ever been before. When they'd sung that final ballad, he'd ached to make it real, to give her his heart, to declare his love for her, to shower her with kisses.

He'd nearly accomplished that last bit before the crowd had oh-so-rudely interrupted. He chuckled. Much as he hated delaying that first kiss, he had to admit the timing wasn't right. He'd gotten too far ahead of himself. There'd be plenty of time for kisses later, once he knew for sure that Tara loved him like he loved her.

The time for heartfelt declarations wasn't in the middle of the Smith reception, though. Not with everyone and their brother looking on. Sweeping his hat from his head, he bowed low to Tara. "M'lady," he intoned. "Methinks the bride and groom would have a word with us."

"Aye, Captain." Tara tossed out a saucy grin that made his pulse race.

He leaned in to whisper in her ear. "We'll just pay our respects and then we'll slip away." He nodded to a side door. His heart warmed another degree or two when her eyes sparkled in agreement.

An hour later, he and Tara were still no closer to making their escape than they'd been at the close of their set. First, the bride and groom had insisted on posing for photographs with the Captain and his Lady. After that, practically every guest at the wedding expected their turn.

"The downside to a job well done is that everyone wants to thank you for it," he whispered to Tara while yet another guest snapped a few pictures.

"It's part of the job, isn't it?" Shrugging, she hid a yawn behind one gloved hand. "I don't mind. Really, I don't." She yawned again.

Sympathy tugged deep in his chest. He'd say one thing for the woman he loved—when she put her mind to doing something, she stuck with it. But he'd bet a week's salary that the after-effects of an adrenaline rush were hitting her hard right about now. "You know what?" he said, wrapping his arm around her waist. "It's time we got you out of here."

Treating the rest of the guests to a broad smile, he gently but firmly guided her to the exit. There, he snagged two glasses of champagne from a passing waiter. He handed one to Tara. The other, he raised high above his head. "To Mr. And Mrs. Smith," he said, letting his voice carry throughout the room. "Best wishes for a Heart's Landing love for the ages!"

While glasses clinked and voices raised in a hearty, "Hear, hear!" he whisked Tara through the door and down the hall. "Thanks for sticking in there as long as you did. You have to be worn out."

Tara's skirts swished against the risers as they mounted the stairs to her room. "I'll admit I'm beat. But I was glad to be a part of it. I'll never forget how happy it made the bride and groom to have us there."

"It was perfect. You were perfect." He could've said more. Could have pointed out that tonight she'd experienced first-hand what Heart's Landing was all about. But he had other things—more important things—on his mind.

At her door, he propped his arm on the jamb over her head. He wished the night could go on forever. He longed to tell Tara how much she meant to him. He needed to find out if she felt the same way toward him. If she did, they had a future to plan.

But one look at Tara, and he knew any serious talk of love or hopes and expectations would have to wait. Fatigue had tightened the faint lines at the corners of her eyes. The strain of smiling for hours on end had carved furrows around her mouth. He let his arm fall to his side. "It's not every night you get to wow the crowd. You definitely did that tonight. Now, get a good night's rest. You deserve it."

Confirming his decision, Tara stifled another yawn behind her gloved hand. "Sorry," she whispered. Fatigue etched itself a little deeper into her features.

"We'll talk tomorrow." A smile loaded with promise stole across his face. "What do you say to taking a walk together first thing in the morning?"

"Sounds good. I'll meet you downstairs around seven?"

"I'll bring coffee. We can follow the bike path along the cliffs behind the Cottage."

Wishing he could kiss her properly but all too aware that the time wasn't right, he touched his lips to one finger and pressed it against the tip of her nose. "Good night," he said and forced himself to walk away.

Seconds later, he bounded up the stairs to the third floor where, no matter how exhausted he felt, he was sure he faced a sleepless night.

Chapter Fifteen

"*E*VELYN AND I TALKED EARLIER. Or I did, anyway. She still can't do anything more than whisper." Jason's shirt tail flapped in the breeze that blew off the ocean. Below them, the outgoing tide lapped at the sandy beach. At the point where the blue water met the pink-tinged sky, a ship steamed along the horizon. "She wanted me to tell you she was sorry for roping you into playing Mary last night. She hopes you aren't too mad with her about it."

"I'm not." Although she didn't think for a second that his cousin had laryngitis. Not that it mattered. Considering the way things had worked out with Jason, she owed Evelyn a debt of gratitude. Tara sipped piping-hot coffee from the travel mug Jason had handed her in the foyer. He'd doctored it just the way she liked it.

"I knew you didn't like crowds. I never dreamed you'd have stage fright." Sympathy laced Jason's voice like the cream in her cup. "I'm so sorry."

"It's okay." At his doubtful look, she added, "Honest. It was good for me to step out of my comfort zone. Yeah, I froze for a second there, but thanks to you, I got past it. I'm going to push myself to do more of that." The next time the church choir director asked her to sing a solo part, she wouldn't be so quick to turn him down.

"For purely personal reasons, I'm glad to hear it. I was hoping you'd fill in for Evelyn in the pageant tomorrow night."

She nearly stumbled over a pebble on the cement walkway. Catching herself, she gazed up at Jason. "You want me to play Mary's part?"

Okay, that wasn't what she'd had in mind at all. Singing was one thing, but acting on stage? When she thought about it, though, she supposed that was what happened when you vowed to press your limits. The next thing you knew, someone came along and asked you to do exactly that. "Who's playing Thaddeus?"

"I am. I have to warn you, though. The play ends with a kiss."

At Jason's shy grin, her heart skipped a beat. This was one opportunity she couldn't pass up. "I'll need the script so I can learn my lines."

"I'll have a copy delivered to your room," Jason promised. "It's not complicated. Rehearsals are tomorrow afternoon at two in the Blue Room."

She chewed softly on her bottom lip. The pageant was the last big event on her schedule before she returned to New York. And then what? She hadn't told Jason that she'd developed feelings for him, but what was the point if all too soon she'd be forced to move a thousand miles away? So far, she hadn't found a single entry in Mary's diaries that would save her job.

"Is something bothering you?"

"Why do you ask?"

"You have your hand pressed to your throat. You do that whenever you're worried or upset." Jason drank from his coffee cup.

Deliberately she lowered her fingers. "You know me so well."

She stopped by a rocky outcropping. Above them, sea birds wheeled and turned, riding the thermals that rose off the cliffs. Her gaze fell to a lone figure on the beach below. Swinging a metal detector in slow arcs, he worked the water's edge. He stopped every now and again to dig up a scoop of sand and let the grains sift through his fingers into the gentle waves. She sighed. The secrets she'd kept from Jason weighed heavily on her. She needed to get some of them off her chest. She owed him that much.

"I probably shouldn't tell you this, but I'm in trouble at work. My editor hasn't exactly been pleased with how I've handled this assignment." She paused to fortify herself with coffee. "I wasn't supposed to fall for my host and tour guide." Her fingers crossed, she let that last part hang between them.

Jason was beside her in an instant. A questioning glint filled his eyes. "Handsome, dark-haired fellow? Runs the most popular wedding venue on the East Coast? Poor man. I've heard he's head over heels for a journalist from New York."

Tara's breath caught. "Really?" she whispered.

"Yeah, really."

He wrapped his arms around her. "I know this happened fast, but when you know, well, you know. I love you."

"I was hoping you'd say that. I love you, too." She stepped into Jason's embrace. Resting her head on his chest's broad plane, she sighed. In the movies, this was the part where the hero plied his beloved with kisses. But this was real life, not some made-up fantasy. Before she and Jason could pledge their hearts and lives to each other, they had some things to figure out. "So what does that mean for us? Where do we go from here?"

"This is all new to me. I have to admit, I don't have all the answers. At the moment, I'm still trying to figure out how we got lucky enough to find each other."

"It is a lot to take in, isn't it?" She tipped her head to get a better look at his face. "I keep pinching myself to make sure this isn't a dream."

He snuggled her closer. "If it is, we're having the same one." His fingers traced lazy circles on her shoulder. "I hope it never ends."

Which, when she stopped to think about it, was at least a big part of their problem. His life, his future, lay in Heart's Landing. But by this time next week, she'd be in New York. There was no telling where she'd end up after that. She couldn't let their feelings for one another grow without telling him the rest, starting with the real reason she was in Heart's Landing. That wasn't something she could do when he held her like he never wanted to let her go. Already regretting the loss of his warmth around her, she untangled herself from his hold.

"There's a couple of other things you should know. I told you this assignment was my last chance to make a name for myself at

Weddings Today?" Her voice rose, questioning.

"Your review of Heart's Landing for America's Top Wedding Destination." Tension tightened the lines around Jason's mouth. "That's what you've been working on so hard ever since you arrived. I hope you aren't going to say we've failed to live up to your expectations."

"You surpassed all of them, and more," she assured him, glad she could ease at least that one doubt. "I firmly believe Heart's Landing is the ideal place to get married." From the lowliest sales clerk to the owner of the Captain's Cottage, everyone took their mission of providing the perfect wedding for each bride and groom very seriously. The town offered such a wide variety of venues—from rustic barns to grand ballrooms—that even the pickiest bride could hold her wedding in her ideal setting. Not only that, but the stores in town provided a wealth of choices sure to satisfy a wide range of couples. Those who'd chosen to elope on the spur of the moment were just as pleased here as discriminating brides who demanded perfection in every detail.

"Well, that's a relief." As quickly as they'd appeared, the lines around Jason's mouth softened. "We work hard to make sure everything goes smoothly for all our brides and grooms."

"I know. I've given the town top marks. If the choice was entirely mine, Heart's Landing would definitely retain its ranking. But my editor expects something more than the usual fluff piece."

"You said as much, didn't you?" Jason's brows knitted. "I thought that's why you've spent so much time digging into Captain Thaddeus's past. You wanted to tell the history of Heart's Landing from his perspective."

"That's part of it." She took a breath. Keeping secrets from Jason was killing her. She wanted to tell him everything. How she'd been pressured to undermine the town's chances in the contest. How Regina blamed the people here for ruining her wedding. But what was the point in admitting that she'd been less than honest with Jason if she didn't have a future with him? Before she could tell him the whole story, she had to find that out. "The thing is, despite all my digging, I haven't found a hook to hang the story on. My editor's getting antsy. She's given me the rest of my time in Heart's Landing to come up with something. If I can't, I probably won't have a job at *Weddings Today* to go back to."

Jason stilled. "And that's always been your dream."

She nodded, miserable. "Ever since I

bought my first copy with money I'd saved bussing tables at the restaurant." She sought his eyes, pleading with him to understand. "It's not just my job or my career that's at stake. If *Weddings Today* lets me go, I won't be able to stay in New York. I'll probably have to go back to Savannah and work in my parents' restaurant."

There. She'd said it. It had been bad enough that she lived and worked in the city. Now, she'd told the man who'd made it perfectly clear he wasn't interested in a long-distance relationship that there was a very good possibility she'd be moving a thousand miles away.

For several long seconds, Jason stared at the horizon while she held her breath, certain that this would be the end of things between them before they even got started.

"Look." Jason's eyes met hers. "You're smart. You're capable. I refuse to believe you can't make things work at *Weddings Today*. You'll just have to dig in, find what you're looking for. You'll see. You have two days to give your editor what she wants. Buckle down and do the very best you can." Jason nodded like he understood.

How could he, when she hadn't told him the rest of it? Doing her best would mean destroying his livelihood. Their love couldn't survive that. He deserved to know everything. No matter what it cost. "There's more. I—"

His phone chimed.

Relief swelled in her chest. Jason was right. She wouldn't have to tell him the rest after all. She'd find a way to resolve things on her own so he never had to know how close she'd come to destroying the town he loved. When Jason didn't move a muscle but continued to look at her expectantly, she asked, "Don't you have to get that?"

He grimaced. "I should've shut off the ringer. If it's important, they'll leave a message."

Less than thirty seconds later, a different, more insistent alarm bell rose over the sound of the wind and the surf.

"Guess it was important, after all." He withdrew the phone from his back pocket and glanced at the screen. "Duty calls." He sighed heavily. "Walk back with me?"

"You go on ahead. You probably have things that need your attention." She lifted her travel mug. "I'll stay here and finish my coffee." She had problems of her own to resolve. Chief among them, how she was going to save both her job and Jason's love when having one would destroy the other.

Tara uncapped a bottle of water and took a drink. Stretching, she worked the kinks out of shoulder muscles that had stiffened during the hours while she'd sat, hunched over the desk in her room, paging through Mary Heart's diaries. With lunch only an hour away, she hoped to finish reading by the time she went downstairs. She re-capped the bottle and set it aside, ready to get back to work.

Fifteen minutes later, a phrase leaped off the page. Tara rubbed her eyes. The words written in Mary's elegant script remained the same. She started over at the beginning of the entry from October 17th, 1897. Unable to believe what she was seeing, she traced the lines with her finger. It took three tries before she convinced herself she'd read it right the first time.

> *The Mary S dropped anchor in Heart's Cove this evening. Praise be to God for delivering my husband's ship and crew home once more.*

Her pulse kicked up a notch. With a reminder that now wasn't the time to jump to conclusions, Tara checked the date she'd written after reading Captain Thaddeus's account of the storm he'd encountered on his way from New York to Heart's Landing.

Same year. Same month. Same week. Her heart skipped a beat.

Her movements slow and methodical, she pulled up the hurricane tracking information she'd downloaded onto her laptop. None of the massive, swirling storms that had originated off the coast of Africa had been given names until the 1950s. Before then, they'd simply been referred to by number, and in 1897, the fifth storm of the season had been the only one to rage along the entire East Coast. On October 9th, 188 crewmen had died when their ship had been swamped by high winds and sank off the coast of Cuba. From there, the hurricane had churned northward in the Atlantic. Ten days after it had struck Cuba, the storm had roared ashore at Cape Hatteras, then bounced back out to sea. It made landfall only once more, striking Rhode Island's Block Island with gale-force winds on the twentieth. After that, it had dissipated entirely.

She pushed away from the desk, her thoughts in as much turmoil as winds in a hurricane. She'd traced the paths of every major storm to make landfall in the U.S. during the years Captain Thaddeus had plied the seas. Storm Number Five was the only one that fit all the criteria. The legend of Captain Thaddeus had to have been built around it.

But there was a problem—a huge, glaring problem. According to Mary's diary, the *Mary S* had reached port on October 17th, two full days before Number Five had made landfall in North Carolina. With the hurricane still that far south, Thaddeus couldn't have sailed through it on his final leg of an ocean voyage that had taken him from London to New York, and then home to Heart's Landing. He'd been too far north to encounter even one of the storm's feeder bands.

One by one, like pieces of a puzzle, the facts clicked into place. For over a hundred years, people had assumed that the storm Captain Thaddeus had encountered had been a hurricane. They'd described how he'd steered the ship straight up the front of towering waves, only to plunge into troughs so deep they hid the ship's mast from sight. Old seafarers had talked about how the captain had worried about the loss of cargo and lives if the ship swamped. How he'd braved winds that would've knocked lesser men to their knees in order to stand at the helm of the *Mary S*.

But he hadn't done any of that. He couldn't have. Number Five had been nearly seven hundred miles farther south when the crew of the *Mary S* had run into rough weather. Thaddeus and his crew hadn't encountered anything more than your garden-variety storm. And not even a bad one, at that.

Her mouth went dry. This was the proof she needed to save her job, the evidence Regina had asked her to find.

What now?

She twisted a strand of hair. In college, her professors had harped on the need for journalistic integrity. They'd taught that a good reporter revealed the truth, no matter the consequences. Earlier today, when she'd told Jason how much she was afraid of failing, he'd encouraged her to pursue her dreams. He'd told her to dig deeper, leave no stone unturned, which was exactly what she'd done.

All her hard work had paid off. Success was finally within reach.

She wouldn't kid herself. Her success carried a hefty price tag. Revealing what she'd discovered would hurt the people in Heart's Landing, people she'd come to think of as friends. To say nothing of what it'd do to Jason. He'd be devastated when he learned that the legend surrounding his famous relative was a lie. He'd blame her for exposing the truth.

But she had to report what she'd found. She owed it to Regina and *Weddings To-*

day—to say nothing of how much she owed herself—to tell the real story. Unveiling what she'd discovered was her chance to prove, once and for all, that she'd become the journalist she'd always dreamed of being.

Telling herself she had no choice didn't stop her fingers from shaking though. It didn't keep her stomach from turning mutinous as she assembled the data she'd gathered. Once she'd proofed everything—twice—she saved the file to her laptop. She hefted her computer. As much as she didn't want to risk running into Jason or Evelyn, she'd have to go downstairs to send in her report. A quick check of her cell phone told her it was nearly noon. She was in luck. The hubbub of arriving brides and departing wedding parties made the dining room a busy place over the lunch hour. With all the comings and goings, no one would give a second thought to a lone woman sitting in a corner staring at her computer screen.

Though she grew sicker to her stomach with every step, Tara picked her way down the stairs. She made it as far as the dining room without spotting Jason and drew in a relieved breath. A move that backfired when she inhaled the rich smells of quiche, fresh fruit, and coffee. She stashed her laptop on her favorite corner table. Hoping to calm her stomach, she loaded a small plate with items from the buffet and grabbed a cup of coffee. Back at her table, she nibbled on a plain bagel while she waited for her computer to boot up. Snatches of the conversation at the table next door drifted her way while she brought up her email program.

"I, uh… Saundra, there's something I forgot to tell you."

Tara stole a quick glance at the thin young man who'd just rearranged his silverware for the third time.

"There's no other Mrs. Kevin Dobson, is there?" Sitting opposite her nervous groom, Saundra casually straightened the diamond solitaire on her ring finger.

"No. Not ever." His expression earnest, Saundra's fiancé grasped her hand. "You're the only one for me."

"You're the only one for me, too, Kevin." Saundra leaned in for a quick kiss. "Nothing else matters."

"Well, there is this one thing."

Uh-oh. Tara watched out of the corner of her eye as Kevin pulled a flat jewelry box from his back pocket. He slid the thin case across the table to his bride.

"A present?" Saundra's voice filled with breathless expectation. "I thought we decided not to exchange gifts."

At the young man's hurried movements, the frequent clenching and unclenching of his fingers, Tara hoped the bride hadn't set her expectations too high.

"It's not exactly a gift," Kevin said, confirming her suspicions. "It's the Dobson Star. Dad's family brought it over with them from the old country. Every bride in our family has worn it on their wedding day." His voice faded. "It's tradition."

The bride gave the package a skeptical glance. "Honey, we've been planning to get married for over a year. Why am I just hearing about this now?" Saundra smiled through pouted lips.

"I'm sorry. It's my fault." Kevin gulped. "I forgot all about the Star. It honestly never crossed my mind until Dad handed it to me after the rehearsal dinner last night."

Saundra tapped the unopened package. Her smile widened. "I'd be honored to wear it, Kevin."

Across the table, Kevin grabbed a water glass and slowly rotated it. "Wait till you see it. It's a bit, um, overwhelming."

Tara tried not to stare as Saundra carefully untied the ribbon, but her curiosity got the best of her. She crossed her fingers when the box opened with a squeak of tiny hinges.

"It's, um, it's..." Tiny furrows wrinkled the bride's brow. "Well, let's see what we have here." Saundra plucked the jewel out of its case and held it up to the light.

Tara sucked in a breath of air. A good

three inches across and studded with chips of colored glass, the hammered-silver pin reminded her of a starfish. A misshapen starfish that was hardly beautiful.

At the next table, the bride swallowed. "It's not exactly the Hope Diamond, is it?"

The groom's face fell. "It's too much to ask, isn't it?" His shoulders slumped. He stared down at tablecloth. "You don't have to wear it if you don't want to."

"Nonsense." The bride returned the pin to its case with all the tender care she might give the crown jewels. "I know you, Kevin. You wouldn't have asked if it wasn't important to you and your family."

Wonder filled the eyes Kevin raised to Saundra. "They'll all expect to see it."

"That settles it. I'd be honored to wear the Dobson Star on our wedding day."

When the firm lines around Saundra's mouth softened, Tara ducked behind her computer screen to hide her surprise. Dreadful didn't begin to describe Kevin's family heirloom. That Saundra had agreed to wear the piece boggled her mind.

"You will?" As surprised as Tara, Kevin stared across the table at his bride.

"Of course, honey. Just tell me, are there any rules about how it's displayed?"

Tara stole a quick peek while Saundra calmly sipped from a juice glass.

"I'm not sure I know what you mean."

"Is it worn on a belt? Or at the shoulder?"

"Gosh." Kevin brushed a stray crumb from the table. "I don't think it matters as long as you have it on you."

"Good to know." Saundra's smile deepened. "I'll figure it out."

"Thanks. You're the best." The groom heaved a relieved sigh. "I'll go tell Dad. He'll be happy to hear the news."

"Don't forget. We promised the caterer we'd drop off her final check this afternoon. Meet you there in an hour?" Gold glinted from an expensive watch when Saundra checked the time.

After agreeing, the groom hurried off. Seconds later, Tara spied his lanky form striding down the sidewalk.

At the next table, Saundra flipped the jewelry case over and over in her hands. At last she lifted the lid and peered inside. "Nope." The lid closed with a snap. "It's not the Hope Diamond." She lifted one shoulder and let it drop.

From her spot by the window, Tara leaned forward. "I hope you don't mind. I couldn't help but overhear. You're really going to wear the Star?" At Saundra's nod, her respect for the bride grew. "Do you have any idea how?"

Saundra gave her head a sad shake. "Not a clue."

In response to several frantic letters to the editor, the staff at *Weddings Today* had come up with creative ways to display family heirlooms. One or two of those might work in this case. "What kind of flowers are you carrying?"

"Red roses with white anemones. We're holding the ceremony on the veranda."

Tara sighed audibly. Of all the spots on the grounds, that was where she'd choose to get married. "What if you had the florist either nestle the Star in with the flowers or pin it to the wrapping around the stems?"

But Saundra was shaking her head. "Kevin asked me to *wear* the pin. I don't want to disappoint him." She tapped the box with the tip of a well-manicured finger. "My dress is a trumpet silhouette. It's strapless, with a sweetheart neckline. If I'd known about this six months ago..."

"I don't suppose you could pin it where the skirt flares out?"

"I don't think so. Want to see a picture?" Saundra whipped out her phone and quickly found the one she wanted. "Here."

"Absolutely gorgeous," Tara said, looking at the image of Saundra wearing a dress that had been designed with her long, lean figure in mind. Her gaze dropped to the pin in its box. No matter where Saundra attached it, the Star would ruin the lines of the gown. Tara tapped her finger to her chin. She still had a possible solution or two up her sleeve. "Cheri at Dress For A Day could probably create a belt or a sash for you to wear during the ceremony." The bridal salon had been a favorite of the many places she'd visited in Heart's Landing. "If she made it removable, you could take it off for the reception."

"You think?" Saundra's demeanor brightened. "I like the idea of a sash. It kind of fits in with the whole family tradition." Her excitement faded as quickly as it had built. "There's probably not enough time, though. The wedding's tomorrow."

"You'll never know unless you ask. I have Cheri's number in my room. Let me run upstairs and call her. The worst she can say is no. But I'm betting the two of you can work things out." From what she'd heard, Regina had leaned heavily on her position at *Weddings Today* and had demanded special favors from many Heart's Landing businesses. Tara had approached things differently, but the owner of the bridal salon owner would no doubt jump at the chance to fill a request for her.

Tilting her head, Saundra narrowed her eyes. "There must be twenty wedding ceremonies taking place in Heart's Landing this weekend. Why are you helping me?"

Tara took a breath. "Honesty is the best policy, according to my mom. I think it's incredibly sweet of you to wear your fiancé's family pin. That's reason enough." With a couple of keystrokes, she put the laptop to sleep. Confident that her report to Regina would be safe from prying eyes for a few minutes, she stood. "I'll be right back."

"Take your time," Saundra motioned. "I have to stop by Alicia's office for a minute. Other than that, I'll be right here for the next hour or so."

Tara gave a nod to the waitstaff manning the coffee urns. Assured they'd keep an eye on her table while she was gone, she trotted up the stairs to her room. Minutes later, she explained Saundra's predicament to Cheri who, as expected, volunteered to help.

"Have her swing by any time this afternoon. My seamstress does amazing work. Your friend is in good hands."

"Thank you," Tara said, her appreciation heartfelt.

"We aim to please all our brides in Heart's Landing. Welcome to the club."

Warmth flooded Tara's midsection. She swore Cheri was smiling when the shopkeeper ended their conversation. And no wonder. Taking part in the town's tradition felt better than Tara had ever thought it would.

Chapter Sixteen

JASON RAN THROUGH HIS LINES for the pageant. This time, though, he paid particular attention to Mary's role. Just as he'd told Tara, the part was light on dialogue. For someone as smart as her, memorizing the half-dozen lines should be a snap. Not that the character was an easy one to portray. The last scene, especially, required a flair for the dramatic.

He scanned the final page. Having steered his ship through the hurricane in order to reach port, Captain Thaddeus burst onto the widow's walk. Cutlass in hand, he freed Mary from the ropes that bound her to the railing. The kiss that came next elicited cheers from the crowd each year. When Evelyn had played the part of Mary, Jason had always shielded their faces with his feathered hat. Hidden from the audience's view, they'd grin at each other while they counted out ten long seconds. Tomorrow, though, Tara would take on the role. Considering their newly declared feelings for each other, he suspected he'd dispense with the hat.

Blood pulsed at his temples. He hadn't believed in love at first sight before, but now he knew it existed. He'd loved Tara from the moment he'd set eyes on her in his office. His heart thrilled at the idea that she loved him, too.

But was their love strong enough to last? Especially when she lived in New York while his home was here in Heart's Landing? He'd tried and failed to keep the spark alive with Clarissa...and she only lived as far away as Boston. He'd blamed long distance for the failure of their relationship, but that had only been an excuse. The truth was, he'd never loved Clarissa. Not really. Now that he'd fallen deeply and truly in love with Tara, he knew the difference. Whenever Clarissa had earned a promotion or closed a deal, he'd been happy for her, but his heart hadn't swelled with pride the way it had when Tara had overcome her fears to walk out on stage during the Smith wedding. The tiniest bit of irritation had colored his view of the long hours Clarissa devoted to her job. Not so with Tara. With her, he'd rolled up his sleeves and pored over log books for hours on end. Most of all, he'd never dreamed about the future with Clarissa. Sure, he'd been on the verge of proposing to her, but he'd never looked at the years that lay ahead, hadn't dreamed of children and baseball games and ballet recitals. Not like he did with Tara. He wanted all that with her, and more. He could see them in their dotage, sitting beside each other in a pair of rocking chairs on the widow's walk.

He ran a hand through his hair. How, exactly, would he and Tara work out the logistics? They'd each spent their entire lives preparing for their careers. She'd no more ask him to give up the Captain's Cottage than he'd demand that she walk away from her dreams. Especially not now that she was so close to achieving everything she'd set out to do. Yes, he'd heard her doubts about being able to please her boss, but he trusted that she'd find the solution. Why, he'd even regale her with stories of the Captain and Mary's love for one another if she thought it would help.

He could start with their courtship. The year Mary Shelby made her debut into society, she'd been swept off her feet by a handsome sailor who'd happened to be home on leave. Thaddeus had stolen her heart, promised to name his first ship after her, and asked for her hand by the end of the season. Though she'd known his career required him to be at sea for months at a time, she'd agreed to become his wife, the mother of his children.

Jason shook his head. Talk about long-distance relationships. Half the world had separated Thaddeus and Mary for most of their marriage. Yet their love had survived and flourished. Was he honestly willing to let mere miles prevent him from loving Tara? He came from sterner stock than that. His love for her would endure, no matter how far apart they lived.

The urge to see Tara swelled in his chest. He'd promised to have the script for the pageant sent to her, but delivering it himself presented the opportunity to spend more time with her. That was a chance he didn't want to miss. He tucked the thin booklet under his arm and headed down the hall. When he reached Evelyn's door, he paused for a minute to check on his cousin.

"Hey. How are you today? Feeling any better?" Despite her laryngitis, she'd insisted on coming into the office.

Evelyn peered out at him from behind her computer monitor. Her mouth closed, she shook her head.

"I'm sorry. On the up side, Tara said she'd take your place in the pageant tomorrow night." Grabbing the script, he fanned it at his cousin. "I'm going to drop this off with her now. I'll be out of the office for a few minutes. Can I bring you anything?"

Wait. Wordless, Evelyn held up both hands. While he lingered in the doorway, she pretended to eat off an invisible plate.

Jason scratched his head. "You want me to bring you some lunch from the dining room?"

No. Evelyn shook her head. Pointing to the booklet he held, she repeated her motions. She mouthed a silent Tara.

"You saw her in the dining room?"

Tiny laugh lines appeared on his cousin's face. She nodded.

"Thanks. I'll head there first." Whistling the ballad that he'd sung with Tara, he continued on his mission.

A few minutes later, he stood listening to the hum of a dozen conversations, the clink of silverware, the gurgle of coffee pouring into one of an endless number of cups. He didn't spot Tara, but her laptop stood open on the table he'd come to think of as hers. He shrugged. Wherever she'd gone, she wouldn't leave her computer unattended for long. He'd wait for her. Threading his way through the tables, he stopped to welcome today's influx of brides and their parties and extend good wishes to those who were starting their lives as married couples.

When he reached Tara's spot, he circled around to her chair. He'd planned on dropping the script on the table and taking a seat, but he bumped the corner of the table. The screen on her laptop sprang to life. He scowled. He hadn't meant to disturb her work. He certainly didn't mean to pry. He had no business reading what she'd written. Intending to put the computer back to sleep, he'd pressed one finger to the touchpad when a line on the screen caught his attention.

> *The myth that Captain Thaddeus Heart battled a hurricane to make it home for his wife's birthday is a lie. The storm was still hundreds of miles south of North Carolina when his ship, the Mary Shelby, dropped anchor in Heart's Cove.*

He held his breath as he scanned the rest of the article that was obviously meant for Tara's editor. The more he read, the lower his stomach sank. Tara had claimed that access to Captain Thaddeus' logs would provide the interesting tidbits she needed to include with her evaluation of Heart's Landing. But she'd lied. In reality, she'd used the information for an altogether different purpose. One that would not only damage the Captain's reputation, but the town that bore his name.

Had that been Tara's plan all along? It had to have been. Nothing else made sense. He'd say one thing for her, she knew how to get people to confide in her. Based on her encouragement, he'd opened up to Tara, shared his deepest fears, his hopes for the future with her. The whole time, she'd been playing him, letting him think she'd fallen in love with him, when all the while she'd planned to stab him in the back.

He pushed away from the computer. He had to face facts. Tara didn't love him. She never had. People who truly loved one another would never deliberately destroy everything they stood for.

New fears bubbled in his chest like acid. His stomach plummeted even lower. All along, Tara had offered assurances that Heart's Landing was a shoo-in to retain its ranking as America's Top Wedding Destination. But if she'd lied about everything else, the odds were nil that she was telling the truth about that.

What if the real purpose behind her visit wasn't to ensure that his home town retained its ranking, but to make sure it didn't?

Betrayal seared his lungs, his heart. The

pain lanced through his chest. How had he let himself be duped? Tara was the second woman he'd given his heart to and, like Clarissa, she'd betrayed him. Only this time was worse. Clarissa had only hurt him. Tara's treachery would destroy Heart's Landing.

Once *Weddings Today* published her article, brides and grooms all over the country would cancel their reservations. Newly engaged couples would look elsewhere when planning the most important day in their lives. Within a year or two, five at the most, Heart's Landing would become as distant a memory as Paragon Park in Nantasket Beach.

He eyed the computer screen. The temptation to erase Tara's report surged within him. But what good what it do? She'd only recreate it.

Retrieving the script for the play from the table, he rolled it into a thin cylinder. He might not be able to stop Tara from writing her article, but he didn't have to let her on stage. With so much at stake, he couldn't take the chance that she'd announce her discovery in the middle of the pageant.

The heavy weight of responsibility pressed on his shoulders. For a moment, he bowed beneath it. He struggled to draw in a breath of air that had inexplicably thickened around him. Abruptly, he turned. He had to leave. No matter how badly Tara had broken his heart, he wouldn't let anyone see his pain. No matter how badly she'd betrayed them all, he'd stand tall, determined to uphold the traditions of Heart's Landing for as long as possible.

A task that would've been infinitely easier if he hadn't practically run into her at the door.

"Tara." He pulled himself erect. Until her article appeared in *Weddings Today*, the unenviable task of acting like nothing was wrong fell to him.

"Hey. I hoped I'd see you."

Tara's smile was just as bright and honest-looking as it had always been. He'd swear it was the genuine article if he hadn't stumbled over the truth. But he had, and he couldn't go on acting like everything was fine and dandy between them. He stiffened. "It turns out you won't be needed in the pageant after all."

"You're sure?" Tara's smile dimmed. As if she suspected something was amiss, she peered over his shoulder at the laptop she'd left on the table. "Is everything all right?"

"I don't know why it wouldn't be. Do you?" he challenged.

"No," she said, though her brows knitted and guilt stained her cheeks.

Another lie. He'd once considered

her guileless, but he'd misjudged her. He brushed past her. "You'll have to excuse me. I have an appointment with the mayor." Or he would, as soon as he got the man on the phone.

Behind him, Tara's voice called, "Want to meet for dinner tonight?"

"I can't. I'll call you." Eventually, they'd have to talk. He'd have to say the words that would put the end cap on their relationship. But not now, not today. He set off at a brisk pace before she could ask any more questions or, worse, see how badly she'd broken his heart.

What was that all about?

Her feet rooted to the hardwood floor, Tara watched Jason until he rounded a corner and stepped out of sight. She twisted a strand of hair between two fingers. Talk about your classic bad moods—if she didn't know better, she'd guess he was mad at her for some reason.

Was he already having second thoughts about them? If he was, why not talk it out instead of storming off?

Doubts plagued her footsteps as she made her way back to her spot by the window. At her table, a cold shiver of unease passed through her. If Jason had read her article, it would certainly account for his brusque manner. But no. Her laptop was just as dark as she'd left it. Satisfied, she brought up the email to Regina. Her hand hovered above the Send button. Slowly, she lowered her fingers to the table top.

She eyed the empty table next to hers. The Dobson Star left a lot to be desired. *Gaudy* was too kind a word for the jewel that more closely resembled something from a blacksmith's forge than a jeweler's bench. Yet, Saundra had treated it like a priceless artifact. As proof of her love for the man she was about to marry, the bride planned to wear it when she walked down the aisle.

At the bakery, Nick had said that love was a series of compromises. And here she was, about to ruin the future of the man she professed to love. Where was the compromise in that?

When she'd first landed a job at *Weddings Today*, she'd thought she'd soon be attending the ceremonies of movie stars and power brokers. That she'd be sharing the exquisite details of weddings of the rich and famous with the magazine's eager readers. Things hadn't turned out quite like she'd expected.

It had taken two years, but she'd finally realized that to get ahead, she'd have to get her hands dirty. Much as she hated to admit it, she'd intended to do exactly that by exposing Kate Steven's choice of wedding gowns. Okay, so her first big break hadn't panned out, but it *had* led to her first big assignment—to destroy a legend and, in the process, rip the title of America's Top Wedding Destination from the town that deserved it.

She'd justified her actions by telling herself she was only doing what she had to do in order to get ahead at *Weddings Today*. Once she exposed the truth about Captain Thaddeus, that big promotion was hers for the asking. In all likelihood, though, her next assignment and the one after that would just be more of the same. A different town, a different topic, more slinging mud at someone who didn't deserve it. Just like Jason had predicted. Her stomach plummeted.

Was that really the career she wanted?

It wasn't. A single tear rolled down her cheek. She loved Jason more than she wanted to succeed at *Weddings Today*. Deliberately, she moved the cursor to Delete and hit the button. In an instant, the screen went black. The article she'd come to Heart's Landing to write no longer existed.

She sat for a long moment, her head bowed. She'd just ruined whatever chance she had for success at *Weddings Today*.

She ought to feel sad about that. She didn't. Rather, a giddy elation surged through her. When it had come to a choice between love and career, she'd chosen love.

Jason paced the length of his office. Reaching the wall, he pivoted and retraced his steps to the door. A potent mix of anger and betrayal churned in his stomach. Disappointment tightened his chest. He'd been sure Tara was "the one." He didn't deny that they'd faced hurdles, but none of them had been insurmountable. He'd been so sure they'd succeed that he'd allowed himself to dream of the future. Of a boy with Tara's fair hair who'd race through the Cottage and slide down the banisters. Of a little girl with his gray eyes who demanded to go wherever her big brother went, do whatever he did. There'd been times when he'd sworn he'd almost heard the sound of their laughter ringing through the halls. He'd imagined himself following in his dad's footsteps and asking the cooks to stop feeding the children cookies and ruining their dinners...with the same amount of success.

But it had all been a pipe dream. None of it was possible. Not now that he'd discovered the real reason behind Tara's presence in Heart's Landing. Not now that he knew how she'd played him, had used him to get the information she needed to destroy his town. Not now that she'd broken his heart without giving it a second thought.

He mopped his face with his hand. The question was, what did he do next?

According to the plan, he should already be on the phone with the mayor. The man might be under the weather, but his instructions had been clear. Jason was supposed to contact him the minute he ran into a problem he couldn't handle.

Tara's betrayal certainly qualified. So, why hadn't he picked up the phone?

He wasn't hoping Tara would change her mind. One of the things he'd admired most about her was her insistence on seeing a project through to the end. By now, her article sat on an editor's desk at *Weddings Today*. He wasn't waiting for an apology. He couldn't demand one when she'd been doing a job he'd encouraged her to pursue. He wasn't waiting for her to come crawling to him, begging his forgiveness and asking for a second chance. There weren't enough "I'm sorry"s in the world to undo the harm she'd done, or would soon inflict, on Heart's Landing.

He might as well face it, he wasn't waiting on anything from Tara. Or anyone else, for that matter. No, there was only one reason he hadn't called the mayor or confided in any of the other members of the review team—this fiasco fell squarely on his shoulders.

His job had been to show Tara the best parts of Heart's Landing. He'd been asked to introduce her to the shopkeepers who made their town special. He was supposed to make sure she understood how every resident would go to practically any lengths to ensure that every wedding went off without a hitch.

Maintaining a polite, but professional, relationship with her had been part of the plan. Falling for her had not. But he'd trusted her when he shouldn't have. He'd been wrong to give her access to the ship's logs or Mary's diaries. In doing so, he'd handed her the means of destroying the legend of Captain Thaddeus and ruining the town's reputation.

For that, he had no one to blame but himself.

Worse, he'd given Tara his heart, and she'd smashed it into a million sharp-edged shards that she'd plunged straight into his chest. Was it any wonder he didn't know what to do next? How could he explain his actions to the mayor? How could he stand in front of the people of Heart's Landing and tell them he'd single-handedly brought about the ruin of everything they'd worked for all their lives?

A tapping sound echoed in the hallway. The footsteps halted outside his door. His chin resting on his chest, Jason continued pacing. He didn't need to look up to know that Evelyn stood in his doorway, concern etched on her elfin features. If there was one thing in this life he could count on, it was his cousin. She showed up whenever there was trouble. Normally, he confided in her. Not this time. He couldn't share Tara's betrayal with anyone.

"What's wrong?" Evelyn's hoarse whisper cut through the silence.

He pointed to the furled script for the pageant lying in his desk. "I need someone to play Mary's part tomorrow night."

"I thought Tara was going to do that."

"She's not available." He stopped himself. He might not be up to baring his soul, even to his cousin, but he couldn't lie to her. He sighed heavily. "It's over between us." He made a chopping motion. "Done. *Fini.* Over."

"What happened?"

"I can't talk about it right now." He turned dampened eyes toward her. "It hurts too much."

"Got it." Evelyn cleared her throat. Her voice perfect, she said, "Looks like it's you and me on stage, same as always."

That got his attention. He stared at her, his mouth open. "I thought you had laryngitis."

Evelyn rolled her eyes. "I thought you two deserved a chance."

"Guess we were both wrong."

"I guess so."

Now, all he needed to do was tell the mayor that he'd single-handedly destroyed the future of Heart's Landing. Something he'd do as soon as his heart quit hurting long enough for him to make a phone call.

Chapter Seventeen

*T*ARA TRUDGED THROUGH THE SAND, her feet kicking up a shower of tiny grains with every step. She'd hoped to have the beach all to herself. No such luck. On the far side of the cove, the stranger she'd spotted earlier worked his metal detector along the damp strip at the water line.

Had it really been this morning that she and Jason had stood above this very spot? With all that had happened since then, it seemed like a lifetime ago. She'd unraveled the truth behind the myth of Captain Thaddeus. Lent a hand to a bride in need and learned how much she enjoyed doing her part to make someone else's dream come true. As if that hadn't been enough, she'd polished off the morning by deleting the article she'd been sent here to write. The one that would have all but guaranteed the big promotion she'd spent the last two years trying to nail. Toss in Jason's surprisingly bad attitude, and it was no wonder she'd needed a break.

Shallow waves rolled onto the shore. Bending, she plucked a small cone shell from the wet, gray sand. The tiny creature who lived inside didn't have to worry about where it would lay its head next week. It carried its home with it wherever it went. Unlike her. Now that she'd decided to keep silent about Captain Thaddeus, she'd need to start packing as soon as she got back to New York. What came next was anybody's guess.

Carefully, she returned the shell to the spot where she'd found it. The man with the metal detector had worked his way closer. Nearing, he planted the device in the sand and leaned his forearms on it.

She offered him a smile. "Did you find any buried treasure today?"

"Nah. Need a good storm to stir things up." A strong Rhode Island accent muted the r's in his words. "You from around he-ah, missy?"

"No, sir." Tara brushed her hands.

"Tide's comin' in. It's gonna get wicked deep in a few. You and I, we'd best be getting off this beach."

He was right about the tide. She stood

ankle-deep in water that had barely brushed over her toes five minutes earlier. "Thanks for the warning. I'll move to higher ground."

"Ground nothing. You need to be climbing them steps. Unless you like swimming with the fishes, that is." With that, he hefted his metal detector over one shoulder and shuffled toward the rough staircase that led up to the bike path.

Shading one hand over her eyes, she squinted at the granite outcropping that formed the cove. On three sides, the cliff towered high above her head. Bits of seaweed clung to the jagged rocks about halfway up. "Hang on," she called, eyeing the high tide mark. "I'll walk with you."

The man didn't break stride. She thought he called, "Best keep movin'," but the wind whipped his words. Another wave rushed ashore. This one splashed her thighs. She bolted from the water.

"I see you took my advice," the man said when she fell in beside him. "I'm Walter. Used to own the Honeymoon Hotel on the north side of town."

"I know the place. Nice little bungalows and a cute diner." She'd stopped by one afternoon, looked at the rooms, and taken pictures for *Weddings Today*. She hadn't seen Walter, or Wal-tah, as he said it, though. "I'm Tara, by the way."

He nodded. "My son and his wife took over when I retired a few years back. These days, I comb the beach for lost earrings and bottle caps when I'm not playing with the grandkids. You know the best thing about being a grandparent?"

"No."

"You get to send the little darlings home when you want to take a nap."

She joined in when Walter laughed to himself. For someone who'd left retirement age in his rearview mirror, he amazed her by jogging up the steep steps.

"You sticking around for the pageant tomorrow?" he asked while they climbed.

"I was planning on it." She was supposed to be in it, but for reasons she still didn't understand, those plans had changed.

"It's a good one." Without pausing to look over his shoulder, he nodded toward the beach. "You know, Captain Thaddeus dropped anchor in that very cove each year before his wife's birthday."

"I've heard that." She didn't have the heart to tell him that part of the good captain's legend was a lie.

Moments later, they stood by the railing at the top of the stairs while Tara gasped at the rushing tide. Below them, waves had gobbled up half the distance to the bottom

327

step. "That beach was as pretty as a picture. Who would have thought it wasn't safe?"

Walter shifted his metal detector from one shoulder to the other. "Aye-yup. Just goes to show, things aren't always as they seem. You enjoy the rest of your stay, missy."

"Thanks again for the warning."

The portly gentleman whistled a happy tune as he headed toward the north side of town. Staring at the water that was quickly covering the last of the sand, she had to admit that Walter had been right...and not just about the tide. The opportunity to get ahead at *Weddings Today* hadn't turned out like she'd thought it would. And, apparently, her relationship with Jason had hit an unforeseen bump. She'd gone over the abrupt conversation a dozen times, and she still didn't understand why he'd turned taciturn and gruff. Whatever it was, she wished he'd talk to her about it. She wanted him to know he could trust in their love for one another. That whatever was bothering him, they could work it out together.

First, though, they had to talk. Something that was unlikely to happen while she stood here, looking out at the ocean. Determined to get to the bottom of their problem—whatever it was—she pushed away from the railing and headed back to the Captain's Cottage.

But twenty-four hours and a half-dozen phone calls later, she was no closer to figuring out where things had gone wrong with Jason than she'd been in the dining room. Except, now at least, she knew for sure their relationship was in trouble. What other explanation could there be? No one spent a day and a half avoiding all contact with the woman he'd professed to love. Not unless there was a problem. A big one. She'd done all she could to reach out to him, to let him know that whatever it was, she was willing to work it out. To talk it over. To compromise.

But each time she called, Jason's phone went straight to voice mail. She'd roamed through the Cottage looking for him without success. Finally, she'd swallowed her pride and climbed the stairs to the family living quarters where she'd knocked on the door of his suite. Another wasted effort.

Tears stung her eyes as she descended the stairs once more. She had no choice but to accept the truth. Though she didn't understand why, she'd gotten his message loud and clear. He didn't want to see or speak with her.

Her heart heavy, she retreated to her room. With nothing better to do, she spent a sleepless night working on her final presentation for *Weddings Today*. Though her heart was breaking, she poured her soul onto the page, crafting an article that sang the praises of Heart's Landing. Starting with the hearts-and-flowers trim on buildings and ending with the magnificence of the Captain's Cottage itself, she presented the strongest possible argument that the town should retain its standing as America's Top Wedding Destination.

When she finished, she checked her phone for the umpteenth time. She'd turned the ringer all the way up to be sure she'd hear it if Jason called. He hadn't. The screen remained dark, the icon for text messages empty.

Her heart sank even lower. She was willing to do her share of the work in resolving whatever problem Jason had with her. But she wasn't a mind reader or a magician. She couldn't fix things on her own. She'd given him plenty of time to come to his senses and talk to her. He obviously hadn't. Given that he'd chosen to cut off all communication with her, she didn't see much point in staying in Heart's Landing a minute longer than necessary.

The decision to skip the pageant came easily enough. She swapped her return reservation for an earlier one with a single phone call. Retrieving Chuck's business card from her purse, she arranged for the cab driver to pick her up in front of the Captain's Cottage an hour before the departure time. The glint of afternoon sunlight streamed through the windows by the time she finished packing. All that remained was to return Mary's diary to the library, power down her laptop, and leave.

A dull ache started at the center of her chest and spread outward as she lifted the thin book from the desk. Flipping through the pages one last time, she spotted the slip of paper she'd used as a bookmark. Idly, she passed the diary from one hand to another. Considering her own broken heart, learning more about Captain Thaddeus and Mary's love was the last thing she felt like doing, but leaving without finishing the journal felt like too much unfinished business. With a sigh, she sank onto the chair and found the point where she'd left off. Her breath stalled on the next entry.

> *The homecoming celebration I planned for Thaddeus must wait. Word came by way of his steward that my husband left the Mary S in New York. He assumed command of the SS Pentaur, bound for North Carolina, after the ship's captain suffered a grievous injury. God willing, the P*

*shall drop anchor in Heart's Cove
by next week's end.*

Tara gasped. Clamping one hand over
her mouth, she read the passage and several
of the entries leading up to it again. Her own
surprise about the captain's delay matched
Mary's. Her fingers shaking, she turned to
the next page.

> *This may be my last entry for
> several days. My heart trembles
> with fear for my husband.
> I received word today of a
> monstrous storm churning the
> waters to the south. Pray God
> that Thaddeus has learned of it
> as well and chosen to ride out the
> storm in safety. I have instructed
> the servants to watch over the
> children with all diligence while I
> remain on the lookout for the P.*

Taking command of the *Pentaur* had
no doubt delayed Captain Thaddeus in New
York. It wouldn't have taken much—a day
or two—and he'd have sailed his new ship
straight into the hurricane on his way to
Heart's Landing. Tara held her breath as she
turned the page.

> *Oh glorious, glorious sight. Her
> sails tattered and torn, one
> mast broken, the P. nonetheless*

*survived the storm and has at
long last anchored in Heart's
Cove. Never has there been such
a joyous celebration as when
Thaddeus arrived home last
evening. Repairs to the P will
require at least two weeks, which
shall make my birthday a grand
affair indeed.*

Tara slumped against the chair back.
The legend of Captain Thaddeus was true.
She tapped her finger against her chin.
A heady joy bubbled up inside her. She
couldn't wait to tell Jason. She could practically picture his face when she gave him the
news. He'd be thrilled.

She gulped.

The truth was, Jason wasn't speaking
to her. Even if he were, he'd never understand her excitement...unless she told him
the whole story. Closing Mary's diary, she
bumped the laptop with her elbow. Her heart
hammered as the screen sprang to life.

"Oh, no! The sleep mode." The day she'd
had so much trouble sending her report to
Regina, she'd deleted the password protec-
tion.

Suddenly, Jason's change-of-heart made
a lot more sense. He must have stopped by
her table while she was upstairs yesterday. A
little nudge was all it would have taken, and

he'd have been staring at the article she'd written for *Weddings Today*. The article that called the legend of Captain Thaddeus a sham.

Guilt tightened her throat.

Thank goodness she'd changed her mind before she'd sent that report. As for Jason, she had to make this right. Had to let him know she'd chosen love—for him and for Heart's Landing—over her career.

Picking up her phone, she hit redial. In seconds, she'd arranged for Chuck to pick her up earlier and make an extra stop on the way to the train station. The pageant was due to start in an hour. Now that she knew the truth, she couldn't leave without at least trying to speak to Jason. She crossed her fingers. Though her heart cried out to fix things between them, she didn't dare hope for more than the chance to apologize.

The curtains on the temporary stage in Thaddeus Park rippled in the cool breeze that swept in from the ocean. Through a gap, Jason caught a glimpse of the gathering crowd. It was larger than he'd expected, much bigger than when they held the pageant in the fall. Today, most of the folding chairs had been filled by casually dressed

A Cottage Wedding

couples who sat in neat rows. A few sipped icy beverages or snacked on items purchased from the food trucks that lined the nearby streets. Moms and dads had taken advantage of the summer weather to spread blankets on the grass, where they doled out animal crackers to toddlers who were eager for the show to start. Stragglers continued to arrive. Some carried lawn chairs. Others sat cross-legged wherever they could find a vacant spot.

Jason stuck one finger inside his stiff collar and tugged. Although he donned the replica of Captain Thaddeus's uniform for a half-dozen appearances each month, today the fabric felt tight enough to choke him. The cape he wore around his shoulders weighed him down. His shoes pinched. His skin crawled.

"Argh!" He knew himself well enough to rule out stage fright as the cause. No, this was all Tara's fault. Before she'd arrived in Heart's Landing, he'd been content with his life. Things hadn't worked out the way he'd thought they would with Clarissa, but he'd known that someday he'd find the girl of his dreams. Only, when he had, she'd ruined everything, broken his heart, and shaken his faith in the tales of his swashbuckling ancestor.

How was he supposed to go on stage,

pretend to sail the *Mary S* through a hurricane, and declare his undying love for his "wife" when he questioned every word in the script?

From out of nowhere, Evelyn appeared at his side. "You have company." She nodded toward the wings where the rest of the cast waited for their cues to go on stage.

Tara. It had to be. She was the last person he wanted to see right now. Groaning, he forced his attention in the opposite direction.

Evelyn squeezed his forearm. "You need to talk to her. Whatever's going on between the two of you, you can't simply ignore her and think the problem will go away."

"It will, though," he insisted. "She's headed back to New York tomorrow." After that, maybe his heart would begin to heal. Who knew—one day he might be able to walk along Procession Avenue without imagining her standing on every corner, without seeing her in every shop. Maybe someday he'd roam about the Captain's Cottage without sensing her presence in every room.

"Don't look now, but she's headed over here."

At Evelyn's warning, he stiffened, but Tara's insistent "Jason, we need to talk," still punched him in the gut.

He wheeled on her. He thrust one arm

toward the crowd that waited beyond the curtains. "I'm a little busy at the moment. Can't it wait?"

"No. I've done enough of that already." The sound of Tara's foot striking the floorboards echoed through the back stage. "Why haven't you returned any of my calls? I've left you a dozen messages."

"Seven, actually." He'd listened to every one of them. Her forlorn voice had torn him apart, but he couldn't reply. Not without breaking down completely, and that was something he'd sworn he wouldn't do. "I read your article."

Beneath her summer tan, Tara paled. Her blue eyes watered. "I was afraid of that. I want you to know, I deleted it. That article will never appear in *Weddings Today*."

Steeling himself against her tears, he shrugged. "It doesn't matter whether you filed the report or not. You wrote it."

"I did." Tara hung her head. "But that was before I read the rest of Mary's diary and learned the truth. Or realized I loved you more than anything. More than my job. More than my future at *Weddings Today*."

He brushed invisible lint from his cape. "You expect me to believe that? How can I when you've been telling one lie after another from the moment you came here?"

Tara's voice dropped to a dead calm. "I didn't lie. I never lied."

"Oh, no?" Heat built within his chest. He wanted to rail at her, to show her how badly she'd broken him. He needed her to feel his pain. "You *said* you were here to evaluate Heart's Landing when, from the very beginning, your real goal was to ruin the reputation of Captain Thaddeus. You knew good and well what that would do to the town, how it would destroy any chance we had of retaining our standing as America's Top Wedding Destination."

His words struck home, and she gasped. Though he told himself he was only giving her what she deserved, payback didn't feel nearly as good as he'd imagined.

"It was my job, Jason." Her fingers splayed, she pushed the air between them as if she were trying to stem the tide of his words. "Regina threatened to fire me if I didn't give her what she wanted."

"And that's supposed to make it all right?" He steeled himself and forced the words from his lips. "You betrayed me, Tara. You've been using me this whole time. Me and everyone else you met while you were here. Congratulations. I hope that promotion was worth it."

Judging from the tears that gleamed wetly on her cheeks, he'd made his point.

But his words had been a double-edged sword that hurt him as much as they hurt her. He'd expected to feel vindicated. Instead, he only wanted to take her in his arms. He swirled away from her.

On the other side of the stage, the pageant director lifted a megaphone. "Places, everyone!"

"I'll tell you one thing," he said, moving toward center stage. "You've got what it takes to make a name for yourself. You played me like a fool. I didn't even see it coming."

"You need to leave." Evelyn grasped her elbow. With a thin, firm line replacing her usual, elfin smile, Jason's cousin guided her to the edge of the stage.

"I'm so sorry," Tara whispered. She reached into her purse and pulled out the leather-bound volume she'd intended to give Jason.

"What is this?" Evelyn backed away as if Tara was the wicked witch, trying to give her a poisoned apple.

At center stage, actors and actresses took their places for the opening act. She had seconds to say what needed to be said. "It's Mary's diary. I've marked the key entries.

The bottom line is, the legend is true—Thaddeus did sail through a hurricane to reach Heart's Landing before his wife's birthday, only he wasn't aboard the *Mary Shelby*."

While the director issued the final call, Evelyn eyed the thin volume with outright skepticism. Long seconds passed before the redhead plucked the booklet from Tara's outstretched palm. Without another word, she stashed the diary in a duffel bag and took her place on stage.

Tara breathed in a thready breath. Captain Thaddeus had been a true hero. To help a fellow seaman, he'd given up his berth on the *Mary Shelby*, a move that had forced him to battle a hurricane in order to keep a promise to his wife. The passages she'd marked, along with the research she'd left in the library, would put an end—once and for all—to the whispers and doubts that had swirled around the century-old legend.

Too bad she couldn't sway Jason's opinion as easily. No amount of research would ever change his mind about her. No matter how strongly she'd believed in their love or how much she'd sacrificed for it, she'd heard the death knell of their relationship in his bitter accusations. She'd seen it in his blank stare. She'd hoped to fix things between them, but it wasn't possible. She saw that now.

Breath-stealing pain sliced through her chest. She pressed a hand over her heart. She'd had a chance at love, and she'd lost it, along with everything else she valued. Her job, her career, any chance of success— she'd risked it all on love and failed.

What little self-pride she had left helped her keep her tears at bay during the ride to the station. Once she boarded the train and found her seat, though, she couldn't fight her tears any longer. Turning her back on the rest of the car, she pressed her forehead against the window and gave in to the heart-break.

Chapter Eighteen

THE FIRST STARS OF THE evening twinkled in the sky overhead. In the deepening twilight, birds flocked to their nests in the trees along Procession Avenue. Jason caught his reflection in the window of the first shop he strode past. He'd lost weight. His clothes hung from his frame with unfashionable bagginess. Dark circles had formed under his eyes. *Hmph.* And people said love was a good thing. They couldn't prove it by him. His broken heart hadn't healed nearly as quickly as he'd thought it would. Two months had passed since he'd learned the truth about Tara, and she was still his first thought when he woke in the mornings. He couldn't walk into a single room in the Captain's Cottage without picturing her smiling face or reliving a joke they'd shared. As for sleeping, forget about it. She haunted his dreams. No wonder Doc Adams had warned that he was on the verge of developing an ulcer.

"I wish I'd skipped this and stayed home," he muttered.

"You can't hole up in your office for the rest of your life. You've barely poked your head out ever since Tara left." At his side, Evelyn hurried to match his sidewalk-eating pace. "It'll be good for you to be with friends tonight."

"I guess. If nothing else, I'll give them someone to blame if things turn out the way I expect."

"No one said anything to you about the results?"

"No. *Weddings Today* has held their cards pretty close to the vest." The whole town had been on edge, waiting for the big announcement. "Greg received the FedEx package this morning, but he didn't want to open it until we could all be there. I heard Bar Harbor got theirs yesterday. They made it to fourth place."

"Ouch! They've always come in second, haven't they?"

"Yep." Judging from the hatchet job he'd read on Tara's computer, Heart's Landing wouldn't even make it into the top ten. The stomachache that had been a near-constant companion of late flared.

"Don't worry, Jason. Everything will be all right." Evelyn's voice dropped to a low whisper. "She said she gave us top marks. Maybe it'll be enough. And remember, she did do right by Thaddeus." The information Tara had left in the library, combined with the entries in Mary's diary, had finally settled the questions surrounding the Captain's legend.

"One thing doesn't have anything to do with the other. She lied before. We can't trust her to keep her word. She could've changed her mind and sabotaged our entry after she left here." He didn't want to believe that Tara would stoop so low, but what choice did he have? He couldn't let himself believe in her. If he did, he'd expose the frayed nerves of the heartache that had barely begun to heal. "I wish I knew what she put in her final report."

"You're sure no one else even suspects she had a hidden agenda?"

"You and I are the only people who know why Regina really sent Tara here. I haven't told a soul." He'd planned to. But, as it turned out, the mayor's cold had developed into full-fledged pneumonia that had landed him in the hospital for ten days. It went against Jason's moral code to hit a good man while he was down, so he'd held off on sharing his news until Greg had fully recovered. By then, too much time had passed. Whatever Tara had decided to do, she'd already done it.

Reaching I Do Cakes, Jason pulled open the door and held it while Evelyn entered. Unlike the excited chatter that had greeted him on the eve of the *Weddings Today*'s review, tonight a subdued hush lay over the bakery. Here and there, muted conversations barely rose to a whisper. Not exactly eager to talk with anyone, he exchanged a quiet word with Mildred Morey and nodded to other friends he hadn't seen much of recently. His social obligations out of the way, he headed to the chairs Evelyn found for them in the back of the room. They took their seats just as the clock struck seven.

Greg approached the hostess stand that had been pressed into service as a podium. A hollow sound echoed through the room when he rapped on it.

"Well, this is it, folks," he began, holding the much-ballyhooed envelope aloft. "The results are in, and tonight we'll learn if all our hard work over the last year has paid off. We'll get to that in just a minute. Before we do, I want to give a quick thanks to everyone who helped us get ready for the competition. Heart's Landing wouldn't have a chance of retaining its number-one rating if it weren't for the dedication you've all shown our town."

Polite applause rippled through the room when Greg stopped to sip from his water glass.

"Special thanks to our renewal committee," he continued, naming three of the four members one by one. Each stood to a round of applause.

"Last, but certainly not least, the whole town owes a huge debt of gratitude to Jason Heart. When I fell sick on the very day the rep from *Weddings Today* arrived, Jason stepped up to the plate. No one could've done a better job. Jason, stand and take a bow."

In his chair, Jason tried not to squirm. Praise was the last thing he deserved. If the town lost its leadership position in the competitive wedding destination arena, the fault was his alone.

Evelyn's elbow delivered a sharp jab to his side. "Up."

He gave in, standing to heartfelt applause. Unable to accept praise when, in all likelihood, his failed relationship with Tara had only made things worse for the town he loved, he sank onto the chair like he had lead weights tied to his ankles.

If anyone other than Evelyn noticed his

discomfort, Greg didn't give them a chance to comment on it. At the podium, the mayor raised the envelope. "Here it is, folks, the moment we've been waiting for. Just remember, no matter where we land on the scale, I'm proud of each and every one of you for making Heart's Landing the perfect place to get married. Let me hear it now."

Someone up front shouted, "The best is yet to be!"

Disappointment wreathed Greg's face. "Okay, folks. You can do better than that."

"The best is yet to be!"

While the cheer echoed off the walls, Greg ripped the padded envelope open. Shielding the magazine from prying eyes, he stared down at the cover. "Well, would you look at that."

"What is it, Greg?" Mildred called from her aisle seat.

"Did we win?" Tom Denton leaned forward.

A wide grin broke across Greg's face. He held up the magazine for all to see. Pandemonium erupted as the business owners got their first glimpse of the glossy cover featuring the Captain's Cottage. Beneath the masthead for *Weddings Today*, bold print named Heart's Landing as America's Top Wedding Destination.

Leigh Duncan

"I knew we could count on her," Evelyn whispered at his side.

"How is that even possible?" Jason shook his head.

The mood in the room shifted from quiet desperation to controlled bedlam, taking on the air of a victory party on election night. Shop owners hugged one another. Tears of joy streamed down Mildred's face. Meanwhile, Jason was treated to so many enthusiastic pats on the back he was pretty sure his shoulders would be black and blue by morning. While Kool and the Gang's "Celebration" poured through overhead speakers, Ashley and Alexis popped bottles of champagne they'd secretly had delivered from Favors Galore. Nick ducked into the bakery's massive kitchen and reappeared moments later, carrying trays of cupcakes adorned with #1 flags.

During a rare moment when he wasn't being pummeled by well-meaning friends, Jason nudged the baker. "What would you have done if we hadn't landed in first place?"

Nick grinned. "I guess everyone at the soup kitchen would get a double-portion tomorrow. Jimmy already dropped off our usual delivery."

"You were a whole lot more confident than I was," Jason admitted. He shrugged a non-committal answer to Nick's questioning

348

gaze before searching out the mayor to offer his congratulations and get a closer look at the magazine. By the time he reached Greg, though, the special edition was making its way around the room.

It took an hour or more for the party to wind down. Another half hour passed before Jason finally got his hands on the copy of *Weddings Today*. He stared at the cover, still unable to wrap his mind around the idea that, despite all that had happened between them, Tara had written a favorable report on Heart's Landing. Or that she'd convinced her bosses to once again hand their town the title. Hoping to learn her reasoning, he flipped through the four-page spread, but the article focused solely on what made Heart's Landing so special.

The magazine was a dead end. He wasn't going to find the answers to his questions there. He'd nearly closed it when a photo on the next page caught his attention. He stared at himself dressed as Captain Thaddeus. A quick read of the column above it told him the piece marked a decided departure from the puff and fluff people were used to seeing in *Weddings Today*. Couched as marriage advice, the author had used a hurricane as a metaphor for the troubles couples truly in love might have to overcome.

He stilled, knowing in an instant that

Tara had written the article. He read the column through again, this time absorbing every word. When he finished, dampness clouded his vision. Tara had loved him. The accusations he'd flung at her had ruined things between them; the bitter words he'd said to her had pushed her away, but she'd loved him enough to share their story with the world. When he finally wrenched his focus off the page, Evelyn stood beside him.

"Wow," she said reading over his shoulder. "She must have really loved you."

"Not as much as I loved her," Jason murmured. "And still do. I've been such a fool." He stared at the picture, resigned to spending the rest of his life with a gaping hole in his heart.

Evelyn's eyes searched his face. "You're going to leave things like this? That's nuts. You know that, don't you. You have to talk to her."

Could he?

Like Captain Thaddeus and Mary, he and Tara were made for each other. If he had the chance to make things right between them, he had to try. He whipped out his phone. Her number was seared into his memory. He punched it while he strode out the door. In seconds, he was listening to a recorded message.

"You've reached Tara. If you're calling

about the apartment, you're too late. It's already rented. Otherwise, leave a message at the beep."

Jason lowered the phone. Was *he* too late as well? He dug in his pocket for the business card he'd tucked into his wallet. Somewhere in Manhattan, a phone rang... and rang...and rang. He groaned, certain he'd missed his chance. He was just about to give up when an unfamiliar voice came on the line.

"Tara Stewart's desk. This is Van. May I help you?"

Vanessa Robinson. Tara's office mate. He straightened. "This is Jason Heart. I'm trying to reach Tara."

"You're the guy who broke her heart."

The ice in Van's voice knocked him back a step. Jason swallowed. If the situation called for it, he'd grovel. "I know I don't deserve it, but I need to talk to her. At the very least, I owe her a huge apology. More than that, I—" On the verge of confessing how badly he'd messed things up with Tara, he stopped. He'd shout his love for her to the world if it would bring her back to him, but he thought—maybe—she should be the first to hear him say it.

Silence stretched until he thought Van had hung up on him. At last, she sighed. "I shouldn't tell you this, but..."

But what? Had she moved on? To Savannah? To someone else? He winced. There'd never be anyone else for him but Tara.

Van's breath whispered through the receiver. "She has a meeting with Regina Charm tomorrow at ten. If you want to catch her, that's your best chance."

"Thank you. From the depths of my heart." Jason's voice wavered.

"Don't make me regret this," came a warning he didn't need.

"I won't," he swore and ended the call.

Minutes later, he pulled Evelyn aside. "I'm going to try and get her back. I need your help. Can you call the train station? Get Georgia to book me on the 10:15 to New York. If I leave now, I'll just have enough time to swing by the Cottage and grab a bag." He had to retrieve the ring that had been handed down from one generation of Hearts to the next. Nestled in a velvet-lined box, it sat in a safe in his room. If Tara forgave him, if she'd have him, he'd never let her go again.

"What are you waiting for?" Evelyn had already pulled out her cell phone. "Go. Go." She waved her fingers in the air.

Tara glanced at the wall calendar that hung beside the sink in her tiny apartment. The ominous red circle around today's date hadn't disappeared since the last time she'd looked at it. She sighed. All good things came to an end, and her time was up at *Weddings Today*. She stretched the tape over the cardboard, ripped it from the dispenser, and dusted her hands. That was it. The last of them. She surveyed the meager pile of boxes in the one-room apartment. To save moving costs, she'd sold or given away most of her furniture. Later this morning, after the fateful meeting with Regina, she'd begin the arduous task of loading what she could into the small truck she'd rented. By this time tomorrow, she'd be on to the next chapter of her life.

Where that chapter would unfold, she had no idea. The thought of returning to Savannah, of moving back into her old bedroom, working in her parents' restaurant, and giving up on her dreams made her stomach hurt. But she couldn't afford to stay in New York, not even in a tiny, fifth-floor walk-up.

Lately, she'd been thinking about Heart's Landing. A lot. She'd fallen in love with the town, with the people there, with the dedication they poured into providing the perfect wedding for every bride. She wanted to be a part of that somehow. To contribute to making other brides' dreams come true, even if her own had shattered.

She wiped tears from her eyes. There wasn't a whole lot left in her savings account, but it, along with her severance pay, should be enough to see her through a couple of months until she got on her feet again. She supposed she could go freelance—write articles touting the area and submit them on spec to various newspapers and magazines. Eventually, that might lead to a permanent job with the Heart's Landing Gazette.

But could she live in the same town as the man she'd loved, would always love? One day in the not-so-distant future, Jason was bound to start dating again. Her heart clenched. He might have already. Could she handle meeting him on the street, greeting him with the casualness of an old friend, making the next Ms. Potentially Right feel welcome? She'd have to if she followed her heart, and right now, it was leading her to Heart's Landing.

She sighed. It was time to go into the office and face the music. The last two months had been quite the roller coaster ride at work. She'd been certain she was about to get fired when Regina had called her into her office the day she'd returned from Heart's Landing. But no. Though her boss had clearly been unhappy with the decision, the senior editor had explained that upper management had chosen Heart's Landing as one of the top ten finalists in this year's competition. It had fallen to Tara to polish her presentation for the final round, a task she'd worked on day and night for four solid weeks. Which hadn't been easy, considering that every picture, every line of text, reminded her of Jason and the love she'd had and lost. In the end, it had been worth it. She hadn't been able to contain herself when word had come down that Heart's Landing had retained its number one ranking as America's Top Wedding Destination.

Her first impulse had been to call Jason and deliver the good news personally. She'd stopped herself. Wiping her eyes, she'd let her coworkers think she was crying tears of joy as she stepped away from the phone and accepted their good wishes.

Regina, though, hadn't been among the many people who'd stopped by her cubicle to offer their congratulations. The night before, she'd flown to London for a preview of Sophie Olson's spring line. From England, the senior editor had gone to Paris, where she'd consulted with that country's top designers in bridal wear. After a lengthy stay in Milan, she'd polished off her month-long sojourn by attending the royal wedding of the prince of

Belgium at the Cathedral of St. Michael and St. Gudula in Brussels. The editor was due back in the office today, and Tara harbored no doubts about the topic of their ten o'clock meeting. She checked her phone. She'd have to hustle if she was going to make it across town on time.

Two hours later, she marched into the lobby of the magazine's headquarters wearing the only pair of designer heels she owned and a slim-fitting suit that usually bolstered her spirits. A task that became infinitely more difficult when silence fell over the bull pen the instant she stepped out of the elevator. Her knees went weak. The quiet created the distinct impression that she was running a gauntlet. Except, in this case, she was on the receiving end of furtive peeks and sidelong glances instead of sticks and stones.

She squared her shoulders. Ahead, Regina's office door yawned open. She pressed toward it. Passing her own cubicle, she caught Van's thumbs-up sign. She managed a shaky smile in return.

"Ms. Charm?" She stood in the hall.

Not much had changed in the weeks since she'd last set foot in her boss's office. If anything, the piles of paper on Regina's desk were higher, the frown on the editor's face more deeply etched. Her glasses, purple this time, twirled from the ends of her fingers.

"Yes, Tara. I appreciate your coming in to the office today. I hope it wasn't too much of an inconvenience."

"None at all." Getting fired, though, that was a huge pain.

"Have a seat."

She slid onto the guest chair, her back stiff.

"Let's get right to it, shall we?" Laying her glasses aside, Regina flexed her fingers.

Figuring it might be her last for a while, Tara sucked in a breath.

"You did an excellent job with the Heart's Landing proposal. Although, I must say, I was surprised by your continued support of the town, considering all you went through there."

Tara cocked her head. *Say what?*

In answer, Regina made a dismissive gesture. "Please. I might be in management, but my investigative skills are still as sharp as ever. I know I'm not the only one who lost the love of her life in Heart's Landing."

Tara fought an urge to scratch her head. She *had* fallen in love with Jason. Their relationship *had* shipwrecked. She was pretty sure she'd *never* get over losing him. But how had Regina found out about it? Did she have other spies working for her? Whether she did or not, there was no point in denying the truth. "I don't know where you got your information, but you're right. My love life aside, though, I still believe in the town and what it stands for."

Regina's features, always so stiff and formal, softened. "You're a better person than I am, Tara. When Robert called off our wedding, I let it color my opinion of Heart's Landing. I'm glad you didn't do the same thing." She picked up the issue of *Weddings Today* that featured the Captain's Cottage on the cover. "It is such a pretty little town. You were right to advocate for it."

Wow. The admission was so far out of Regina's character, Tara didn't know how to react. "How long does it take before your heart stops feeling like it's being ripped to pieces every day?" she whispered.

Regina's dark eyes watered. "I'll let you know when that happens." Perching her glasses on her nose, she assumed her usual distant demeanor. "There was a reason I wanted to meet with you, and it wasn't to reminisce." She cleared her throat. "We— and by that I mean myself as well as the powers that be upstairs—were impressed by the work you did on the Heart's Landing proposal. Your attention to detail, your ability to work independently, your creative flair are exactly the attributes we want in our staff at *Weddings Today.*"

Tara slowly exhaled the breath she'd

been holding. A tiny spark of hope lit in her chest. Regina made it sound like she wasn't getting fired.

"In addition, your article using a storm as a metaphor for true love was brilliant. Response has been extremely positive. We want to see more of that. That being said, we'd like to offer you the newly created position of Senior Columnist."

Tara's breath stalled. This was more than she'd dared hope for. "What, exactly, would my responsibilities be?"

"You'd write a monthly advice column for the magazine. The topic can be anything you like. Subject to my approval, of course."

Tara nodded. She could live with that. No editor in her right mind would give a brand-new columnist carte blanche.

"A thousand words, max. You'd have your own byline. The offer comes with a commensurate salary bump. You'll have your own office." Regina slid a slip of paper across the desk.

Tara stared at the number, her eyes widening. The amount was more than she'd imagined in her wildest dreams. The raise meant she could afford to move to a more spacious apartment. With an elevator. Maybe even a view. But she wouldn't kid herself. Writing a monthly column about some aspect of love was going to be difficult given the current shattered state of her own heart.

"Well, what do you think?"

Before Tara had a chance to answer, the intercom on Regina's desk buzzed. "Ms. Charm. I'm sorry to interrupt, but there's a Mr. Heart here to see Tara. He's, um, quite insistent on speaking with her right away."

"Jason? What's he doing here?" The questions flew from Tara's mouth. Hope leaped to her throat. Her heart thudded.

Regina's glasses slid down her nose. She looked over the tops of the frames. "I take it he's *the one*?" At Tara's speechless nod, she asked, "Do you want to see him?"

It took less than a split-second for her to decide. "Yes."

Regina pressed a button on the intercom. "Show him in."

Agreeing to see the man who'd ripped her heart to shreds was one thing; deciding how to greet him was something else again. Remaining seated felt too cold and impersonal. Standing might send the message that she was glad to see him. Which, after all the pain and heartache he'd put her through, shouldn't be the case. She crossed and recrossed her legs. In quick succession, someone rapped on the door, which sprang open, and there he was, the man of her dreams. The man who'd been her every-thing...before he'd broken her heart.

As if she realized Tara might need a mo-ment to pull herself together, Regina sprang from her seat and came around the desk to greet him. "Mr. Heart. Welcome to *Weddings Today*. I'm Regina Charm, Executive Editor for the magazine."

Tara's gaze had locked on Jason's the moment he'd entered the room. When his attention shifted to the diminutive woman in his path, the loss felt like a body blow. From the mournful look she glimpsed in his eyes, he must have felt the same way. Neverthe-less, he extended a hand in greeting.

"Ms. Charm. It's a pleasure. On behalf of all of Heart's Landing, I'd like to thank you for the honor you bestowed on our town."

Tara watched the interplay, her mouth dry. It was a good thing Regina was handling this part of things. She didn't think her lips could form a single word.

"Our magazine was thrilled with this year's selection. Of course, a lot of the credit goes to Tara here. Though Heart's Landing is indeed the perfect location for a wedding, it was her presentation to our management team that sealed the deal."

Jason swung to face her. "You did that for us after...after everything?"

Tara found her feet. "I wouldn't let my

personal feelings interfere with the job I was sent there to do." Jason had broken her heart, but she wasn't vindictive or petty. He needed to know she was tougher than that. "I fell in love with Heart's Landing. I wanted the world to see it the same way I did."

Jason pressed one hand to his chest. "Thank you. The whole town thanks you."

"That's one of the reasons we've just offered Tara a promotion. Senior Columnist," Regina interrupted.

Jason's focus shifted to the editor. When he looked at Tara again, equal portions of happiness and regret swam in his eyes. "A promotion? That's, uh, that's great news. Congratulations." He shuffled his feet.

"Thanks." Tara hid a smile. The man who never lost his cool was clearly ill at ease. She wondered why.

The imploring look Jason tossed in Regina's direction all but demanded the editor leave her own office. But Regina wasn't going anywhere. Her arms folded, she leaned against a nearby bookcase as if she didn't have anywhere better to be. Jason shuffled sideways until his broad shoulders blocked as much of the editor's view as possible. "There's, uh, there's something else I wanted to tell you. The last time we spoke, I said some things I shouldn't have." With another glance at Regina, he moved closer to Tara. "I wanted to tell you how sorry I am."

Tara sliced a hand through the air. "Apology accepted. You weren't the only one in the wrong. I should've been honest with you from the beginning." If she had one misgiving—other than how things had turned out—it was that she hadn't confided in him, trusted him, earlier. She wouldn't make that mistake again. Not ever.

Jason bowed his head. "In the future, I won't be so quick to judge."

"See that you don't...the next time you fall in love." Whoever she was, Jason's next girlfriend would reap the benefits of the mistakes they'd both made.

Jason slowly shook his head. "I'm never going to fall in love again."

"Don't be so sure." It was bound to happen. For him, at least. As for her, there'd never be anyone else like him.

"Because I never fell out of love...with you."

Tara's heart skipped a beat before stalling out completely. The air in her lungs escaped in a long hiss that ended with, "Me, neither."

The tiny lines around Jason's mouth and eyes smoothed. His feet lost their nervous shuffle. "That's the best news I've heard in two months." A wistful smile slanted across his face. "That's saying something."

When she stopped to think about everything else that had transpired, it was actually saying quite a lot.

His mouth opened and closed, leaving whatever else he'd planned to say unfinished. Her eyes watered. He didn't have to speak. She understood. Relationships were tough enough when the two who loved each other lived within hailing distance. With more than two hundred miles separating them, theirs would be a constant struggle.

Jason's expression firmed. "If you think there's even a chance for us, I'll move to New York. There's an opening at the Beacon Theater. I've already applied for the position."

"Wait. No." That wasn't what she'd had in mind. She couldn't let him move away from Heart's Landing. Not for her. "What about the Captain's Cottage?"

"Evelyn has agreed to take over. She's not thrilled with the idea, but once she gets her feet wet, I'm sure she'll be fine."

But there was something he didn't know.

"Jason." Stepping forward, she placed her hand on his broad chest. Through the rough weave of his shirt, she felt his heart beat. "My promotion—I'll be a columnist. I can do that job from anywhere." She glanced at Regina for confirmation. "Isn't that right?"

Lingering by the door, Regina swiped a finger under her eyes. "I don't see why not. You'd need to come into the office once or twice a month, but everything else can be handled by phone or email."

Longing to put the confusion she saw there to rest, she stared into Jason's eyes. "I was actually planning to make my home in Heart's Landing."

"Really?" Jason stilled. "You're moving... there?"

She shrugged, the worries of the past few months slipping from her shoulders. "My bags are already packed. I was going to load the truck tonight, hit the road first thing in the morning."

"That puts a different spin on things. I hadn't considered..."

When he wavered, her entire body went cold. She'd seen the possibility of a second chance in his presence here. But maybe she'd gotten it all wrong. Maybe that wasn't what he wanted at all. She drew in a calming breath. "Jason. It's okay. If we're not on the same page, I don't have to move to Heart's Landing. I can stay, find another apartment in New York. The city's not such a bad place."

She'd never feel at home here, though.

Not like she did in Heart's Landing. A part of her would always belong to the small, seaside town where brides went to get married.

"I'm not saying that. In fact..." Jason shoved one hand in his pocket.

Before Tara could draw a breath or form a cogent thought, he sank to one knee. "I love you more than I ever thought possible. I will regret to my dying day the words I said to you in anger, and I'll spend the rest of my life making it up to you, if you, Tara Stewart, will do me the honor of becoming my wife and accept this ring as a token of my love."

The world came to a full stop. Her heart stammered. She thought she'd lost him. She thought she'd lost everything. Instead, she'd gained her heart's desire.

"Yes!" The word whispered across her lips. When her thoughts caught up, she knew she'd said the right thing. Her heart belonged to Jason. It always would.

Her fingers steady with the firm belief that she'd made the right choice, the only choice, she watched as Jason slipped a circle of emerald and diamonds on her finger. She sucked in a gasp. She'd have worn the ring even if it were as ugly as the Dobson pendant, but it was truly a work of art.

"My great-great-great-grandfather gave this to his bride. It's been worn by Heart women for generations. If you want something more modern..."

"Never. It's a treasure. I'm honored to wear it." She pressed Mary Heart's ring to her lips.

She tilted her face to his. Eyes the color of unbreakable steel, as deep as the ocean's depths, as impervious as slate, stared back at her in a steady gaze that told her Jason's love would never falter. That it was, indeed, a love for the ages.

Regaining his feet, Jason drew her into his arms. Tenderly, almost reverently, he cupped her chin in his hands. Her breath steadied as Jason leaned toward her. He shifted closer, drawing out the moment with gentle strokes of his fingers against her throat until she couldn't stand it. She ached to feel his lips against hers. Rising on tiptoe, she met him as, at last, he dipped down until their lips touched. A soft moan rose in her throat and she knew, once and for all, she'd found her home. He was what she'd been searching for her entire life. He was where she wanted to be more than anywhere else.

All too soon, they pulled apart at Regina's not-so-gentle throat clearing. "I think that's my cue," murmured the misty-eyed editor. An instant later, she slipped out the door. It closed firmly behind her retreating figure.

"I thought she'd never leave," Jason whispered.

Tara leaned against him. Eager to start her new life in Heart's Landing with the man she loved, she lifted her lips for another of Jason's amazing kisses. In an instant, she pictured the future they'd have in one another's arms, the years they'd spend at each other's sides. She and Jason would grow old together. One day, they'd have matching rockers on the veranda of the Captain's Cottage, where they'd sit side-by-side and regale their sons and daughters—the next generation of Hearts—with stories of Thaddeus and Mary and their very own Heart's Landing love for the ages.

"Let's go home," she whispered.

Epilogue

"A LITTLE HIGHER. HIGHER. YOU ALMOST have it," Alicia Thorne directed from beyond the first row of chairs in the side yard of the Captain's Cottage.

"Now, don't you boys crush my flowers." Mildred Morrey fretted beside her.

"Not a chance." Ryan Court's head swung toward the helper he'd conscripted minutes earlier. "Jason, you good on your end?"

Jason tightened his grip on the rope they'd used in assembling the backdrop. Purple hyacinths swayed as the final piece of the wooden frame slid into place over his head. "Got it," he said through gritted teeth.

As if there were a chance in the world that he'd let go and have the whole thing come crashing down. Not after all the hard work Ryan had poured into building the bower. Not after Mildred carefully covered every inch with ribbons and bows before tucking flowers into niches. Not with half of Heart's Landing slated to arrive at the Captain's Cottage in a matter of hours. Certainly not with Tara's happiness at stake.

His heart hammered. In just a little while, in front of family and friends, he and Tara would say their vows and begin their new lives as husband and wife. He could hardly wait. He'd thanked God every day in the weeks that had passed since he'd sworn to love and cherish her for the rest of his life. Beginning today, he'd prove to her that he was a man of his word.

"Jason! Are you daydreaming again?" Hammering a nail into place with one blow, Ryan shook his head. "Serves me right for asking the groom to lend a hand."

Startled, Jason gave his friend his best aw-shucks smile and tightened his hold on the rope. Lately, he hadn't been able to think about anything but Tara. "Falling in love should come with a warning label like some medicines. 'Don't operate heavy machinery. Stay away from sharp objects.'"

"Oh, man. You've got it bad." Ryan said, but a smile accompanied his grumbles. He sank a few more nails. "Okay. You can let go now. Stand over there with Mildred and Alicia, and tell me how it looks."

Jason didn't need a second invitation. While Ryan tucked his hammer into his tool belt, he trotted down the stairs and took his place between the florist and the event planner. On the side porch, tall pots of purple hyacinths stood against a backdrop of gauzy white curtains. More flowers dripped from the archway that he and Tara would pass under when they mounted the steps to join the minister on the veranda.

"I think you nailed it—pun intended," Jason declared. The day they'd held the taste testing at I Do Cakes, Tara had been crushed when he'd pointed out the problems with using her favorite flowers in a wedding at this particular location. For today, though, he'd wanted, more than anything, to fulfill her every wish, even if it meant taking gardening shears to the rose bushes. With a lot of help from friends like Ryan, Alicia and Mildred, that hadn't been necessary. Now, with the trellises tucked behind sheer drapes and folding chairs arrayed in rows on the lawn, the stage was set for the wedding of Tara's dreams. He took a deep breath. "What do you think, ladies?"

"She'll love it! Does she know about any of this?" Mildred's gesture encompassed row upon row of white chairs, the flower arrangements beside each aisle seat, the white runner Tara would walk down.

"It's the best-kept secret in Heart's Landing," Alicia answered. "We waited till she left for the spa before we began setting up." She tapped her watch. "She should be back soon."

"We'd better wrap this up, then." Tool box in hand, Ryan joined them. Turning to give his creation one final look, he whistled. "This is the first one of these I've built. I have to say, it's not bad."

"It's perfect." Mildred plucked at Ryan's shirt sleeve. "Backdrops and arches are the next big thing in weddings. If you want to expand your business, that might not be a bad way to go."

The man whose family owned one of the largest construction companies in Heart's Landing gave a noncommittal shrug. "I have my hands full renovating the old boat works. It's slow going, but it'll be worth it when I'm finished."

"This town could always use another wedding venue," Jason pointed out. Reservations at the Captain's Cottage had soared lately.

Ryan nodded. "That's what I think. Well, I probably ought to get moving if I'm going be back here on time."

Jason shook Ryan's extended hand. "Thanks for everything. I owe you."

"Consider it my wedding gift for a lady who's lucky to have you."

Thinking of Tara, Jason shook his head. "I found my soul mate, a true Heart's Landing love for the ages. I'm the lucky one."

"Oh! My! Word!" Evelyn exclaimed as Tara stepped from behind the dressing screen. "Is that— It can't be. Is that my great-grandmother's dress?" The redhead's voice trailed upward.

Tara spun in a slow quarter turn. Silver fringe rippled over the bodice and swished along the hemline. The beads sown in swirling patterns rustled softly. "It is. I sent it to the same restorer who handles the Mary Heart gowns. Isn't it fabulous?"

She swallowed past the tiniest doubt. She'd fallen in love with the 1920s flapper-style dress the instant she'd taken it from the chifferobe her first day in Heart's Landing. But had borrowing it from the attic been a mistake?

"You look amazing. Jason is going to lose his mind," Evelyn stated with firm conviction.

Tara exhaled the breath she hadn't realized she'd been holding. "I wanted to wear something tied to the Captain's Cottage, something that would reflect Jason's love of history and sense of place."

Tears welled in Evelyn's eyes. She swiped at them. "Well, you certainly did that. He'll love it, and he'll love you all the more for it. If that were even possible." Her gaze swept upward. "Oh, and that veil! It's stunning. Where on earth did you get it? I know we didn't have that in the wardrobes upstairs."

"No, that was Ames's doing." Three short strands of pearls hung from an ornate button adorning the Juliet cap. The beads swung when Tara ran her fingers over the gossamer fabric. "He had it delivered to the Captain's Cottage. I hadn't even told him what I was wearing."

"He definitely has a knack," Evelyn answered with stars in her eyes. "I want him to design my veil when I get married. If that day ever comes."

"It will. Be sure you stand up front when I toss the bouquet." Evelyn was the closest thing to a sister-in-law she'd ever have. Tara shot her a conspiratorial smile. "Maybe you'll catch it."

Evelyn shook her head. "Finding my special someone isn't in the plan anytime soon. I'll be too busy running things here at the Captain's Cottage while you and Jason are on your honeymoon."

"You never know. Look at Jason and me. We certainly didn't plan on falling in love. But when it's right, it's right."

Tara pressed one hand over her heart. She'd always wanted a summer wedding, but the thought of waiting till next June had nearly driven her to distraction. Fortunately, Jason hadn't wanted a long engagement any more than she had. With a droll expression that still made her laugh, he'd assured her he had an "in" with the best venue in town and insisted on handling all the arrangements. She'd snuck a peek at the veranda on her way back from the spa. The backdrop he'd commissioned had turned the space into a fairy tale setting for their wedding and taken her breath away. It was just one more in a long list of reasons she'd love him forever.

She straightened her engagement ring, eager to have Jason slip a plain gold band on her finger. "Speaking of honeymoons—a month visiting all the great cathedrals in Europe. Isn't that the best ever?" As was the custom, they'd spend their first night in the Azalea Suite. Tomorrow, they'd board a flight to London and, from there, she and Jason planned to visit all the sites on their list.

"I don't know who's looking forward

to the trip more—you or Jason." The clock over the mantle in the bridal dressing room chimed softly. "Okay, it's almost show time. Final check. You have your something borrowed, something blue, something old, and something new?"

Tara skimmed one hand over the antique dress. "Borrowed *and* old. Alicia gave me a hanky embroidered with blue flowers. As for new..." Lifting the hem of the ankle-length gown, she balanced on one foot while she held out the other. The jewels in one of the Sophie Olson high heels caught a ray of light and reflected a thousand sparkles.

"Oh! Those are to die for!" With her typical candor, Evelyn gasped, "They must have set you back a pretty penny."

"Actually, no. They were Regina's gift. My something new for the wedding." Lately, her boss had been full of surprises.

"I guess she's not the cold fish everyone made her out to be," Evelyn mused. "She and Robert make a nice couple."

No one had been more surprised than Tara when Regina had announced that her ex-fiancé would be attending the wedding as her plus-one. "I guess seeing Jason and me together, watching him go down on bended knee—"

"—I can't believe he didn't propose at a

nice restaurant, someplace romantic," Evelyn protested.

"It was plenty romantic for me." Her heart still went pit-a-pat when she thought of that moment. "Anyway, Regina had always said true love was only a fairy tale. But we convinced her otherwise. She called Robert the very next day. They've been seeing each other ever since." And, according to Van, the temperature at the office had thawed considerably over the last month.

"Maybe they'll try again for a Heart's Landing wedding," Evelyn said, hopeful.

"Maybe." Stranger things had happened. But that was down the road a bit. Right now, there was a man and a minister waiting for her at the altar. "Are we all set? Are Lulu and Maggie ready?"

Her family had closed the restaurant and flown in earlier in the week. Not that they'd lounged around since they'd arrived. Taking time off wasn't in their nature. Instead, Maggie and her mom had taken over the job of decorating the dining room for the rehearsal dinner, while her father and Lulu had worked with Connie and her staff, preparing their signature shrimp 'n grits. Last night, a few of the locals had turned up their noses at such "Southern fare." That was, they had until they'd tasted the dish. Then, her father had sworn he'd never seen so many plates come back to the kitchen licked clean. He was still proudly chuckling about it when she and Evelyn had whisked her mom and sisters off to the Perfectly Flawless Day Spa this morning.

"Alicia and Jenny have everything under control." Evelyn had no sooner offered the assurance than a light tap sounded and the door eased ajar.

Tara cocked her head as Jenny stepped into the gap. "Your bridesmaids will start down the aisle in a minute. Your dad's waiting right outside. Are you ready?"

Tara inhaled a deep breath. "Ready." She'd been waiting for this since the moment she'd first looked into Jason's eyes.

Jenny nodded, her mouth gaping open. "I know you think I have to say this, but this time I really mean it—you look absolutely stunning. The most beautiful bride I've ever seen." The opening notes of "Pachelbel's Canon" drifted into the room. Straightening, Jenny resumed her usual businesslike manner. "It's time."

While Evelyn slipped past to claim her seat before the ceremony started, Tara stepped from the room.

"There's my girl." Above a bowtie and starched, white collar, her father's ruddy face broke into a wreath of smiles. "Honey, you look gorgeous. The first of my daughters to get married." His chest swelled, and he kissed her cheek. As they started the short walk to the ceremony, he grinned. "I guess this means you're not coming back home to join the family business."

"No, Dad." Tara patted his arm. "You aren't too disappointed, are you?"

"Never! Your mother and I, we knew the restaurant wasn't in your blood from the time you were just a little girl. All those wonderful stories you used to tell over the dinner table—that's where your passion was. Honey, all your mom and I have ever wanted is your happiness. If that means living in Heart's Landing and marrying Jason, if he makes you happy..." He halted, waiting for an answer.

"He does, Dad." Tara squeezed her father's arm. "I've never been more certain of anything in my life."

"That's good enough for me." He stood straighter. "What say we get you married?"

Arm-in-arm, they stepped onto a white runner that led them to the aisle. Tara lifted her head as Lydia, Greg Thomas's daughter, played the opening bars of the "Wedding March." Skirts rustled. Men cleared their throats. The gathered crowd rose. Two months ago, she would've trembled in fear at the sight of even a hundred people watching her. The three hundred who stood now barely caused a flutter. Jason had helped her with that. Among other things, he'd shown her that by putting the one she loved first—whether it was a man or a town—she'd banish her fears. She barely leaned on her father's arm as, carrying a single purple hyacinth, she walked down the aisle to the man she loved.

And there he was, looking magnificent in a tux and tails. A giddy frisson ran through her, and she nearly pinched herself. Jason's eyes widened, his lips parted the moment he caught sight of her. She knew in that instant she'd been right about the dress. Then his gaze locked on hers, and she lost herself in the gray depths of his eyes.

"The best is yet to be," she whispered, grateful for all that had led her to Heart's Landing, where she'd discovered her very own love for the ages.

The End

Orange Balsamic Roasted Carrots

A Hallmark Original Recipe

In *A Cottage Wedding*, Tara attends a cocktail party in her honor, catered by a chef who trained at Le Cordon Bleu in Paris. All the food is amazing, including the balsamic-glazed carrots, and Tara savors every bite... until Jason sweeps her off her feet to dance. Our Orange Balsamic Roasted Carrots add a dash of panache to any menu, and they're as easy as they are elegant.

Prep Time: 5 minutes
Cook Time: 45 minutes
Serves: 10

INGREDIENTS
- 20 organic whole carrots with greens, trimmed
- 2 tablespoons olive oil
- 1 tablespoon balsamic vinegar
- 1 tablespoon orange juice concentrate
- 4 cloves garlic, minced
- 1 tablespoon thyme, fresh, chopped
- Kosher salt and pepper, to taste
- Italian parsley, chopped, optional, garnish

PREPARATION
1. Preheat oven to 375°F.
2. Clean and trim carrots and place on a lightly greased baking sheet.
3. In a small bowl, whisk olive oil, balsamic vinegar, orange juice, garlic and thyme.
4. Season with salt and pepper to taste.
5. Pour the mixture over the carrots and gently toss to coat.
6. Roast 40-45 minutes or until tender. If desired, garnish with parsley.

Thanks so much for reading *A Cottage Wedding*. We hope you enjoyed it!

You might like these other books
from Hallmark Publishing:

A Simple Wedding
Country Hearts
A Country Wedding
Beach Wedding Weekend
Love On Location
Sunrise Cabin

For information about our new releases and
exclusive offers, sign up for
our free newsletter at
hallmarkchannel.com/hallmark-
publishing-newsletter

You can also connect with us here:

Facebook.com/HallmarkPublishing

Twitter.com/HallmarkPublish

Turn the page for a sneak peek of

A Country Wedding

Based on the Hallmark Channel Original Movie

Leigh Duncan

Chapter One

*B*RADLEY SUTTONS TWIRLED HIS STETSON on the tips of his fingers. Light glinted off the buckle on the fourteen-hundred-dollar hat that had been a gift from his agent. In the shadows beyond the cameras that tracked his every move, someone made a chopping motion, meaning *Stop that.*

Bradley stilled. He traced his fingers over the brim and gave himself a stern reminder to keep his trademark smile in place while he willed away the urge to squint or squirm or stand and walk straight out of the studio.

Quit your bellyaching. He wasn't really going to complain about the dizzying heat or the blinding glow that came from all the spotlights aimed at him, was he? Not when he'd spent the past ten years working to get where he was. Every step he'd taken, every stage he'd stepped onto in the bars around

Nashville, every mic he'd poured his heart and soul into—they'd all led to this moment.

He glanced at the incredibly talented, beautiful woman seated next to him on the couch. Catherine tipped her head toward his. The smile she always wore in public, the one that rarely touched eyes the color of fine cognac, deepened as she met his gaze. A long, blond curl slid over her shoulder. Bradley's fingers ached to reach out, tuck the errant hair back into place. Aware that millions of viewers were watching, he merely cupped his knee. He was a lucky, lucky man. He'd landed the girl of his dreams, signed a recording contract, amassed a fortune, and now, finally, had the fame that guaranteed the fulfillment of his every wish. Not too bad for a kid whose whole world had come tumbling down around him at thirteen.

The final chorus of "Love Don't Die Easy" bounced off the walls of the studio. He looked up as the hit that had catapulted him into stardom came to an end.

"I love that song." The host of the nation's most popular morning talk show tapped his fingers on the armrest of his chair. Seated to give viewers the full benefit of the panoramic view of Hollywood over his shoulder, Stan beamed a dreamy smile straight into the cameras. "How did it feel to win Album Of The Year at the Grammys?"

Surreal. Bradley glanced down at the toes of his shoes. The Italian leather boots probably cost more than he'd earned in the entire year he'd written that song. He leaned forward, directing his answer at the blinking red light on Camera Three rather than their host, just like Catherine had coached him to do. "Well, not too long ago I was playing in bars and clubs around Nashville. So, winning a Grammy has been quite a change." Thanks to the award, he had the life that, a few years ago, he'd only dreamed of living.

Not that everything was perfect. All the newfound fame and fortune had placed so many extra demands on his time that he was way behind on the new album. Between his schedule and Catherine's work on what was sure to be another blockbuster movie, the two of them rarely spent any time alone together. When she'd called last night and asked if he could free up his morning, he'd had a momentary vision of the two of them eating breakfast and trading kisses over orange juice and coffee. Instead, they'd spent the last two hours in makeup and rehearsals before they were ushered onto the set.

But no one turned down the opportunity to appear on Stan's show. No one. Not unless they wanted to watch their careers sink below the horizon like the setting sun. Careful not to let even the slightest hint of frustration show, Bradley eased back into the plush leather couch when the host's attention shifted.

"Catherine Mann." Stan's dark eyes lit with the fervor of a true fan. The coppery brackets around his mouth deepened as, exuding confidence and poise, he crossed one long leg over the other. "It's a real thrill to have you in the studio today."

"Thank you, Stan." Catherine's perfectly modulated voice caressed the mics while she gave the shy smile that had first delighted movie goers when she was a child, turned her name into a household word as a teen, and stolen his heart the moment Bradley had met her. "It's a pleasure to be here."

"You discovered Bradley, didn't you?" The consummate morning show host, Stan dove straight into the meat of the interview. "I mean, he was already well known in Nash-ville. But you brought him to Los Angeles and got him a recording deal."

Bradley felt his shoulders stiffen. Sure, things had begun to change for him once he and Catherine had started seeing each other. Her name had opened a few doors. But it had been his talent that had propelled him upward and gotten him where he was today.

"I introduced him to a few people," Cath-erine admitted. She slipped her perfectly manicured fingers over his knee and stared deeply into his eyes. "But he's a pretty talented guy. He got himself a recording deal."

Her firm answer shut down Stan's line of questioning and soothed the acidic burn in Bradley's stomach. Undaunted, the talk show host smoothly changed subjects. "And the two of you have been inseparable ever since?"

The melodic tones of Catherine's laugh echoed through the small space. "I think the first time I heard Bradley sing"—emotion flickered in her eyes for an all-too-brief moment before she turned to face Stan—"I fell in love with him."

As if he sensed a story, Stan leaned forward. "Are you saying the two of you might have some news for us one day?"

Bradley straightened and said, "We like to keep our private lives private." In rehearsals, Stan had offered repeated assurances that his guests' personal lives would remain off-limits. Yet less than five minutes into the interview, the host was already prying into matters Bradley and Catherine had decided they'd rather not have aired on national TV. He looked to Catherine for support.

"We're engaged to be married," his bride-to-be blurted.

Despite the countless stage appearances and a thousand-and-one coaching sessions where he'd learned to keep a carefully crafted façade in place, Bradley couldn't even begin to hide his surprise.

He and Catherine had talked about this. They'd decided to keep the depth of their feelings for one another hidden from their adoring—but demanding—fans who'd insist on knowing every detail of their wedding plans. She knew how important it was to him to keep their relationship to themselves. So why had she just shared the news of their engagement on national TV?

"Now, I know we agreed not to share this publicly, but..." Catherine patted his arm. The wattage on her signature smile increased to the point where it practically guaranteed to turn her fans' hearts all aflutter. "I just want the whole world to know how happy I am."

"Well, you heard it here first, folks." Stan's pleased grin announced to viewers everywhere that he'd just scored the scoop of the century. "Catherine Mann and Bradley Suttons are engaged to be married!"

Bradley took a deep breath, steadied his nerves, and aimed a loving look at his fiancée. There really wasn't anything else for him to do, was there? He couldn't very well shut the door now that the horse had already bolted out of the barn. Besides, if he knew anything about his fiancée, it was that Catherine never made a move in public without having a very good reason for it.

Now, he just needed to figure out what that reason was.

Sarah Standor dusted her hands on the back of her well-worn jeans as the screened door she'd been walking in and out of her entire life swung shut behind her. Voices came from the corner of the roomy ranch house. She'd left the TV on to keep her rescue dogs company while she fed and watered the horses this morning. When she glanced at the screen, her footsteps slowed.

The devastatingly handsome cowboy on the talk show sat next to Catherine Mann, America's reigning box-office queen. Sarah resumed her march to the coffeemaker and poured herself a much-needed cup. The starlet on TV giggled like a schoolgirl, tossed her long blonde curls, and announced their engagement. The groom-to-be looked as if he'd just swallowed a canary.

Sarah shook her head and laughed. *Bradley Suttons.* Along with every other person who lived within a fifty-mile radius, she'd followed the meteoric rise of Mill Town's favorite son. It didn't seem to matter to anyone that Bradley had moved clear across the country when he was thirteen and never once returned for a visit. Or that the house he'd lived in as a child had sat vacant all these years. The good citizens of the town and surrounding areas had claimed him as their own, and that was that.

And now, he was engaged to be married to Catherine Mann, America's sweetheart. Talk about power couples. Their union was sure to top all the Who's Who lists from Nashville to Hollywood, and everywhere in between.

"Well, congratulations, Brad-Bird." Sarah smiled.

A noise from the other end of the house interrupted before she'd finished doctoring her coffee with cream and sugar. She glanced down the hallway that ran as straight as a shotgun from the back door to the front of the house. A familiar figure stood on the wide porch. Sarah noted the suit and tie the banker wore beneath his Stetson and sighed. She'd hoped to put off the inevitable just a little while longer, but it looked like the day she'd been dreading had arrived. Forcing a cheery note into her voice, she called, "Mornin' James."

"Mornin'." Without waiting for an invitation, James let himself in.

"What brings you out here so early?" Sarah took a steadying breath and prepared for the worst. She'd known she couldn't dodge the banker forever. In a place the size of Mill Town, there really wasn't anywhere to hide.

"Well, I had to come out here to see you since you won't answer any of my phone calls or emails." His boot heels rattling against the hardwood floors, James swept the wide-brimmed hat from his head and ran a hand over his sparse hair.

Sarah propped one hand on the kitchen table and leaned on it for support. She was pretty sure she was going to need it. Still, it wouldn't do to let the banker see her sweat. Not quite sure how she did it, she managed a teasing smile. "Well, I don't got time for phone calls and emails. I got a ranch to run." Hoping she'd guessed wrong about her visitor's intentions, she asked, "How's your mama?"

"She's...she's real good." His expression far too serious for a social call, James moved closer.

"She get those garden roses I sent over?" It really was a shame that her boarding stables didn't produce revenue as well as her flowers did. When it came to those, she was known throughout the county for her green thumb. She grabbed the remote control and turned down the volume on the television set.

"She did, and I thank you." James rocked his hat back and forth, talking with his Stetson like people back East spoke with their hands.

"She is such a sweet lady." Uncertain how much longer she could stall, Sarah sipped from her mug. "James, you want some coffee?"

"I'd love a half a cup of coffee." James parked his hat on the kitchen table. He rubbed one finger down his equine nose and straightened the strings of his bolo tie. "But you need to quit changing the subject, 'cause we need to talk about your finances."

Sarah heard the frustration in his voice. It pained her to put her friend in such an awkward spot, but what else was she supposed to do?

She'd grown up in this house. She knew every creaking floorboard. She knew the way to twist the handle in the shower to coax the most hot water from the ancient boiler, and that she could cool the entire house by propping open the front and back doors on a summer's evening.

Still, even though the ranch had been in her family for generations, she could've walked away from it if she only had herself to think about. But there was far more to it than that. If she lost the ranch, what would become of the horses she cared for? Of the dogs she'd rescued and who now served as her surrogate family? Who would tend to the gardens that provided flowers for weddings and funerals and high school proms and, yes, brought such joy to people like James's mother?

She couldn't lose the ranch. She just couldn't. The ugly fact was, though, she didn't have the money to pay off all her debts.

Hoping to stall, she resorted to the one thing that had worked so far—she hedged. "Now, my mama told me never to talk about politics or money in mixed company," she said as she poured James's coffee and topped off her own cup.

"There's no getting around this, Sarah." James held out his empty palms. "I'm going to have to foreclose on you and sell off this ranch if you can't find a way to make the mortgage payments. If it were up to me—"

"It is up to you, Jimmy." With more firmness than she'd intended, she handed him his cup. "You're the president of Mill Town Bank."

James's voice rose in protest. "I don't *own* the bank, Sarah."

Her shoulders slumped. As desperate as she was to hold on to the ranch, she wouldn't beg, wouldn't put her childhood friends in an awkward position.

One final chance existed to salvage her situation. She crossed her fingers. "I'm just waiting to hear if I got this grant from the Equine Rehabilitation Fund." With the money from the foundation, she'd be able to bring her mortgage up to date and buy enough feed and hay to see her stock through the winter. Without it, though... She stopped her train of thought. She had to get that grant. She had to.

James's voice dropped to a near whisper. "I've given you six months more than I have any right to, and now I have no choice."

Sarah stared at the floor. She'd exhausted all her other options. The Equine Rehabilitation Fund was her last hope. They'd already had her application for far too long, but any day now, they had to approve her request and send the money she needed. She lifted her head and looked James in the eye. "One month," she pleaded. "That's all I'm asking."

A long minute stretched out while she held her breath and prayed. At last, the bank president held up a finger. "One month, Sarah. That takes us to June first."

Deliberately, she straightened her shoulders. James was going pretty far out on a weak limb to give her this last chance to balance her accounts. She had to make sure he didn't regret it. "I will tell you what," she began. "If I don't have the money by June first, I will walk into your office, I will shake your hand, and I will sign this ranch over to you."

"Well, that's—that's fair." To free up his

right hand, James shifted his coffee mug into his left.

Sarah took the hand he extended and gave it a firm shake. "You need me to sign something?"

James lifted the hand she'd just shaken. "You just did."

Sarah hefted her mug. A warmth that had nothing to do with the coffee she swigged spread through her midsection. Despite all her financial woes, returning to Mill Town after graduation had been the right decision. Where else would the president of the bank do business on a handshake?

The reason for his visit concluded, James pointed over her shoulder to the television where the morning talk show had continued. "That guy grew up here," he announced.

Sarah took a second to swallow her coffee. "Bradley Suttons." She nodded. "He used to live next door. Moved away when he was about thirteen. But I believe he still owns the house."

"I remember." Sympathy tugged at the corners of James's lips. "His parents were killed in that car accident over in Greenbrier."

"Yep." Propping her elbow on the arm she'd folded across her chest, she tipped her coffee cup toward the screen. She'd never known there was such sadness in the world before the day that word of the Suttons' deaths spread through the town. But, as bad as their loss had been for her, it had been so much worse for the boy next door. One minute, her best friend had been a normal kid growing up in a small town with his whole future laid out for him. The next, everything he'd ever known—his parents, his home, his friends—had been stripped away from him.

"He must be about the most famous resident to ever come out of Mill Town." James lifted one eyebrow. "I guess you knew him pretty well?"

"Knew him?" She took a long swallow from her mug. "I was married to him."

Read the rest!
A Country Wedding is available now!